AFTER SAPPHO

Selby Wynn Schwartz holds a PhD in comparative literature from the University of California, Berkeley. She is the author of *The Bodies of Others: Drag Dances and Their Afterlives*, a finalist for the Lambda Literary Award, and the forthcoming novella *A Life in Chameleons*.

Praise for *After Sappho*

"A poetic patchwork of fragments of literary history that together take shape as an intergenerational tale of the Lesbian family. An ancestry eruditely, playfully recovered."

Booker Prize Judges

"Highly original, practically uncategorisable... an entrancing choric collage of a novel."

Daily Mail

"A sparkling, imaginative gem… A gorgeous celebration of pioneering thinkers who rejected docility and self-abnegation… Enthralling."

Independent

"Bold... radical... artful... this fine novel is an inspiring and witty ode to sisterhood and sapphism… I haven't read anything I've loved so much in a long time."

Literary Review

"A glorious, genre-expanding work of fiction… Spell-binding."

Telegraph

"What a wonder. This book is splendid: impish, irate, deep, courageous, moving, funny… and truly significant."

Lucy Ellmann

Booker Prize-shortlisted author of *Ducks, Newburyport*

"*After Sappho* is superb. Mesmerizing. Such incredible writing. And thinking. Selby Wynn Schwartz tips everyone out of the water."

Deborah Levy

Booker Prize-shortlisted author of *Swimming Home* and *Hot Milk*

"It's brilliant, an unobtrusive, quietly mesmerizing, imagined collocation of linked feminist lives that succeeds in delineating a movement bigger than all of them without diminishing any one of them… An inspiration."

Ian Patterson

poet and reviewer

AFTER SAPPHO

SELBY WYNN SCHWARTZ

PICADOR INDIA

First published in 2022 by Galley Beggar Press Limited, United Kingdom
First published in India in 2022 by Picador India
an imprint of Pan Macmillan Publishing India Private Limited
707 Kailash Building
26 K. G. Marg, New Delhi 110001
www.panmacmillan.co.in

Pan Macmillan, The Smithson, 6 Briset Street, London EC1M 5NR
Associated companies throughout the world
www.panmacmillan.com

ISBN 978-93-90742-22-6

4

Typeset in Adobe Garamond Pro by R. Ajith Kumar, New Delhi
Printed and bound in India by Repro India Ltd

FSC www.fsc.org
MIX
Paper from responsible sources
FSC® C047271

A tuttə voi che siete Lina Poletti

which means, to all of you
who are Lina Poletti.

The problems of Albertine are
(from the narrator's point of view)

a) lying
b) lesbianism,

and (from Albertine's point of view)

a) being imprisoned in the narrator's house.

—Anne Carson,
The Albertine Workout

PROLOGUE

SAPPHO, c. 630 BCE

The first thing we did was change our names. We were going to be Sappho.

Who was Sappho? No one knew, but she had an island. She was garlanded with girls. She could sit down to dine and look straight at the woman she loved, however unhappily. When she sang, everyone said, it was like evening on a riverbank, sinking down into the moss with the sky pouring over you. All of her poems were songs.

We read Sappho at school, in classes intended merely to teach poetic metre. Very few of our teachers imagined that they were swelling our veins with cassia and myrrh. In dry voices they went on about the aorist tense, while inside ourselves we felt the leaves of trees shivering in the light, everything dappled, everything trembling.

We were so young then that we had never met. In back gardens we read as much as we could, staining our dresses with mud and pine-pitch. Some of us were sent by our families to distant schools to be finished, so that we would come to our proper end. But it was not our end. It was barely our beginning. Each one lingered in her own place, searching the fragments of poems for words to say what it was, this feeling that Sappho calls *aithussomenon*, the way that leaves move when nothing touches them but the afternoon light.

At that time we were not called anything and so we cherished every word, no matter how many centuries dead. Reading of the nocturnal rites of the *pannuchides* we stayed up all night; the exile of Sappho to Sicily turned our eyes to the sea. We began writing odes to clover blossoms and blushing apples, or painting on canvases that we turned to the wall at the slightest sound of footsteps. A sidelong glance, a half-smile, a hand that rested on our arms just above the elbow: we had not yet memorized the lines for these occasions. Or there were only fragments of lines that we could have offered, in any case. Of the nine books of poems written by Sappho, mere shreds of dactyls survive, as in Fragment 24C: *we live/... the opposite/...daring.*

ONE

CORDULA POLETTI, b. 1885

Cordula Poletti was born into a line of sisters who didn't understand her. From the earliest days, she was drawn towards the outer reaches of the house: the attic, the balcony, the back window touched by the branches of a pine tree. At her christening she kicked free of the blankets bundled around her and crawled down the nave. It was impossible to swaddle Cordula long enough to name her.

CORDULA POLETTI, c. 1896

Whenever she could, she took a Latin primer from the Biblioteca Classense and went to sit in a tree near the cemetery. In her house they called, Cordula, Cordula!, and no one would answer. Finding Cordula's skirts discarded on the floor, her mother openly despaired of her prospects. What right-minded citizen of Ravenna would marry a girl who climbed up the trees in her underthings? Her mother called, Cordula, Cordula?, but there was no one in the house who would answer that question.

X, 1883

Two years before the christening of Cordula, Guglielmo Cantarano published his study of X, a twenty-three-year-old Italian. In excellent health, X went whistling through the streets and kept a string of girlfriends happy. Even Cantarano, who disapproved, had to admit that X was jovial and generous. X would throw a shoulder to a wheel without complaint, could make a room roar with laughter. It wasn't that. It was what X was *not.* X was not a willing housewife. X remained unmoved by squalling infants, would not wear skirts that swaddled the stride, had no desire to be pursued by the hot breath of young men, failed to enjoy domestic chores, and possessed none of the decorous modesty of maidenhood. Whatever X was, Cantarano wrote, it was to be avoided at all costs.

Thus X was locked away in an asylum and Italian mothers were instructed to watch for signs of deviance in their daughters. Even those who had normal breasts, Cantarano cautioned, might turn out to be like X, whose apparently standard genitals had not prevented the attempt, late one night, to set the family home on fire.

C – POLETTI, c. 1897

She shut the insistent voices of her family inside the house and went up her tree. From a haven of leaves she looked out over the cemetery. The tombs of poets were wreathed in laurel and etched in glorious verses, while the graves of the ordinary listed as their only accomplishments the names of children produced or a spouse bereaved. So many dead in childbirth, she observed, and so few by shipwreck.

Her mind was a tangle of lyric odes and unconjugated verbs. Each line of Ovid demanded an unspooling of which object bore the action, and by whose brave hand. Each epithet traced to its source showed the divine moving behind the scenes of human life: in her tree was a great rustling of gods, owls, winged serpents. As soon as she finished the Latin primer she went on to the Greek. She stayed up late, rapturously late. It became apparent that she wasn't Cordula at all.

LINA POLETTI, c. 1899

Towards the end of the century she changed names. Cordula sounded anyway like a heap of rope. Lina was a swift, sleek line, a hand brushing a row of buttons. Lina was the one who would read Sappho.

Lina lived with her family on Via Rattazzi, not far from the tomb of Dante. A tomb is a dead place in the ground. There is a rock on top of it, covered with tiny nicks that are words. Lina stayed up late writing verses for the tomb. Not for Dante himself, who had been dead since 1321, but for the incisions that words make on immutable substances.

It would be many years before we learned of Lina Poletti. In her childhood she dwelt alone, her only companions the solemn constellations of the night sky. The refrain rang through her house, Cordula, Cordula!, but Lina listened only to the silence of stars. Eventually she would learn to translate Sappho without a dictionary. She would find that she was one of us. But in those years it was a great wonder that Lina, unlike X, did not set fire to the family home.

LINA POLETTI, c. 1900

As the century turned, Lina Poletti outpaced her classmates in classical subjects from elocution to the elegiac mode. Moreover she kept her distance when they paired off to walk home or passed each other scraps of crude rhymes. Lina walked alone to the Biblioteca Classense and noted various uses of the genitive.

The genitive is a case of relations between nouns. Often the genitive is defined as possession, as if the only way one noun could be with another were to own it, greedily. But in fact there is also the genitive of remembering, where one noun is always thinking of another, refusing to forget her.

SAPPHO, FRAGMENTS 105A AND 105B

Sappho writes of many girls: those who are pliant and bind up their hair modestly, those who are golden and go willingly into the bridal chamber, and those *like the hyacinth in the mountains that shepherd men/with their feet trample down*. An entire book of Sappho is made of wedding songs; like the hyacinth in the mountains, none have survived.

For the girl who wishes to avoid being trampled down by the feet of men, Sappho recommends the farthermost branch of the highest tree. There are always those rare few, Sappho notes, that *the applepickers forgot—/no, not forgot: were unable to reach.*

Lina's father made his living selling earthenware pots. With four daughters to maintain, he saw the necessity of their marriages like the exchange of dry goods. A line of daughters was already a liability, and there was no market for girls who were not pliant.

Whenever Lina's mother called her, Cordula, Cordula!, to embroider the trousseau of linens for her dowry, Lina was already elsewhere. She was at the very end of the Greek primer, she was ensconced in a far corner of the Biblioteca Classense, she had gone out of the back window and into the pine tree to read poems from a century less muffled in fabric.

We could picture Lina in those years: her high buttoned boots, her erudite citations. Above her boots she seemed hardly to be wearing skirts. Lina Poletti was like that, she could make visible things seem scant and unremarkable. She had her own ways of escaping the century.

SAPPHO, FRAGMENT 2

A kletic poem is a calling, both a hymn and a plea. It bends in obeisance to the divine, ever dappled and shining, and at the same time it calls out to ask, When will you arrive? Why is your radiance distant from my eyes? You drop through the branches when I sleep at the roots. You pour yourself out like the light of an afternoon and yet somewhere you linger, outside the day.

It is while invoking the one who abides and yet must be called, urgently, from a great distance, that Sappho writes of *aithussomenon*, the bright trembling of leaves in the moment of anticipation. A poet is always living in kletic time, whatever her century. She is calling out, she is waiting. She lies down in the shade of the future and drowses among its roots. Her case is the genitive of remembering.

LINA POLETTI, C, 1905

Lina Poletti fought to sit in a chair at the library. She fought to smoke in the Caffè Roma-Risorgimento. She fought to frequent literary gatherings in the evenings. She did up her cravat with determined fingers and presented herself in public, over and over, to murmurs in Piazza Vittorio Emanuele II.

She went on, against the wishes of her family, to the university in Bologna. She studied under the esteemed poet Giovanni Pascoli, who was surprised to find her there. He peered at her, although she was sitting clearly in the front row of the lecture hall with her pen ready. There weren't many women who wanted to write a thesis on the poetry of Carducci. People were always saying that about Lina Poletti: they were surprised to find her, there weren't many like her. It was true that she had very striking eyes, with golden rims around her pupils. She seemed volatile, alchemical. Something might flash through her and change everything. As Sibilla Aleramo would say to us later, Lina was a violent, luminous wave.

TWO

RINA FACCIO, b. 1876

As a girl, Rina Faccio lived in Porto Civitanova and did what she was told. Her father told her to work in the accounting department of his factory, and she did it. She was twelve years old, dutiful, with long dark hair.

In the factory glass bottles were produced, thousands every day, tinting the air with ferrous smoke. Rina was charged with the figures, how much sodium sulphate was carried to the furnace on the shoulders of how many *portantini*, the boys who worked eight hours a day for one lira. There was no school in Porto Civitanova, so Rina tried to teach herself how to account for all of this.

RINA FACCIO, 1889

In 1889 Rina's mother told her something wordlessly that she never forgot. Her mother was standing at the window, looking out, in a white dress that hung off her shoulders. Then suddenly her mother went out of the window. She plummeted, her dress trailing like a scrap of paper. Her body landed two floors down, bent into a bad shape. That was what Rina Faccio's mother had to say to her.

NIRA AND RESEDA, 1892

Nira was the first time Rina changed her name. She wanted to write for the provincial local papers, but she was afraid that her father would find out.

When Rina Faccio turned fifteen, she grew out of anagrams. She chose the name Reseda because it reminded her of *recita*, a verb for actresses: it means, she plays her role, she recites her part. When her father thundered in the drawing room about the opinions of these hussies, whoever they were, appearing in print, Rina Faccio looked up from her needlepoint as blank as a new page.

RINA FACCIO, 1892

Despite having been warned wordlessly by her mother, Rina Faccio didn't foresee her fate. She was obediently adding and subtracting numbers about the factory, keeping the ledgers in straight lines. A man who worked at the factory was moving in circles around her. He had brute hands that fastened on levers, a breath that crawled up the back of her neck. She didn't see him until the circles were very tight, and then it was too late. Her dress was shoved up. She cried out, but only the brute palm of his hand could hear her.

RINA PIERANGELI FACCIO, 1893

Once Rina's father learned that she had been possessed by that man, there was nothing to do but transfer her to him in name and deed. Articles of Italian law bound a daughter into becoming a wife at the word of her father. In particular Article 544 of the Penal Code was like an iron lever, manoeuvring girls of sixteen into position as brides to the very men who had trampled them down.

In the winter Rina was handed from one household to another, sallow and dazed. In the house of Rina's father, her two sisters sat silently at their needlepoint while her mother, or what was left of her, was consigned to the asylum at Macerata. There were no words for what happened in the house of the husband to whom Rina now belonged. After Rina Pierangeli Faccio had been delivered to him, along with some dining-room furniture, the curtains were drawn. When in the early months she miscarried in a feverish rush of blood, she did not ask why. But she felt welling up in her a tumultuous hatred of life, this life, her life.

THE PISANELLI CODE, 1865

The politicians hailed the Pisanelli Code as a triumph of the unification of Italy. The new state was eager to grow into its full shape, stretching the length of the entire peninsula and covering the populace with its laws. As one politician said, We made Italy; now we have to make the Italians.

Under the Pisanelli Code, Italian women gained two

memorable rights: we could make wills to distribute our property after our own deaths, and our daughters could inherit things from us. Our writing before death had never seemed so important. Those of us in Italy considered whether we might bequeath to our daughters some small gift that could be pawned for a future.

RINA, 1895

In 1895, amid laundry and bruises, Rina Pierangeli Faccio gave birth to the child of that man. It was a son. When the infant turned two, she found the bottle of laudanum and wordlessly took all of it.

The laudanum didn't kill Rina Pierangeli Faccio, but it ended her days as a dutiful wife. The woman she had been until that night was dead, she said. The doctor prescribed bed rest, the husband reproached her. But Rina would only speak to her sister.

Often that was the first thing we did when we were changing: we would find a sister and stay with her, taking breakfast in our room. Or we would find someone in her room and stay with her, pretending if needed that we were sisters. The housekeepers would widen their eyes, but if we prevailed, milky tea and toast were served in our room, on trays that spanned the whole width of our bed.

DR. T. LAYCOCK, *A TREATISE ON THE NERVOUS DISORDERS OF WOMEN*, 1840

The eminent Doctor Laycock of York, writing on the nervous disorders of women, could not help but notice that the more young women consorted with each other, the more excitable and indolent they became. This condition might strike seamstresses, factory girls, or any woman who associated with any number of other women.

In particular, he cautioned, young females cannot associate together in public schools without serious risk of exciting the passions, and being led to indulge in practices injurious to both body and mind. Novels, whispers, unsigned poems, general education, shared sleeping compartments: no sooner were girls reading in bed than they were reading in bed together. What might look like sisterly affection or a schoolgirl's fancy ought to be diagnosed as the pernicious antecedent of hysteric paroxysms. In the throes of it they were highly contagious and might throw whole households into disorder.

AMENDMENT TO THE PISANELLI CODE, 1877

The rights we didn't have in Italy were the same rights we hadn't had for centuries, and thus not worth enumerating. But in 1877, a modification to the Pisanelli Code allowed women to act as witnesses. Suddenly, legally, we could sign our names to what we knew to be true. Our words, which had always before been seen as gauzy and frivolous, gained a new weight as they settled on the page.

Then, too, we were beginning to notice how the outlines of our doorways and dowries were matched up, so that one box could be carried through another, signifying the transfer of a bride. No one could leave a marriage, but some of us could discern the shape that it made of our lives. As one politician said at that time, In Italy, the enslavement of women is the only regime in which men may live happily. He meant that we ourselves were the small gift, pawned for the future of the fatherland.

THREE

ANNA KULISCIOFF, B. *c.* 1854

Before Anna Kuliscioff spent her life fighting for the rights of Italian women, she was born in southern Ukraine. As soon as she was old enough to grasp the basic idea of humanity, she began explaining its principles to those around her, for which she was exiled, arrested, and imprisoned across Europe.

In 1877 she sang for her supper in a public park in Kyiv, then fled the country with a false passport. Hardly had she arrived in Switzerland in search of a clandestine printing press when the police swarmed in, asking pointed questions about her revolutionary belief that women ought not to be held as property.

She was expelled from France, she was arrested in Milano, she was jailed in Firenze although there was no evidence for her guilt except that she was clearly incorrigible. By 1881 she had a daughter, fathered by an Italian anarchist. Anna Kuliscioff was careful not to marry the man, she had other ideas.

ANNA KULISCIOFF, 1886

Anna Kuliscioff was so often the object of outcry and imprecation that by 1884 she scarcely registered an insult. She enrolled in the University of Napoli to study medicine, despite the fact that no woman had ever done so before. She was interested in epidemiology and why on earth so many Italian women were permitted to die from puerperal fevers. At her graduation in 1886, when she was decried as a pathological perversion of femininity, Anna Kuliscioff paused briefly to recite the correct medical definition of 'pathogenesis'. Then she took her degree.

THE *PATRIA POTESTAS*

On the grounds of sheer human life, Anna Kuliscioff opposed the Pope, the Russian tsar, and most of the Italian socialists. It was ludicrous, what these men busied themselves with instead of preventable post-partum infections. What was worse, what was *truly* malignant, was the casual breaking of bodies in the back rooms of a household, nearly always the bodies of women, authorized under a civil law called the *patria potestas*.

Patria meant both 'the father' and 'the fatherland', and *potestas* was the thick knot of their power to dispose magisterially of women, children, and domestic goods. *Patria potestas* had been handed down from father to father since the Roman Empire. In the Pisanelli Code of 1865 it was wedded to the *autorizzazione maritale*, which authorized the husband to treat his wife as a child forever: no matter how she grew in mind and body, she would never be fully a person in the fatherland. As soon as she could, Anna Kuliscioff became a doctor, specializing in gynaecology and anarchism.

DOTTORESSA ANNA KULISCIOFF, *IL MONOPOLIO DELL'UOMO*, 1890

In 1890 the Dottoressa Kuliscioff somehow got herself invited to lecture at the Philological Society of the University of Milano, where no woman had ever lectured before. She chose for her talk the title *The Monopoly of Men*. On a bright day in April, Anna Kuliscioff seized her chance to explain to those assembled how marriage was fundamentally a humiliation of women. The philologists should know full well, she pointed out, that *patria potestas* was nothing but Latin for fathers who sold their daughters cheaply to the very men who had violated them.

DOTTORESSA ANNA KULISCIOFF, *CRITICA SOCIALE*, 1899

Condemned by a military tribunal to several months in prison, the Dottoressa Anna Kuliscioff was freed on the first day of 1899. She came home to the dust on her books, to the winter light through the windows, to the white-spired spectacle of the Duomo of Milano preaching its dominion over the piazza. For the length of a coffee Anna Kuliscioff allowed herself to sit on the green divan. It was a new year; it would soon be a new century; even if half of the radical socialists who wrote for *Critica sociale* were still imprisoned, Anna Kuliscioff reasoned, publication could not be delayed.

In a rush of ink and dust, Anna Kuliscioff wrote to everyone who might help with the next issue: comrades, revolutionaries, socialists, feminists, writers, editors. Among the comrades of Anna Kuliscioff was the socialist revolutionary whose feminist journal was now edited by a young writer named Rina Faccio.

RINA, 1901

In the evenings Rina could read freely and go to the theatre. In the north then we were beginning to hear the word *femminista*, which sounded like the French *femme*, meaning both 'wife' and 'woman'. Much preferring women over wives, we watched closely for signs of what was to come. For example, the theatre in Milano was so crowded that Rina could barely find her seat. The play was Ibsen's *A Doll's House*, the story of a woman named Nora who ceases finally to be a wife. In the last act, Nora leaves her house, her husband, and her children, clicking the latch of the door behind her with a sound like a century snapping shut.

ELEONORA DUSE, *NORA*, 1891

A Doll's House had first come to Italy in the form of the actress Eleonora Duse. She was already famous when she swept into a theatre in Milano in 1891, thirty-two years old, melancholy and determined. On the cold stage she took off her hat and furs and, bowing her head, had a chain put round her neck with heavy keys on it. The tines of the keys hung down to the tops of her thighs, so that every step she took made the sound of keys and chains, chains and keys. On opening night, tickets to see her cost twice what they should, and still the theatre was creaking with bodies all the way up to the balconies. Then the curtain went up, and Eleonora Duse became Nora.

RINA, *SIBILLA*, 1902

In 1902 Rina left that man, the child, and her name. She escaped to Rome and rented a tiny room with a writing desk. Between giving private lessons and volunteering in a dispensary for poor children, she fell in love with a distinguished novelist. When the novelist asked her name, Rina said it was Sibilla, like the Sibyl of Delphi. A new name was like a blank notebook; Rina could write herself into it. With a folio of fresh pages she could write herself into becoming Sibilla, enigmatic and sibilant.

Under the Pisanelli Code her conduct was inexcusable: no one could leave a marriage, but especially not a wife and a mother. A lawyer would barely take her case out of the charity of his heart. The problem of Mrs Pierangeli Faccio was hopeless, he said; she would never see her child again. Her old names would drag after her like chains. As she left the lawyer's office, Sibilla made a sound in the back of her throat like vapours escaping from cracked earth. Then she went back to her writing.

SIBILLA ALERAMO, B. 1906

In later years, Sibilla Aleramo would say that she had been born in 1906 when the first copy of *Una donna* was printed in Torino. She held the book in her hands. It was not like a baby. It was not like a bottle of laudanum. It was a solid object, the volume of a life. It bore her new name on its spine. Whether it was a novel or an autobiography no one could say, but its pages were the sustenance of Sibilla as she came into the world, unblinking, thirty years old. It was the story she told herself of herself, like a sibyl who eats her own words.

SIBILLA ALERAMO, *UNA DONNA*, 1906

The manuscript of *Una donna* had initially been rejected by a set of editors in Milano because it was too boring. It was only the story of a woman, they said. It was a story that they already knew, there was only one story. It had no dramatic tension.

Una donna was the story of a woman whose mother goes out of the window in a white dress like a scrap of paper, whose body is trampled down like a hyacinth, whose father delivers her to that man, whose son is born amid laundry and bruises. It was the story of a woman not named Nora who ceases finally to be a wife.

Una donna was published instead by a small typographical agency in Torino, and almost immediately throngs of readers bought up all of the copies. The editors in Milano were greatly surprised, but as reasonable businessmen they acquired the rights for reprinting the book. Perhaps there was a new market in boring stories about women, they remarked, or perhaps the women who read such stories found them of some unfathomable interest.

CONGRESSO NAZIONALE DELLE DONNE ITALIANE, 1908

The Queen Elena herself, in a bold blue skirt and feathered hat, attended the first National Congress of Women in Italy in the spring of 1908. The price of train tickets had been reduced so that schoolteachers, postmistresses, and the matrons of foundling houses from all over Italy might converge upon Rome, ascend the hallowed steps of the Capitoline Hill, and mingle with countesses and infamous *femministe*. More than a thousand women watched the Countess Gabriella Rasponi Spalletti preside over the inaugural ceremonies in the frescoed Sala degli Orazi e Curiazi; there was a tea in the gardens, and then, together, they took up the question of women.

In fact there were many questions of women; the demands of immigrant women were not the same as those raised by countesses. Suffragists wanted the vote; schoolteachers wanted literacy campaigns; the matrons of foundling houses wanted aid for unwed mothers. And yet two propositions were universally affirmed: an end to the odious *autorizzazione maritale*, and a rule that any man attending the Congresso should be denied a vote on its proceedings.

SIBILLA ALERAMO AND LINA POLETTI, 1908

By 1908 Sibilla Aleramo was a famous writer and an infamous *femminista.* Lina Poletti was a golden-eyed poet of twenty-three who stood in the marble doorway of the Sala degli Orazi e Curiazi, watching her. They were in Rome, in April, and there were women everywhere. Women were in hot rooms together discussing the rights they should have. Even the queen had come, and the princess Maria Letizia with her, to hear about the education of girls. Anna Kuliscioff was there, exhorting everyone not to content themselves with the mere education of girls when they could seize the right to vote down the *patria potestas* and the autocratic men who upheld it.

A poet is someone who stands on the door sill and sees the room before her as a sea whose waves she might dive through. Lina took her breath in and then strode into the crowd, the shoals of jutting shoulders, the swelling of conversations and the sweep of skirts all around her; finally, arriving at Sibilla, she exhaled, triumphant. At the rush of breath on the back of her neck, Sibilla turned, and there was Lina with her eyes molten. A poet is someone who swims inexplicably away from the shore, only to arrive at an island of her own invention.

SIBILLA AND LINA, 1908

This time it was Sibilla who stayed up all night, feverish and poetic. From the moment she had walked out of the Sala on Lina's arm, the air around her had been stirred by a sound of leaves massing like tiny wings on every branch, turning to feel on all surfaces what had set them trembling. Lina was that sound in the air, Sibilla wrote, or perhaps Lina was the light soundlessly touching all of the leaves at once. Lina spoke in a very low voice and was difficult to explain in words. While the rest of Rome lay silent and hollow in its sleep, Sibilla was writing to Lina, You are a violent, luminous wave.

R, c. 1895

R was distinguished by her mania for writing letters, Cesare Lombroso reported, and by the way she strolled under the windows of women. As a child, R had fancied herself a brigand, a bandit, a captain of the trees at the edge of the park. Now thirty-one years of age, R was an artist. R cropped her hair decisively and painted in the mornings. It was noteworthy that R could not be bothered to chatter or ornament herself, and in general found men empty. Cesare Lombroso, who was a criminologist in the positivist vein, put this down to the fact that R's father was a neuropath and her mother a verifiable lunatic. Her brother, too, was very queer, Cesare Lombroso noted, pleased to have discovered such a good case study.

R appeared on pages 423 and 424 of Cesare Lombroso's *La donna delinquente, la prostituta e la donna normale*, published in 1893 in Torino. Translated into English in 1895 as *The Female Offender,* the book did not reach to pages 423 or 424, because any mention of sexual practices or non-mammary organs had been cut out by the translator. It was thus a short book that offered little practical guidance on delinquent women, but those of us in England read it avidly anyway. Most of us were artists, and we were all guilty of writing too many letters.

ARTICLE 339

We still lived in a little hollow between laws. What we wrote to each other and where our beds were, in which rooms, was not prohibited exactly. In Italy the unification had swallowed up some regulations, and others had gone out with the Savoy kingdom. It was a time of uncertainty, despite the efforts to catalogue almost everything and set it into typologies and monographs.

In fact the fixity of some things was the cover for others. For example, there was an extreme reticence in the nineteenth century when describing women together. The English dictionaries used shy Greek terms, or omitted the possibility entirely. Only the criminologists wanted to discuss it, and only in order to chronicle the interiors of insane asylums, brothels, and unnatural mothers.

In 1914 an anonymous book called *Tribadismo, saffismo, clitorismo: psicologia, fisiologia, pratica moderna* appeared. It was promptly censored under Article 339 and its publisher Ettore Cecchi put in prison for three months, since the author, the anonymous tribade, could not be punished for her obscene existence. Of the many ways in which we could be together, tribadism and clitorism were merely two of the more externally visible. But still we felt a little thrill, which we left unspoken in our room together, for fear of the housekeeper. It was there in plain script on the title page: sapphism was a modern practice. Now that we had become a book of our own, we studied the diagrams intently. We needed a great deal of practice before we could become Sappho.

FOUR

ANNA KULISCIOFF, 1912

When all of the citizens of a kingdom are men, they very often elect a series of men to rule it, sometimes even a series of the same man. Italy was such a kingdom, and thus in 1906 such a man was ruling for the third time. His name was Giovanni Giolitti, and the Dottoressa Kuliscioff had some sharp words for him. Anna Kuliscioff had sung for her supper in the parks of northeastern Ukraine, she had survived tuberculosis and childbirth and exile: the only thing she feared was compromise, the soothing voice that licks down rage until it is nothing but a small smooth lump in your hand.

When she went to hear Giolitti speak in parliament, he was extolling the prudent progress made by the kingdom of Italy. He said, soothingly, Would you not admit our benevolence in housing the poor, pensioning the aged, protecting the children from working before they attain the proper age of twelve? And soon, too, every man will have his vote. The country of Italy will be a model of mankind!

Silently Anna Kuliscioff clenched her rage jagged and

whole in her heart. In the spring of 1912, Giovanni Giolitti was speaking in parliament, alongside the man who was Anna Kuliscioff's lover, on the issue of suffrage for women. She wrote to her lover, I will try to arrive in time to hear you speaking. Please, do not betray me. Her lover spoke to parliament in the smooth, sonorous tones of a reasonable socialist. The men of parliament voted. Affably, Giovanni Giolitti announced the results: women had failed to achieve the right to vote. Or, as Anna Kuliscioff put it, Now any Italian who wishes to become a citizen must do only one thing: be born a man.

SIBILLA ALERAMO, *CIÒ CHE VOGLIAMO*, 1902

In 1902, Sibilla Aleramo wrote an article called *What We Want*. What did we want? To begin with, we wanted what half the population had got just by being born, and then we wanted to change how it had got that way. We wanted lives that did not lead us so directly to laudanum and asylums and puerperal fevers. As Sibilla Aleramo wrote in her article, We want women to become human beings: to be at last as free, autonomous, and fully alive as we have until now been subjugated, oppressed, and kept quiet.

In 1902 we would put that proudly in print for anyone to read. But it was not the only thing we wanted. We also longed for writing tables that were not in the kitchen, stained with onions; we wanted to read the novels kept from us because they were decadent and suggestive; we wanted to exchange the finger-pricked linens of our trousseaus for travel guides and foreign grammars; we wanted to meet each other in rooms and discuss the rights of women, we wanted to close the doors to the rooms and lie in each other's arms, the light pouring in the window, the curtains drawn back, the view over the bay running in cerulean and azure swaths into the open sea. We dreamed of islands where we could write poems that kept our lovers up all night. In our letters, we murmured the fragments of our desires to each other, breaking the lines in our impatience. We were going to be Sappho, but how did Sappho begin to become herself?

LINA AND SIBILLA, 1908

On the first postcard that Sibilla sent to Lina was a scattering of pines on vast plains, a sky cast open. Thus in the first reply from Lina to Sibilla was a deft and courteous allusion to the enigmatic Sibyl of antiquity. Therefore in the third and fourth letters there were references to those lonely hours when you gaze across the tawny fields to the edge of the sea, pricked by the tops of the pines, and scry the marvellous new thing that will grace and harrow your life. By the fifth letter Lina had rented a modest flat in Rome that could be reached on foot from Sibilla's and, by the sixth, had also bribed the *portinaio* to overlook any woman who might pay her a nocturnal visit.

NORA, 1879

In 1878, Henrik Ibsen was invited to lecture at the Scandinavian Club of Rome. His plays were of great interest to the members, who discussed them vociferously over cognac. While presenting his theory of human drama to the Club, Ibsen introduced a motion to allow women to become members. Vociferously, the question of women was discussed, and then a vote was held: women failed. Ibsen stalked out of the Scandinavian Club without finishing his cognac.

In 1879, Ibsen was convalescing on the Amalfi coast. The light breeze of orange blossoms and honeyed pines, the sea dissolving into shades of blue: he had a writing table set out on the terrace and began a new play. He called it *A Doll's House,* and he put into its protagonist Nora all of his observations about the wretched state of women in marriages, how they were chained round the neck by their households, how they were cossetted with sweets and dresses until they became exactly the frivolous, flighty playthings that men liked to see dancing in drawing rooms. At the end of the play, when Nora's husband insists that above all she must be a wife and a mother, Nora replies, I believe that I am first and foremost a human being, just as much as you – or, at least, that I'll try to become one. Then she leaves.

When Rina Faccio saw *A Doll's House* in Milano in 1901, tears came to her eyes and stayed there, stinging. Rina Faccio never cried at plays. But Nora, a woman of nerves and bones consigned to the life of an object with its smile painted on, made her weep. Or perhaps it was the moment when Nora left that so moved her: that a woman *could* leave, even in a play, moved Rina Faccio towards becoming Sibilla Aleramo.

LAURA KIELER, 1874

The end of the play, however, was not the end of the story of Nora. What Ibsen did not mention is that *A Doll's House* recounted the life of a woman he knew named Laura Kieler, who was also a writer. The events of *A Doll's House* are wrought from the fabric of her existence; there onstage, twisted into being, thrown into hot relief by the gaslights, are her children, her debts, her lies, her dresses, the sententious pronouncements of her husband, her cowering and miserable dependence upon a household that would grant her no more than pocket money to buy sweets.

Once when Laura Kieler needed money, she sent a manuscript of her novel to Ibsen, beseeching him to recommend it to his publisher. Ibsen disliked her novel and did not see, moreover, why her desire was so desperate, why she was always so fretful and secretive. Receiving Ibsen's refusal at her onion-stained kitchen table, Laura Kieler flung her manuscript into the fire. Unlike Nora, Laura Kieler could not leave: instead, pregnant and terrified, she was sent to an insane asylum.

Ibsen felt badly about this. But still, sitting on his beautiful terrace in Amalfi, he took her life for his play.

SIBILLA AND LINA, 1909

In 1909 Sibilla was not sleeping well. She went to the sea at Santa Marinella, she went to the mountains and tried to look peaceably out over the pines. But the pines were tilting at jagged angles out of steep rock faces, their limbs hanging over the ravines, and the sea was crawling with tiny salt waves, each overlapping another in dizzying succession. Sibilla would stay up all night writing yet another letter to Lina about the rosy touch of dawn on the horizon, only to discover that the sky was already smeared and livid with sunset. Somehow the indescribable parts of Lina made the earth itself falter and skip.

Lina on the other hand slept marvellously. She was barely twenty-four and the world was a fount of lyric images. For every moment of romantic melancholy, there were lonely copses of pines; for every delight, there were swallows reckless in the sky, riverbanks fresh with ferns and violets. You could hardly have a walk without the world suggesting an ode, an elegy. Even upright in a chair in the Biblioteca Classense, Lina would be taken by the green leather spine of Ragon's *Grammaire grecque*, or by dust motes in the light, anything really, a word in Aeolian dialect was enough to set her off. For example, the lexicon of Pollux mentions Sappho's use of the term *beudos*, a short and transparent dress. Who would not desire to sleep for endless hours, dreaming of *beudos*?

SIBILLA ALERAMO, *LA VITA NELLA CAMPAGNA ROMANA*, 1909

Yet in 1909 the world was not made of pressed violets; Sibilla took Lina to the Agro Romano, a miasma of mud and smoke and malaria in the fields surrounding Rome. Charitable and gaunt, Lina walked from village to village, distributing books to peasants who ate nothing but a broth of weeds and maize and called it soup. Sibilla helped in the infirmary for impoverished children, administering vinegar and gauze with her hair pinned up. Folded into the arms of their mothers, Sibilla wrote, the infants seemed to be little packets of exhausted flesh, already bent into the shape their lives would take.

What more could be written about bodies, Sibilla said to Lina that winter, than what was already etched into the faces of the mothers of the Agro Romano? By twenty-five they were toothless, none could read, they lived in reeking huts scrabbling for food. They would never see the stone steps of the Capitoline Hill, much less take up the questions posed at the National Congress of Women. Sibilla shuddered in pity over their unimaginable lives, the blur of their hungry sallow faces. Then she rose to dress for dinner.

SIBILLA ALERAMO, *L'ASSURDO*, 1910

The play *L'assurdo* was never finished. The manuscript tells a snarled story of lovers: Lorenza, Pietro, and someone named Arduino who is described sometimes as a masculine girl, sometimes as a girlish youth, sometimes as a dream made to seem real. Once Arduino appears, Lorenza is no longer content to stay with Pietro: she wants both of them, she is hesitant, she desires Arduino, perhaps Arduino does not exist, Lorenza cannot explain him exactly, except that he is like a sudden springtime, her lap is full of violets.

When Sibilla Aleramo wrote *L'assurdo*, she was writing her own life. After leaving her husband in 1902, she had fallen in love with a dignified novelist from Torino. He was earnest and modern, he believed in the free union of men and women. But Lina Poletti was a brash young poet who believed that if you wanted someone, you wrote verses that poured violets into her lap. You led her down to dewy riverbanks in the evening and you made sure that when she arose again, mosses feathery in her hair, she would never be the same.

Sibilla Aleramo dedicated the play *to the one who made me/believe that it was true,/ this dream.* That was Lina Poletti, ardent and indescribable. Even those who loved her were not sure she was real.

SAPPHO, FRAGMENT 147

For *someone will remember us/I say/even in another time*, Sappho wrote. She was writing of the woman who would lie back with her in the cress and moss at the river's edge, how darkness would gather in her lap as evening came over them, the melting from that darkness. One of the epithets of Sappho that is difficult to translate, even for a poet, is this darkly bright hollow of the body. It might be a fold of cloth or flesh, the shadow between breasts, or the surprise of twilight. It might be a sharp, haunted longing that surges in the viscera, or it might be your lap heaped with violets. Whatever it is, Sappho writes, it lasts all night long.

SAPPHO, FRAGMENT 31

Was this what it was, then, to love a woman? Sibilla wrote to Lina. Although Lina was hardly a woman like any other. Striding around in her high buttoned boots, leaning her elbows on the balustrade while she smoked, writing of aviation and the eulogies of Carducci: Lina, ineffably, was Lina.

The man who had been Sibilla's lover for eight years looked on as their free union began to dissolve. He was dignified and modern, a man of the new century: when Sibilla left, he let her go. She went with Lina to a villa by the sea where they threw open the windows and closed the doors, foregoing breakfast because there were so many poems and hollows of the body. The man who had been Sibilla's lover faded into a distinguished outline.

Sappho writes in Fragment 31 of the triangulations of lovers. The lover sits and watches while the beloved turns her rapturous smile to someone else; now the new favourite moves close enough to touch her. *All is to be dared*, Sappho writes; then the poem breaks off.

WILLIAM SEYMOUR, 1875

William Seymour was a cabman whose only flaw was a rheumatic knee. He was congenial, clean-shaven, and an asset to the streets of London and Liverpool, where lady bicyclists were often imperilled by rash hansom drivers and runaway horses. Moreover Bill Seymour had a sweet wife who brought his dinner to the cab stand and rubbed his rheumatic knee. In 1875 he was accused of daring to steal two pieces of meat from a butcher's shop in Liverpool, which as an honest man he denied.

When brought to trial, William Seymour was accused of crimes beyond the theft of meat: he was found to be one Margaret Honeywell, who, having been married off at fourteen, had brazenly left her husband, dared to run away to London, and conspired to earn her living independently as a cabman. In other words William Seymour threw into question what was a woman like any other.

SIBILLA ALERAMO, *A PROPOSITO DI UNA VOTAZIONE*

Lina could translate Sappho without a dictionary, but she could not attend the meetings of the Philological Society of the university of Milano, because the philologists had voted not to admit women. Anna Kuliscioff, who had lectured the Society with such furious asperity in 1890 on the monopoly of men, said that the philologists had badly confused the transitive and existential modes of the verb 'admit'. Lina Poletti said that if the philologists of Milano looked at her and saw only a woman, they could go hang themselves. Moreover, Lina could not resist adding, did they not know Pollux the lexicographer, who praised Sappho as the most marvellous chiseller of words from the raw stuff of Aeolian dialect?

Sibilla did not much care for philology, but she could tell a monopoly of men when she saw one. She devoted her next article to explaining that as long as men were the only ones voting, frankly the proper term was not 'democracy' but 'tyranny'. In the margins of Sibilla's article, Lina wrote, *N.b.*, from the Greek *τύραννος*, cf. Aristotle, *Pol. 5.11*; Thucydides, *Hist. 1.13*. Lina Poletti liked to have the last word.

ARTICLE 544

The philologists were mulish and exasperating, but Article 544 of the Italian Penal Code would lead you straight down to laudanum. Article 544 would not be repealed until 1981; Sibilla did not live to see its death. It was a law about the verb *impadronirsi*, which binds together so many forms of power that it is difficult to translate. *Impadronirsi* means to become the patron and possessor, the proprietor and the patriarch; to conquer, to overmaster, to take charge, to gain ownership; to act with the impunity of a father who, according to Article 544, may expunge the crime of the rape of his daughter by marrying her off to the man who has raped her, without a dowry. This is called a 'marriage of reparation', because it satisfies both men involved.

In *Una donna*, Sibilla Aleramo recounts how the man who has raped the young woman tries subsequently to caress her, to flatter her, to put his mouth over hers so that no interrogation or protest can escape from her lips. He declares pompously that nothing can compensate her for the gift she has given him, and at that very moment, *tentava impadronirsi di nuova della mia persona*, she writes, he attempted once again to become the patron and the possessor and the proprietor and the patriarch of my person. That is, while he was thanking her for having been raped by him, he tried to rape her again. It was some months later that Sibilla Aleramo's father, in accordance with Article 544, gave her to that man in marriage.

SAPPHO, FRAGMENT 16

Whenever we could leave these marriages, we fled. Those of us who had nothing in our pockets but our own badly stitched handkerchiefs scraped together what we could. Some of us gave piano lessons on dull afternoons and others dusted the parlours of ladies until we could buy our passage. There were those like William Seymour, industrious lads in the trousers of their brothers, and there were those who might have idled their lives away on estates had they wished. But none of us wished to live overmastered. Always, however we left the verb *impadronirsi*, we went with no return: thus we embarked, each in her own way, on the voyage out.

We arrived in unknown cities, in the ports of southern islands, at the houses of anyone appearing to be a sister. We shuddered and threw off our names. We began to find each other, slowly at first because we were so new. You would see someone in the street, someone like X, and wonder and know at the same time. Or there would be a glance like R's, wondering and knowing, rising to meet you on the balcony where you were standing because it was the farthest limit of your father's house. Then we would write our first uncertain letters to each other, hesitant to ask, to tell, with what words, stretched over silences; we took a little false courage in seeing our lines torn and gasping on the page like Sappho's: *to pray for a share/...towards/...out of the unexpected.* Afterwards we sat very still waiting for a response, hoping for a correspondence of fragments.

FIVE

THE LANTERN BEARER, 1899

In slivers and starts the lantern shone out and then faltered. It was evening in the English garden, it was summer in late childhood; the lantern bearer came third in a procession of excitable siblings all hushing each other across the tennis lawn. The eldest brother held the glass jar and explained the system while the youngest brother wandered off towards the pond. It was in the hands of the lantern bearer to illuminate what it all meant.

Twice the wick went out, but the lantern bearer persevered. She was seventeen and accustomed to the caprices of bicycle lamps. At last her moment arrived; she raised the lantern to search out every shadowed crevice of the tree; the light caught triumphantly upon two night-moths, drunk on the rum and black treacle smeared on the tree trunk. A cheer went up, the glass jar went down, a vague tipsy flutter was offered in protest by the Yellow Underwings, and the episode concluded.

Very late that night the bicycle lamp could be seen flickering through the window of Miss Adeline Virginia

Stephen, who was writing the episode into her journal, for as she noted with satisfaction, the lantern bearer was none other than the present writer.

LESLIE STEPHEN, *DICTIONARY OF NATIONAL BIOGRAPHY*, VOL. I, 1882

The year when Virginia Stephen was born also marked the birth of her father's *Dictionary of National Biography*. He edited every article in the first twenty-six volumes and wrote hundreds of lives of notable British men, complaining of violent headaches for the entire nine years thereby consumed. For in fact the National Biography of England could not be cured with a mere ammoniated tincture of quinine drops.

The notable deceased men of England and its colonies marched onwards after Leslie Stephen resigned as editor. They were innumerable, insatiable in the service of empire; their ghosts whined for glory. The *Dictionary of National Biography* trudged on until it reached sixty-three volumes, and the century was finished.

VIRGINIA, 1895

Leslie Stephen's study was at the top of the house, over all of the rooms of women and children. One floor down in the night nursery, a fire burnt through long winter evenings; Virginia watched the nervous, flighty shadows flung on the walls. As the firelight came in flickers and glimpses, her thoughts flared and fell into a charred confusion. Voices were coming and going like shadows, muttering at her, leering, crackling, casting themselves at the windows. She could hear them mouthing burnt words at her. There were evenings in the night nursery when these voices came on viciously. There were nightmares.

CASSANDRA, 1895

Nightmares are the visits of what has come before you undead. They claw into the seam that should sew up your life. They hiss the ancient fates that will have undone you in your very bed, how you could not move while the whole city was falling around you in blood and firelight. The entrails of birds will lie on the stones of your dreams, making signs.

It is the task of sibyls and prophetesses to host these visits. But Cassandra was a prophetess who did not hold her nightmares on her tongue. One poet says of Cassandra that when she stood up to prophesy she shone like a lamp in a bomb shelter.

In fact we observed that Cassandra shone like a lantern bearer, like someone who had lived our lives before. She had seen all of the ashes we might be burnt down to and she had heard all of the jeering at her madness. What then were the nightmares of 1895 to Cassandra?

What Cassandra knows, Virginia wrote much later, is that Virginia Stephen was not born on the 25th January 1882, but was born many thousands of years ago; and had from the very first to encounter instincts already acquired by thousands of ancestresses in the past. We took this to mean that both nightmares and sibyls have many lives.

LAURA STEPHEN, 1893

Laura Stephen, half-sister to Virginia, was called myriad names. Her father deemed her fiendish, wicked, perverse, dreadfully passionate, extremely disturbing and extremely pathetic. She stammered and shrieked at a pitch that penetrated the upper floors of the house at Hyde Park Gate. To Virginia she was a vacant-eyed girl who could hardly read.

At first Laura was put in a device called a Rational Corset. This did nothing, and by 1893 she was put away into an asylum in Redhill. For the rest of her life she was kept in institutions, babbling to herself. One of the Stephens reported back to the others in 1921 that Laura was still jabbering constant nonsense; the only intelligible phrase she uttered was, I told him to go away.

FLORENCE NIGHTINGALE, *CASSANDRA*, 1860

By the time the nurse Florence Nightingale was ready to pronounce her thoughts on the fate of Victorian women of the upper classes, her pet owl Athena had died. Florence had grown used to having little Athena in her pocket, a steadfast companion who observed everything sagely. Athena observed that Florence's parents willed her a wife and a mother. But their wilful, dreadfully passionate daughter embarked on her own career, alone except for Athena.

In 1860 Florence Nightingale published *Cassandra*, an account of what drove young women mad in Victorian families of a certain class. It was not their fragility, it was not their caprices. It was not that they lacked doting mamas or proper chaperonage or private lessons. It was what they were willed into, Florence wrote, that gave them nervous disorders. They stammered and screamed because there was no language in their own language for what they knew.

Florence Nightingale published her *Cassandra* solely in private editions. In 1860 it was dangerous to speak too openly of these things, and there were no goddesses or familiars left to protect her.

VIRGINIA STEPHEN, *LOGICK: OR, THE RIGHT USE OF REASON WITH A VARIETY OF RULES TO GUARD AGAINST ERROR IN THE AFFAIRS OF RELIGION AND HUMAN LIFE AS WELL AS IN THE SCIENCES, BY ISAAC WATTS D. D.*, 1899

Without reverence for the late Mr Watts or the sanctity of his philosophy of *LOGICK*, Virginia Stephen replaced the pages of the entire volume, acquired second-hand for thruppence, with those of her own journal. Thus in 1899 *LOGICK* was upended by the thoughts of a girl of seventeen, who gained for her musings a handsome, solid binding in tooled calfskin.

Many of us had desecrated our schoolbooks with scribbles and sketches, but until Virginia we had not conceived of such a breathtaking subversion of non-fiction. Moreover we admired the practicality of her art: with paper, leather, and glue, she had converted the stolid Rules of Mr Watts into her own private memoirs.

SAPPHO, FRAGMENT 133

For classical Greek poets, it is a rare thing to address oneself as another. In fact perhaps the only surviving instance is Sappho, who apostrophizes herself in Fragment 133. She says her own name in the vocative, which is the case of calling upon someone directly. For this reason the vocative is sometimes translated as O….!, followed by the name of the invoked.

But Sappho does not exclaim herself. She does not lecture, incite, curse, implore, or harangue her own person. Instead, like Virginia Stephen writing the earliest pages of her journals, she enquires. She wonders of herself, without yet knowing the answers; she delves and reflects from line to line. The light is always changing on the page, on the sea, on the thought as it comes arrowing from a mind strung taut: *Sappho, why?*

VIRGINIA, 1903

In 1897 Virginia began to study Greek at the Ladies' Department of Kings College. Verb by verb she went on, until in 1903 she was reading Euripides and Aeschylus and finding them beautiful. She waxed rhapsodic with her Greek tutor Miss Case about the way a girl perched on a branch in the orchard, aloft in the primaveral air. How poetically the Greeks could hang a maiden on a branch, ripe for the plucking! But Miss Case did not permit rhapsodies without grammar; if one wanted to read the Greeks like the boys of Cambridge, one could not be caught up in mere literary value. Instead, Miss Case said, let us note a very rare sort of genitive in the third line.

MISS CASE, 1903

A very rare sort of woman, Miss Case had been among the first to graduate from Girton College, itself the first college for women at Cambridge. In university dramas she took the role of Athena: she was wise in matters of translation and the rights of women. Sometimes Virginia Stephen wished that she could keep Miss Case in her pocket, to consult in moments of need.

In 1897, while the men of the Cambridge Senate were debating whether women should be allowed to take full degrees, ominous crowds of male students gathered. Upon the announcement that women were not fit for higher forms of education, the crowds roared their victory; bonfires were lit, fireworks shot up, banners were hoisted. Just across from the University Church, the boys of Cambridge thrust out of a window the dangling effigy of a Girton Girl astride her bicycle. How politically the boys of Cambridge could hang a maiden on a pole, ripe for the decapitating and incineration! Here Miss Case noted the extremely common use, or overuse, of the genitive of possession.

VIRGINIA STEPHEN, *THE SERPENTINE*, 1903

Virginia's eldest brother had become one of the boys at Cambridge, and she showed off her verbs to him. In return he brought other boys of Cambridge trooping into the drawing room of their house on Gordon Square, where they stayed until all hours talking of truth and tragic form. Occasionally Virginia would interject, perhaps something had struck her in the papers, for example the body of a woman had been found in the Serpentine, not an unusual occurrence, but in this case the note pinned to her inner pocket stopped one's heart, it was her whole life sketched in two or three lines now blurred by water: No father, no mother, no work. May God forgive me for what I have done tonight.

This was the nature of Greek tragedy as we moderns must understand it, Virginia said. How an Englishwoman of forty-five years could write the truth of her life and then end it; that the volume of her existence was uncontainable by any edition of the *Dictionary of National Biography* thus far conceived by mankind; and what filament inside her had finally dimmed and faltered into darkness on that day, in that hour, when she went down to the Serpentine with death in her pocket: *Sappho, why?*

VIRGINIA STEPHEN, *REVIEW OF THE FEMININE NOTE IN FICTION*, 1905

The Serpentine, an essay on the death note of the drowned Englishwoman, remained privately pasted into Virginia's journal of 1903. But in 1905 Virginia Stephen began publishing her thoughts and compelling newspapers to send her cheques of £5 or more for them.

On her birthday in 1905 her review of *The Feminine Note*

in Fiction came into the world. Unsurprisingly, the book of that title had been written by a man; just as expectably, that man asserted that as more and more novels are written by women for women, they increasingly cause the novel as a work of art to disappear. Furthermore, the man went on, the feminine note when sounded in fiction is a tinny squeak; women get mired in shrill details and have no sense of the great sweeping vistas of art.

Those of us who read the English papers in January 1905 were treated to the extraordinary spectacle of Virginia Stephen raising her eyebrows in print. For here we could see a sceptical black-and-white furrowing on the page, a wrinkling of words as she gathered her incredulous ironic wit. She assembled her thoughts; she marshalled her citations; she reviewed *The Feminine Note in Fiction* like a lieutenant reviewing the shoddy shambling march of a slothful regiment. Given that women have scarcely been granted a score of minutes to write fiction in the centuries since Shakespeare flourished, Virginia Stephen demanded, is it not too soon after all to criticize the 'feminine note' in anything? And will not the adequate critic of women be a woman?

We cheered her on as she demolished *The Feminine Note in Fiction.* If there were faults with women writers, Virginia pointed out, these merely demonstrated the dire need to educate girls as rigorously as the boys of Cambridge; if our novels were to be judged, let the critics wait a century before pouncing. Lastly, as proof that women writers might range freely from poignant details to the vastness of truth and tragic form, Virginia offered the indisputable example of Sappho.

SAPPHO, FRAGMENT 96

In the summer of 1905 Virginia Stephen went to the seashore to rest from her defence of women in fiction. It was a great relief to leave London, with its literary critics and constant threats to the lives of lady bicyclists, and to arrive in a world where nothing was happening except the light on the water.

Virginia arose to a view of boats settled on the bay like gulls with their wings tucked. All morning she turned her pages to face the land around her: how the fishing boats skidded on the froth of waves, how there was a hush before the rains while the light hollowed and dimmed. Virginia sketched what she could in words, inexact perhaps, impressions rather than essays, but attempting always to limn that moment, as Sappho writes, when the *light/stretches over salt sea/equally and flowerdeep fields.*

SIX

ROMAINE BROOKS, *L'AMAZONE*

Romaine Brooks spent her youth in Rome learning to paint sharp grey forms like her own body. She did not see why the class on drawing nudes from life should be filled with only young men: she had charcoal and a steady hand. Therefore she enrolled and ignored everyone but the model. She could not prevent her classmates from remarking aloud on her person, how odd and lanky she was, but she began to wear a top hat that shadowed her eyes. At the Scuola Nazionale d'Arte she got high marks in silhouettes, live nudes, and the first year of poetic metre. After the first year, they stopped reading Sappho and Romaine Brooks failed literature.

Natalie Barney spent her youth in Paris, where her mother was learning to paint. Left to herself, Natalie did what she liked, namely writing poems and meeting girls. One summer she met Eva Palmer, whose long red hair was like a poem Natalie Barney wanted to write: it fell down to her ankles and hung there irresistibly. In the woods they took off their clothes to read Sappho, declined nouns naked in the leaves. They lived together in a vermilion cloud in Paris until Eva went off to Greece and married someone.

It wasn't until the war that Natalie Barney met Romaine Brooks, who painted all in shades of dove and steel. Natalie thought Romaine could be trusted, more or less, to stay in places like Paris where the light was constant and muted. Romaine glanced coolly at Natalie and began to paint her grey before a window, wintry, wrapped in a fur. On the desk at Natalie's elbow was a small jade statue of a horse, prancing over the pile of Natalie's poems. Romaine titled the portrait *The Amazon*. Then she left Paris for the ochre and azure of the south.

PAULINE TARN, B. 1877

Violently Pauline Tarn had extinguished her name. Plain, practical Pauline, and flat yawing Tarn: she burnt them up in the piercing blue fire of her repulsion and then left swiftly for Paris. Her new name would be inky and enigmatic, she vowed, she would make poems like night-blooming violets and emblazon her new name above them. There would be no more Pauline who ate supper, no more Miss Tarn who darned stockings. Instead she would consume nothing but the evening air and stitch together only ragged fragments of verses. She took a room on the rue Crevaux and acquired Ragon's *Grammaire grecque*, bound in elegant green leather. Soon she was piecing together phrases from the Aeolian. By 1899, she was reclining on one elbow in a black frock coat and broadcloth breeches, reading Sappho. In the lamplight she looked like a sleek, dark line. She had become Renée Vivien.

RENÉE VIVIEN, 1899

Renée Vivien barely had a youth. What few years she had were in Paris writing poems and studying Greek. She wouldn't eat, she wouldn't sleep, she wouldn't go out in the daytime. She would only translate Sappho into French. One evening in the autumn of 1899 when the horse chestnut trees were bare of leaves, somewhere between Fragments 24a and 31, she met Natalie Barney.

SAPPHO, FRAGMENT 24A

You will remember, Sappho writes, *for we in our youth/did these things/yes many and beautiful things.* It is true that in the velvety bloom of our youth we met Natalie Barney. But Natalie Barney met everyone who caught her eye. She went riding in the Bois de Boulogne in the mornings, wrote steadily all afternoon by the window, and then settled in her salon to receive us, first in Neuilly with Eva Palmer gracious by her side, and later at 20 rue Jacob, which was famous for Natalie alone.

During the reign of Natalie, we believed that every woman in Paris paid her tribute. In fact our idea of everyone was equal to the number of women it took to fill her house. Only later did we discover women in Paris who were not subjects of Natalie, women who were empresses of their own nightclubs or lived in run-down *quartiers*, fomenting revolution.

But at that time it seemed to us that everyone came to Natalie's: some reading poetry in the salon, some dancing in the back garden, all of us surging in around Natalie wherever she sat princely and pleased. She had taken the ordinary walls of a house with unremarkable elms round it and made them ancient, celestial, sibylline. As the dancer Liane de Pougy was fond of saying in those days, Natalie was an *idylle saphique*.

Thus we in our youth remembered Sappho writing that we would remember. And thus, yes many and beautiful things.

LIANE DE POUGY, 1899

Liane was a dancer at the Folies Bergère and could never sit still in an idyll. At first, dancing the cancan at the Bal Bullier, Liane had whirled past Natalie without a glance. But once Natalie had determined you were worth meeting she would meet you, even if it took all month and astronomical amounts of flowers. She got herself a page outfit made in almond-coloured velvet and fell to one knee in Liane's drawing room. Shortly thereafter in a burst of hothouse lilies commenced the *idylle saphique* of Natalie and Liane.

LIANE DE POUGY, *IDYLLE SAPHIQUE*, 1901

People said that Liane de Pougy hadn't written *Sapphic Idyll* herself. They called Liane a coquette of the most vulgar order, one of *les grands horizontales* who made her way through the world in the arms of others. She might well have been Natalie Barney's lover, they granted her that, but she could not have written her own book.

However, in our eyes no one had written any of this

herself. We were grasping each other by the wrists in a circle. Without Natalie, Liane might never have known she was one of us. Without Eva Palmer, Natalie might never have read Sappho. Without Sappho, Pauline Tarn might have mildewed in London darning the heels of sensible stockings. Instead, here was Renée Vivien, a wraith of incense and violets, translating Sappho into French until dawn. Here was Liane clasping our hands and whirling us round the garden, resplendent, barefoot, laughing.

We gathered around Natalie and gleaned what we needed. She had made a haven from fragments, a garden where sunlight could set the leaves quivering. Thus we thought it fitting and right that in the middle of Liane de Pougy's *Idylle saphique* was a chapter by Natalie Barney. In the middle of Natalie Barney, guarded by Doric columns and garlanded by us, was Sappho.

AUREL, *COMMENT LES FEMMES DEVIENNENT ÉCRIVAINS*

Aurel, like Sappho, had just one name. When Aurel was writing *How Women Become Writers*, she refused to attach to her writing Aurélie, Octavie, Gabrielle, Antoinette, or any of the many other decorative names she had been given. There had been quite enough of women being given, she thought. It was time for women to write into being what they wanted to become.

SIBILLA ALERAMO, *LA PENSIEROSA*, 1907

Reading Aurel, Sibilla Aleramo felt a chorus of voices rising in the air. How did women become writers? There seemed so many answers; each voice would tell its own. Translating Aurel for an Italian literary magazine made phrases fly around in Sibilla's head like birds in a room. Aurel hoped that women writers would disobey the laws that bound men's books. It was time for women to take language for themselves, Aurel said, even one word at a time, to take their own names and become. To become even one word.

By now in Sibilla's room in Rome there was a darting and soaring of voices: how to translate Aurel saying that the intimate letters and journals of women formed their own verbal sensibility, how to translate Renée Vivien invoking the isle of Lesbos in kletic verse: *rends-nous notre* âme *antique*. Years ago the soul was exiled from us? Ours is the isle where once we dwelled? We call out, we are waiting?

Sibilla could not read Greek, but she could translate Renée Vivien's poem *Retour* à *Mytilène* from French into Italian. After Aurel and Renée Vivien, Sibilla went on to translate Colette, Anna de Noailles, and Gérard d'Houville who refused to be called Marie. Sibilla let their voices wing their way through hers, intertwine with hers, rise up on her tongue; they formed a dialogue, to which she gave the title *La pensierosa*, meaning *The Woman Thinking*. Thus Lina, who in 1907 read everything written by Sibilla Aleramo, learned that despite the great distances between women thinking, we might still enter into intimate correspondence.

NATALIE BARNEY, *LETTRES À UNE CONNUE*

In our sapphic idylls we wrote volumes of amorous letters. Even after the idylls ended, we did not sever our communications with each other, but merely changed the key of our intimacy. A friend, a companion, a beloved: for us the tones of amity were many and mutable. For example, after the idyll of Natalie Barney and Liane de Pougy ended, Liane published her *Idylle saphique* and Natalie, by way of reply, wrote a novel made of letters to Liane. She called it *Lettres à une connue*, or *Letters to A Woman I Know.*

Straightaway the same people who said that Liane could not really have written a book said that Natalie's letters were not really a novel. Most of us would have let those words scratch our hearts. But Natalie was so placid and self-assured, as Radclyffe Hall said later, that everyone felt very normal and brave just to gather around her.

In fact Natalie in her salon would exclaim, *Epistolary* novel!, and shout with laughter. She wanted to hear our voices rising around her in unscratched mirth. It was her habit to find the timid and unknown ones, *les inconnues*, and to make of each of them *une connue*. Everyone who went to Natalie's came to be known. She urged us to be unrepentant in our letters, to announce our new names at the door. We had hopes of becoming in all our forms and genres.

LÉO TAXIL, *LA CORRUPTION FIN-DE-SIÈCLE*, 1894

Just after the chapter *Le sadisme* came *Le saphisme;* Léo Taxil thought of us as painful and scandalous, but alphabetical.

In that chapter were described veritable lesbian academies where, Léo Taxil claimed, the Sapphists communally delivered themselves to unnamable orgies. Had there in fact been a Lesbian Academy of any accreditation, we would have valiantly undertaken the curriculum. But Léo Taxil overestimated us. In truth many of us were still struggling with the genitive of possession and Eva Palmer, who could have helped us, had gone off to Greece in 1906 and married someone. Now she was Eva Palmer Sikelianos and wafted around Athens in hand-spun tunics, her flame-coloured hair trailing in the dust.

Léo Taxil, like Guglielmo Cantarano and Cesare Lombroso before him, fancied himself a criminologist. This meant he was uncommonly interested in what women did when unwatched by men. They all wanted to observe, for strictly moral and scientific reasons, exactly what happened on the couches of our carriages, within our back gardens, and in our undergarments. We were deemed notably corrupt specimens of the *fin-de-siècle,* Chapter III, Section 2.

For hundreds of pages Léo Taxil went on about brothels, sadists, *cabotines*, bad mothers, madames, and the salacious turpitude that was allegedly us. The number of women presently in Paris who were taken by other women, Léo Taxil concluded in 1894, was scientifically incalculable. He related as evidence the words of a lesser official of the Préfecture: It was dispiriting, yes, but legally nothing could be done; the crime of Sapphism had not been foreseen by the Napoleonic Civil Code.

As Natalie Barney remarked drily one evening in 1913,

Maybe Napoleon should have asked the Sibyl, *n'est-ce pas*, Sibilla? From the settee where she was reclining, Sibilla Aleramo gave Natalie Barney an enigmatic smile.

SIBILLA ALERAMO, *IL SALOTTO DI UN'AMAZZONE*

For the rest of her life Sibilla Aleramo remembered the Salon of the Amazon at 20 rue Jacob: yes many and beautiful things. In 1913 Sibilla had come to stay in Paris with Aurel who was like a sister to her, and she stayed on for half a year, there were so many women to meet. It seemed that Natalie Barney knew everyone, and in her garden there was an actual temple, modest enough but with four Doric columns supporting the inscription 'à l'amitié'; in its interior, a bust of Sappho kept watch over the private suppers Natalie held by firelight.

Natalie invited Sibilla to everything in that half-year, and so she met nearly all of us. It was in that time, in glimpses and shards, that we first learned of Lina Poletti. Perhaps it was the legend of her molten eyes or the intimacy of firelight, but we felt that even a little knowledge of Lina Poletti might melt us, achingly, and forge us anew, steely and bright in form.

RENÉE VIVIEN, *SAPHO: TRADUCTION NOUVELLE AVEC LE TEXTE GREC*, 1903

Although Renée Vivien set out to translate Sappho with the utmost accuracy, there was always something left out. Renée lit candles, burned incense, washed her mouth out with perfumed water. All night she stayed up pleading with spirits that only she could see, but she could not bring Sappho exactly into the world. For her Sappho was *La Tisseuse de violettes*, the weaver of violets; there was no way for Renée to translate the impossibly delicate phrases without crushing them bruised in her hands. Often Renée looked at the bones of her hands with great repulsion. She began to wear bangles around her wrists to ward off the sound of her mind making the wrong words.

In 1904 Natalie Barney took Renée to the island of Lesbos. For a few sunny months in Mytilene they gazed at the perfect blue of the sea and spoke of nothing but founding together there a school, a salon, a retreat, a temple to the intimacy of women, at last, the *Retour à Mytilène*. Renée felt herself floating in kletic time, swam in the calm Aegean mornings, promised to take less chloral. She could wear rough linen trousers and write her visions untroubled, like an ascetic or an oracle. To return to Mytilene was to go down to the very bone. Once the flesh was sheared away, the lines cleaved truly unto Sappho.

But at the end of the summer when Natalie took her back to Paris, Renée nailed her windows shut against the muted grey sky. She could not bear the return to a place that was not Mytilene.

RENÉ

The year before the summer on Lesbos, Renée had tried to write a book called *Une femme m'apparut*, or *A Woman*

Appeared to Me, about her love for Natalie Barney. Two years before that, Natalie Barney had written a book called *Cinq petits dialogues grecs*, or *Five Small Greek Dialogues*, about her love for Renée Vivien. They were never not writing within a handbreadth of each other. In their intimate correspondence were long letters, poems fondly dedicated, unfinished drafts. *Une femme m'apparut* was an unfinished draft for a long time because while Renée could write a great deal about apparitions, we could see that the flesh of women was difficult for her.

In fact Renée could not finish a poem without slicing down to its blank, ancient bones. Only the changing of her name calmed her; thus she had signed her earliest poems as René. It was a great relief, she explained to us, to see that shorn, clean, masculine form of her name at the top of the page, sheltering the alexandrines from harm. Did we not feel the sloppy, pendulous weight of an extra *e*?

On the whole we did not. But we were reminded of the character San Giovanni in Renée's first draft of *Une femme m'apparut*: androgynous, aloof, terribly pure, a sapphic poet. In that early draft San Giovanni is everywhere, exalting the ecstasies of sapphism. But in the second draft, written after Renée returned from Lesbos, the voice of San Giovanni has been pared to almost nothing, a bare line here or there. We wondered how much could be cut away before Renée disappeared.

TRYPHÉ

At that time there was the *poste pneumatique* of Paris; we could send love notes all afternoon through special tubes that spanned the arrondissements. These pneumatic notes were called *petits bleus* after the colour of the capsules they were sent in. But they also suggested *l'heure bleue*, that lost hour of twilight when the sun has already gone but the sky is still elusively, airily blue. To Natalie that blue was voluptuous and alluring, the skin of the sky stretched bare before her. To Renée *l'heure bleue* was not blue at all: it was the sky stained and sinking into darkness. It was the world always trying to tear her into two thin strips. It was the wrong century. It was the waking of night, the eating of air, the blurring of chloral.

When Natalie Barney wrote *Cinq petits dialogues grecs* about Renée Vivien in 1901, she published it under the name Tryphé. In Greek, *tryphé* indicates a magnificent, almost royal voluptuousness, a great and extravagant love of bodies stretched bare before you, a pleasure in the soft air on your own skin. Natalie Barney was exactly like that. But Renée Vivien, whose name meant something like 'she who is born again and lives', was not. In fact Renée did not live long after that summer on Lesbos. She wrote a poem called *La mort de Psappha*, or *The Death of Sappho*, and began sinking into her darkness. One morning in the autumn of 1909 when the horse chestnuts were bare of leaves, she left her brittle, slight body. At last, Natalie said, Renée Vivien had returned to Mytilene. Every week we brought flowers to her grave in Passy, always violets.

SEVEN

SIBILLA ALERAMO, *APOLOGIA DELLO SPIRITO FEMMINILE*

We were not always able to find each other in time, or in body. By the time Sibilla Aleramo came to Paris in 1913, all she could know of Renée Vivien were the wraiths of words on a page, the numinous spirit that lingered like incense in the Temple à l'amitié. We gave Sibilla what we could of the life of Renée Vivien; we took her to the grave in Passy to lay her posy of violets.

In return, over the course of many evenings, Sibilla told us the story of Lina Poletti. In truth she told us many stories: Lina was molten in form. Like Renée, Lina was a poet in one sleek dark line; like René, she was bold and restless in her high buttoned boots. In Sibilla's stories we saw Lina with her green leather grammar, dreaming of *beudos*, and we heard Lina tell her mother that she would sooner burn the house down than sew her trousseau. Embroidery is nothing, Lina said impatiently, whereas in Greek there is an entire genitive for remembering!

In the house of Lina Poletti this argument was an affront

to femininity. But in those days Sibilla Aleramo believed that women should become poets rather than the seamstresses of their own enslavement, and thus she wrote an article called *Defence of the Spirit of Women.* She dedicated it to Renée Vivien, the San Giovanni of sapphic verse.

LINA AND SIBILLA, 1908

Lina, Sibilla told us, spoke in a low voice and was difficult to explain in words. Moreover, when Lina desired someone, she would often change her name. Ardent, mysterious letters would arrive to you from whoever Lina was, Sibilla said, and you simply had to know. Or you guessed, because it could not have been anyone else. The letters were like hushed breaths on the back of your neck: you wanted to turn around and embrace them, but you also wanted to wait, feeling them arrive one after the other, steady and thrilling.

In 1908, Sibilla felt herself lapped by the warmth of Lina: how constant the succession of letters, how buoyant and amorous their tone. But in 1909 Sibilla sensed that the violent, luminous wave of Lina had crested and rolled back from her. Finally Lina sent a few lines: she was working on a new play. She needed time to think about dramatic action. She was interested in actresses.

TRISTANO SOMNIANS, 1909

It was in 1909 that a certain Tristano Somnians entered into correspondence with a number of actresses, among them the celebrated Eleonora Duse. Tristano, any actress would have known, was the name of the young hero who twines his arms around his beloved like the tightening of a honeysuckle vine in a hazelnut tree. And Somnians means that he is dreaming of her with a half-smile.

To Lina Poletti, actresses were like verbs as yet unconjugated: they contained in themselves the heady potential for any deed, any command, any future. It was by their brave hands that an object would bear its action. What heroic young poet would not linger at the stage door, dreaming of actresses?

ELEONORA DUSE, B. 1858

All through the century of Eleonora Duse's birth, Ibsen noted, every actress in Scandinavia fainted on the same side of the stage every time. If there was a dramatic moment, the handkerchief went to the left hand, the actress went to stage left, and then there was a fainting.

But in Italy, actresses were unpredictable. If they felt the fainting come over them, a wavering took them wherever they stood, and when they sank to the floorboards, tiny cruel splinters went into their palms. Everyone in Eleonora Duse's family was in the theatre. In fact her mother Angelica, seized by labour pangs as the troupe travelled from Venezia to Vigevano, had almost fainted on the train.

Eleonora was barely born in Vigevano, in the middle of the night. She began acting at four years old. Her mother told her, It doesn't matter where you faint, stage left or stage right, but put the handkerchief in the hand you will fall on, to blunt the splinters.

GIACINTA PEZZANA, *MADAME RAQUIN*, 1879

In Napoli the houses were stacked up on stairways that ran with foul water, stray cats, the trimmings of fish and vegetables. Children were called *e' criature*. Everything ran downhill together to the sea, all creatures commingling bones and fur and scales. At least when the alleys reached the sea, *e' criature* could see the sky.

In Napoli Eleonora Duse joined the company at Teatro dei Fiorentini, whose prima donna was the spirited actress Giacinta Pezzana. Eleonora, just twenty-one, was now motherless and given to weeping abruptly. Her father chided her for the bouts of raw nerves. He insisted that here no one could have *la smara*, a dark mood that Venetians got from the chilled fog of the lagoon, because there was no word for it in the dialect of Napoli.

Onstage with the young Eleonora, Giacinta Pezzana began to take on the roles of mothers and aunts. Eleonora was still technically a *seconda donna*, not yet a leading lady, but Giacinta pulled her into the light and stroked her dark hair smooth. In the autumn of 1879, while Eleonora was Thérèse Raquin embracing her aunt Madame Raquin in the second act, Giacinta felt the heavy new roundness of Eleonora's belly under her gown. Neither actress broke character, but both knew: a *criatur'*.

NENNELLA, 1879

The writer Matilde Serao, born in Patras and raised in Napoli, was full of love for any creature that suffered. She would stop well-to-do citizens in the street and berate them about foundling houses. She had opinions about foul water, dank warrens of alleys, and the dubious morals of amorous bachelors. As soon as Matilde Serao met Eleonora Duse, she loved her for the rest of her life. As Matilde often said, If I were a man, there would be no end to it.

Fondly Matilde called Eleonora *Nennella*, which means 'little baby' in the dialect of Napoli. The other person who called Eleonora *Nennella* was the man who had got her pregnant and then refused ever to see her again.

Under Italian law, a woman had no right to ask anything of the man who had impregnated her. A young actress with the barest scrapings of money, her nerves raw and strained, Eleonora prepared to give her baby up to the foundling house.

SS. ANNUNZIATA

In Napoli the saint of *criature* denied by their fathers was SS. Annunziata, for whom the foundling house was named. In the wall of the foundling house a wheel was fixed; it turned only one way. An illegitimate child placed on the wheel was thus turned irrevocably into an orphan.

The mothers who gave up their babies to SS. Annunziata were called unnatural whores with false hearts and painted faces; the fathers were not called anything, because Italian law made no provision for paternity claims. The orphans were called 'children of the Madonna', and half of them died within a year.

ARTICLES 340 AND 341

In France, important men demanded a law to prevent lower-class women, laundresses or actresses or whomever else they had got pregnant, from hounding them endlessly with pleas and tears. What if conniving women, with their false hearts and hungry infants, attempted to insert their bastards into the legitimate French family? Furthermore, the important men cautioned, all of those women who had got themselves pregnant would come crying to married men for money to feed the child, and this was a shame, a crime, a blot on the Napoleonic Civil Code. In 1804 the men passed Article 340, which strictly forbade paternity claims. All children were fatherless at birth, they reasoned, a father is fashioned only by marriage: *pater is est quem nuptiae demonstrant.*

Directly thereafter the men passed Article 341, which stipulated that maternity claims on the other hand were well within the purview of French law. A woman should be held responsible for her immoral carnal conduct, the men said, and such a law would give her pause before she slipped fickle into bed with whomever she pleased. Thereafter an important man need not attend the birth of his illegitimate child, as Article 341 would preside vigilantly in his stead.

ELEONORA DUSE, 1880

Giacinta helped Eleonora conceal her pregnancy onstage until the ninth month, and then Matilde found Eleonora a midwife far out in the countryside where she could go nameless. When the little baby was born, Eleonora sent a photograph to the man who had got her pregnant, her face radiant and drained, the creature weak in her arms. The man received the photograph, wrote one word across it, and sent it back. The word was *commediante,* meaning, you are an actress, no one will believe you.

The little baby died after a few days and Eleonora, who needed money, went back to the theatre in Napoli. She was given to weeping and bouts of raw nerves, but people said actresses were always so emotional; you could hardly believe their tears. Indignantly Matilde Serao retorted that you could have *la smara* even in the brightest blue curve of the sky over Napoli.

ELEONORA DUSE, NORA IN *NORA*, 1891

Eleonora Duse never met Laura Kieler, the woman whose life Ibsen took for his character Nora. But in 1891, when *A Doll's House* premiered in Milano, Eleonora put her own life into Nora's with such force that the keys around her neck jangled violently. Eleanora knew what it was to close the door on a man who doubted that you were fully a person. She was thirty-two and would never be anyone's *Nennella* again. Now she told younger actresses, Our lives are full of tiny cruel splinters, there is nothing that will blunt the fall.

Eleonora Duse never called a play by its title. To her, a play was the woman she would be in it. As soon as rehearsals began, Eleonora condensed herself to make room for the woman who would come over her. She would pile up her hair, clot her own feelings into a side chamber of her heart: anything to make more space for her protagonist to possess. She would shorten her own name. Thus on that wintry evening in 1891 at the Teatro Filodrammatici of Milano, she was Nora who was Nora in *Nora*.

SIBILLA ALERAMO AND GIACINTA PEZZANA, *NORA*, 1901

In 1901, just before Rina Faccio became Sibilla Aleramo, she went to the theatre in Milano and saw Nora. Rina never cried at plays, but that evening her dear friend Giacinta noticed the tears brimming in her eyes. Giacinta understood: Nora was leaving the man who had married her while never noticing she was human. Nora was clicking the door shut on a century of women whose only verb had been to marry. The wet salt burning in Rina's eyes was not crying, exactly. It was the century leaving the body.

The dear friend of Rina who understood all of this was the very same Giacinta Pezzana, now in her sixties and a spirited *femminista*, who had helped the young Eleonora Duse grow into a prima donna. Giacinta Pezzana knew what it was to act. She looked at Rina's eyes glistening in the dim theatre and told her, Now: it is time. Five years later, Sibilla Aleramo was the protagonist of her own life, and *Una donna* was born in a hot smelting rush in Torino.

Giacinta foresaw that Eleonora Duse and Sibilla Aleramo would become their own Noras. Often we discerned in each other the first cue, the opening line. But then we would grow hesitant. We consulted the timetables for trains we intended to take, we bought notebooks and other provisions. We stood on the threshold, the future before us like a sea of ceaseless waves. And now, we asked Sibilla, how to believe that there will be an island of your own invention?

ELEONORA DUSE, *ELLIDA*, 1909

By 1909 Eleonora Duse was exhausted. She had been so many women. She had been working since she was four years old. She had been seen on the stages of Egypt, Russia, and America; in Paris, the divine Sarah Bernhardt had offered to loan Eleonora her own private theatre, which held seventeen hundred admirers. Eleonora had tried strychnine injections and idylls on the island of Capri. But she was in menopause and wanted nothing more now than to lie on the divan of her flat in Rome, reading poetry.

It was an important question, how to leave the stage. Eleonora Duse in 1909 chose as her last role Ellida, which Ibsen called *The Woman of the Sea*. Ellida for Eleonora was, as she said, the liberty of her spirit at last. There was not a man who could impede her, not a law that could keep her from emancipation. Ellida, the daughter of a lighthouse keeper, was a beacon for women who might one day be able to choose who to love and how to live with them. Her silver hair shone in a coil around her head and her neck was free of jewels and chains. To Eleonora, Ellida was who Nora finally became, eighteen years after leaving the man who had kept her in a doll's house. After she left all of the men who were that man.

LINA, *TRISTANO SOMNIANS*, 1909

In the summer of 1909, the mysterious Tristano Somnians paid court to a number of actresses in Rome. Chivalrous notes were perfumed and posted, bouquets of honeysuckle twined in dressing rooms. Without someone to liken to fair Helen, Lina felt, it was impossible to write a play. She was looking for the one who, as Sappho says, *overcame everyone in beauty/left her fine husband/ behind and went sailing to Troy.*

Who would in beauty overcome everyone, who would leave any man that tried to keep her, who would take her life fiercely into her own hands and sail, outwards, beyond the islands?

Eleonora Duse had left the stage and lay on her divan in Rome, reading the poems of Giovanni Pascoli. She roused herself briefly one afternoon to receive a protegé of the esteemed Pascoli, a young poet announced as Tristano. Shown into the drawing room, Lina immediately presented Eleonora Duse with a volume of Sappho, open to Fragment 24C: *we live/...the opposite/...daring.*

LINA, *HELEN*, 1910

Even in winter, the sun in Rome shines like a blessing, Lina wrote in the first letter to Eleonora, and you are among all mortal women blessed, a Helen who overcomes everyone in beauty. O Eleonora, when will you come back to Rome? You are more luminous than the sun; the light of you glitters in the winter sky and falls upon the seas. So you are to me a beacon, Eleonora, in you I see beyond the islands known by any man.

LINA, *ARIADNE*, 1910

Alone in Rome, Lina began writing a play for Eleonora. It was called *Arianna*, after the thread that leads into a labyrinth and the woman who unspools it. A woman, Lina wrote, is someone who gathers the threads of her life into her hands and goes onwards.

You grasp the filament at its heart, Lina wrote to Eleonora. You are Ariadne unravelling all distances, all boundaries, all constraints.

Eleonora Duse lay ill in bed in Belluno, pale as the pillows around her, reading scenes from *Arianna*. It was absurd, she said to herself, at her age, to fall in love with a young poet aflame with visions. But Lina in letters was so warm, so achingly devoted, that Eleonora felt almost like melting.

SIBILLA ALERAMO, *MADAME ROBERT*, 1910

In 1910 Eleonora Duse was fifty-two years old, the same age as the character Madame Robert in Sibilla Aleramo's unfinished play *L'assurdo*. Before the appearance of Madame Robert, *L'assurdo* has only a triangle of characters. At the centre is Lorenza, the woman who must choose between distinguished Pietro and brash, poetic Arduino. Or, seen from another side of the triangle, the worthy Pietro is slowly losing his beloved to a brash young poet named Arduino.

We cannot see this from the third side of the triangle because in Sibilla's play Arduino is indescribable. Sometimes Arduino is a girlish youth, beardless and fey; other times Arduino is a masculine young woman in high buttoned boots. Whatever person Arduino may be, they are irresistible to Lorenza. But Lorenza hesitates. There is something in her desire for Arduino that troubles her sleep. Arduino is hardly a man or a woman like any other, Lorenza understands this, but how can you love someone you cannot define? What if you cannot write a word that captures what your beloved is?

Startled, we looked up from the manuscript of *L'assurdo*. Perhaps Sibilla did not believe that the word 'beloved' was enough in itself? Perhaps in order for Lorenza to love someone like Arduino, she had to solder them to a surface more solid than the side of a triangle? We wondered if Sibilla had ever reproached Lina for being indescribable.

Lorenza never answers these questions; instead Madame Robert appears in the play. Given to bouts of raw nerves, nevertheless Madame Robert exercises the fascination of having lived hundreds of dramatic experiences in her fifty-two years. Arduino is restless, molten; Madame Robert is intriguing, decisive; she takes Arduino as her own lover. At that point, the manuscript breaks off. Some acts can only be written as fragments, Sibilla said with a sigh, they shatter in your hands before the end.

LINA POLETTI, *GLI INVITI*, 1910

All spring letters went from Lina to Eleonora while everything melted. It was then, Sibilla told us, that she felt Lina ebbing away from her. Sibilla tried to write to Lina, tried to write a play like Lina, tried to write about Lina: all the lines broke off on the page.

In that time Lina sent Eleonora a poem that began, Throw open the windows, dive into the sea, come out to the edge of the horizon where the waves melt, where I am waiting for you.

In that time, too, Lina sent a letter to Sibilla that read in its entirety, I may be in Rome soon for a project, greetings to you also from Santi Muratori whom I married last Thursday in Ravenna, I hope that you are well.

AUDOUIN, *ÉTUDE SOMMAIRE DES DIALECTES GRECS LITTÉRAIRES (AUTRES QUE L'ATTIQUE)*

Lina Poletti had affectionately known the librarian Santi Muratori since her earliest days at the Biblioteca Classense in Ravenna. He would loan her any book in the archives and asked for nothing in return. When Lina's mother and father sat her down in the drawing room and said, You must absolutely marry, there is too much talk already, Lina Poletti sought out Santi Muratori amid his beloved bookshelves and explained. Santi of course loaned her Audouin's *Brief Study of the Greek Literary Dialects (Other than Attic)* and agreed to Thursday.

In general they forgot that they were married, except when Lina needed her identity papers for something. It was only then in a dry rage that Lina wrote to Santi, My dear Santi, apparently I cannot in Italy be anything except either Miss Cordula Poletti or Mrs Cordula Muratori née Poletti, please send required papers.

Promptly Santi sent everything to Lina, in double copies. Then he sent a letter to Eleonora Duse, asking her gently to understand that Lina in these dry rages was devoured by a flame, that she burnt and burnt at the injustices done to women until she scorched her own life. It was not only that Santi cared for Lina and did not want to see her charred and bitter, he wrote to Eleonora, but also that he saw, for those of us who are men, how favourable life is, how indulgent society, how easy the honours and how innumerable the rewards. Every step is smoothed for us. But who, who fights for the rights of women? What can men give, from their freedom and ease? Above all, what can be done in Italy?

With the papers sent by Santi Muratori, Lina was free to buy a little house in her own name. Gratefully she replied to him in a letter that he kept in the archives where he spent all of his waking hours, amid his beloved bookshelves, until the war came and they bombed the libraries, burying Santi Muratori under three tons of rubble and paper.

LINA POLETTI, *ARIANNA*, 1910

Together Eleonora and Lina were almost winged. They spent a gossamer summer in Belluno, where the peaks of the mountains kept their sugary snow even in the canicule, and then they alighted in Firenze, at the villa of Mabel Dodge. Mabel Dodge brought them down to earth. She kept dogs and disapproved of almost everything else. Mabel Dodge observed that Lina seemed to be wearing trousers and could not enter a room without imperilling dozens of porcelain pugs.

Lina left the drove of dogs yapping on the terrace and went up an oak tree with her draft of *Arianna*. But her Ariadne kept straying from scene to scene; sometimes she was the fearless weaver of futures, and at other times merely plaintive and forlorn. Lina wanted only the Ariadne who kept the threads tight in her fist. She wanted only the Helen who overcame everyone and left, sailed, outwards, beyond, past even the islands of Skiros and Skiropoula, Psara and Antipsara. That was the beauty of Helen: while she was at sea, you could always hope that she was bound not for Troy but for Mytilene. But it was difficult to write such things, we understood, because it was difficult to live them.

GERTRUDE STEIN, *PORTRAIT OF MABEL DODGE AT THE VILLA CURONIA*

Listening to Sibilla in the Temple à l'amitié late at night, we were like a chorus that does not yet know if this will be a tragedy. By then we knew how to find our sisters and when to evade questions about our beds and undergarments. *Tribadismo, saffismo, clitorismo* had just been published in Firenze, and Natalie Barney lent us many of the other books that had previously been kept from us. But we were afraid that what was to come would be more terrible and inevitable than we could foresee. We asked Sibilla, What will become of Lina Poletti? Sibilla, enigmatic in the firelight, would only repeat to us a line from Gertrude Stein's *Portrait of Mabel Dodge at the Villa Curonia*: So much breathing has not the same place when the ending is lessening.

LINA POLETTI, *ARIANNA*, 1912

When it was ending, Lina and Eleonora went to Venezia. The summer wore on, humid and heavy, while they tried to recover the thread of their life together. Rilke, who lived nearby, read the unfinished draft of *Arianna* and judged it ambitious: certainly Lina was talented, but she was too young, she wanted too much, her Ariadne was too many things at once. As an elder poet he counselled modesty and a more seemly pace of action. My dear, you are only twenty-six, he said; content yourself with small drams of inspiration, do not expect greatness to come upon you. Rilke himself had just written several of the Duino elegies in a matter of days, because the poem had called out to him as he strode lonely along the cliffs, proclaiming his place among the hierarchies of angels.

Lina suspected that Rilke was lying through his teeth. But she wondered if some acts could only be written as fragments.

ELEONORA, 1912

A peacock screamed in the gardens and Eleonora dropped her glass, smashing it. A humid miasma crept over the lagoon and stifled all breath. Gaudy lights went on in the Piazza San Marco and the *gondolieri* cried out harshly like seagulls.

The ending was lessening and Eleonora had some pulmonary illness that kept her from breathing clearly. The ending was lessening and Lina felt a peculiar tightness in her jaw. They had not the same place any more, they had lost the gossamer thread somehow. Lina longed for a Helen who would sail invincibly beyond the dull shores of the known world. She looked at Eleonora wan in her sleep, coughing, her nightdress twisted around her legs.

One of the last things that Lina said to Eleonora was, Let us go away to Paris, I can buy a little house for us, I have heard so many things of Paris, there is Natalie Barney who knows everyone, Eleonora, in Paris I will finish my *Arianna* and you will return to the stage as its star.

But Eleonora was tired and ill, she had already been too many women in her life, she wanted only now to lie on her divan in Venezia and read poetry. Thus Lina Poletti left alone.

She left Eleonora, she left her unfinished *Arianna*, she left Venezia. How we regretted that Lina did not come to us in Paris in the sultry months of 1912! She could have told us everything herself. But instead Lina went back to Rome, where at the end of the summer thunderstorms crack the sky open. Afterwards the air is always dazed and clear, Sibilla said, you can breathe again.

ELEONORA DUSE, *LA DUSE PARLA DEL FEMMINISMO*, 1913

After a year of convalescing, Eleonora Duse returned unexpectedly to the public eye to give a long interview on the subject of women in Italy. First of all, Eleonora Duse said, Italy was indisputably a monopoly of men. Of course women wanted to be human beings instead of little dolls who danced for the pleasure of their husbands, dutifully bore children, and annihilated themselves. Who would not want what half the population had got just by being born? Furthermore, Eleonora Duse went on, if ever a woman wants to work, to write, to think for herself, to take action, to love another woman, she is immediately derided as unnatural and perverse for expressing the very qualities that men hold dear for themselves. It is no wonder, Eleonora Duse concluded, that women in Italy are burning and burning with a dry rage against the long tyranny of men. From the Greek *τύραννος*, she added, explaining to the astonished interviewer that in her long illness she had taken up studying classical grammar. She hoped soon to read the ancients in the original.

EIGHT

EVA PALMER, *SAPPHO*, 1900

Eva Palmer would always remember the first time she had been Sappho. She had stood very still. It was a *tableau vivant.* In half a bed sheet Eva Palmer stretched out an arm, as if in an instant she would begin singing. But she remained silent, her red hair falling to her ankles, the sheet very slowly slipping off her shoulder. In the air around her were the sounds of summer on Mount Desert Island: pine trees creaking with pitch, birds fussing in thatches, a breeze rustling the curtains of the summer house.

Now too a murmur arose from the cluster of spectators watching Eva become Sappho. They were American parents, for the most part, present for charitable reasons. Accustomed to distant orphans and plates of petits fours, they regarded Eva Palmer curiously. She was a striking girl with her cascade of red hair, dreamy, rather a prodigy in classical arts, they had heard. The American parents who summered at Bar Harbor had not heard why exactly Eva Palmer had been expelled for a year from Bryn Mawr. But she was a very queer girl, they could see that. With their eyes they pinned the loose folds of her draped bed sheet more tightly. It was 1900. It was the first time Natalie Barney had seen Sappho in public.

EVA PALMER AND SAPPHO, FRAGMENT 16, 1898

In fact Eva had been practising Sappho for years. In 1898, in a dormitory room in Radnor Hall, Eva had been apprehended while practising with two or three other girls. They had exams in intermediate Greek, Eva protested, and the other girls could hardly manage the aorist tense, she was only trying to help them grasp the concept of past action. But the president of the college would not hear a word of it. Eva and Sappho were expelled for a year. Eva put all of her books into a valise and left for Rome with Sappho in her lap, open to Fragment 16: *led her astray/... for/... lightly*.

ANNA VERTUA GENTILE, *COME DEVO COMPORTARMI?*, 1899

In 1899 there were many Italian books instructing young ladies on proper comportment. Girls were to be noble, nice, industrious, modest, devout, quiet, self-sacrificing, and above all free of vice. Anna Vertua Gentile, who wrote dozens of these books, published *How Ought I to Behave Myself?* just as Eva Palmer arrived in Rome. Eva did not read it.

Instead Eva spent her months in Rome striating the city. She would take a corner, or even a fallen column in the Forum, and work downwards: first the stray cats and moss, then the old Latin names, the large stones cobbling the road underneath, the throngs of sandalled feet that would have trod it; the voices reedy in the ancient air, the songs drifting out from the temple of Vesta like smoke from the sacred flame; at last, imperial Rome laid bare to her. Eva did not read books extolling feminine virtues because she was poring over Virgil, Catullus, Ovid.

It was Ovid, Eva was shocked to learn, who took the voice of Sappho for himself and turned it against her. *Quid mihi cum Lesbo?* Ovid wrote spitefully into Sappho's mouth, What is Lesbos to me now? Eva Palmer could have told Ovid what Lesbos was to Sappho, she could recite the names of Sappho's lovers as if they were her own friends.

NATALIE BARNEY AND EVA PALMER, 1900

In the woods behind the summer house, they slipped off their dresses; naked all afternoon they apostrophized each other in the vocative. When Eva recited poetry, Natalie felt the silent crowd of trees bowing their crowns to listen. After the last verse Natalie took Eva's wrist, led her to the centre of the glade, and stepped back to admire the picture she had made of Eva, regal and naked with the shadows of leaves playing over her.

Those were the earliest days of us, and we regarded with awe the few photographs that remained. Eva appeared as a pale blur trailing her hair in the pine needles, and Natalie was smiling broadly: they were both so young then that they had never met anyone else, except in books. Moreover Eva, having read the *Heroides*, told Natalie that Ovid had taken the life of Sappho and perverted it. Never, Eva swore, never would Sappho have thrown herself from the cliffs for the love of any man! Hearing the tremor in Eva's voice, Natalie embraced her: books, body, pine needles. They were very young, but they were feeling their way towards becoming.

SAPPHO, FRAGMENT 19, 1901

In Fragment 19, no line is complete. It is as if every word is swallowed after a breath. In the early part of the poem Sappho writes of waiting: the tension of time before anything happens. Then the poem is suspended, and for some time there is only nothingness ticking onwards, dot blank dot blank dot, a bleak rhythm. Dot blank dot was Natalie's boat leaving the island, Eva thought, becoming a speck on the bay, vanishing. Blankly in 1900 Eva returned to college while Natalie sailed for Paris.

When at last there is movement, the poem is launched: *but going/...for we know,* Sappho writes. We do not know, but we have heard. We do not know, but despite our uncertainties and ellipses, we are going. Eva is leaving before the final Latin exams. Eva is going to Paris, to Natalie. It is 1901.

Finally Fragment 19 arrives at its destination; from the end of the poem, Sappho looks back: *After/...and towards.* Once in Paris, Eva began training as an actress at the Comédie Française.

An actress, Eva confided to Natalie, is someone who still believes in the ancient rites. There may be electric lights and rigging, there may be satin and cinematography, but an actress herself is always at Delphi. She stands on the splintered floorboards as if amid the great stone circles of seats, the temple of Apollo rising at her back. An actress is like a sibyl, she sees after and towards at the same time.

EVA PALMER AND SARAH BERNHARDT, 1901

In Paris the actress Sarah Bernhardt unpinned Eva's hair so that it fell in one bright cascade to the floor. Sarah Bernhardt was widely known to be divine. Bravely Eva tilted her chin up and asked Sarah Bernhardt about actresses. Sarah, coiling Eva's hair around her wrists like a serpent, laughed and replied that the ancient rites of actresses were not written down on paper, you learned your lines from the page but the rites, ah! the rites you learned only from other actresses.

GIACINTA PEZZANA, *AMLETO*

Sarah Bernhardt, like Giacinta Pezzana before her, frequently performed male roles. These were called 'boy parts' and had the advantage of freedom of movement; in breeches and hose you could stride, lunge, turn suddenly to take action. Sarah Bernhardt particularly enjoyed being Hamlet. There was fur trimming at the thighs and a tapered sword in a jewelled scabbard. Moreover Hamlet was wilful and proud, like Sarah. Her Hamlet went on for four hours.

Giacinta Pezzana as Amleto was less lengthy and more ambivalent. In 1878 Giacinta Pezzana bound her breasts with ten metres of cloth and went to America. She said that she was looking for new horizons, for mobility, for an intelligence without sex. It was not known what she found there. In fact Giacinta Pezzana wrote in a letter to her dear friend Sibilla Aleramo in 1911, *Sulla carta non si dice sempre tutto*: on paper we do not always say everything. In other words we may have learned our lines from the page, but the rites we could learn only from other actresses.

SARAH BERNHARDT, *PELLÉAS*, 1901

Eva Palmer learned from the divine Sarah Bernhardt that an actress could take any shape she pleased: a boy, a queen, a murderer, a saint. A great actress could be two things at once; for example, presently Sarah Bernhardt was rehearsing to be Pelléas, who was both the lover and the brother-in-law of beautiful Mélisande. Yes of course, Sarah said to Eva somewhat irritably, an actress was someone who took the best parts, that was the art of theatre. Boy parts, queen parts, parts of the mind of Hamlet as intricate as lace: Sarah Bernhardt chose the ones she wanted and made them hers.

Your Greeks, after all, Sarah said, jabbing her finger into Eva's shoulder, who do you think they were? Who was Medea, Clytemnestra, Antigone? They were men, *ma chère* Eva! And Ophelia, and Lady Macbeth, and Desdemona! Centuries of men, filling the stages with themselves, every role at their disposal, wearing gowns or breeches as they pleased. And so now, to be a great actress, you must learn: no more shall we be confined to their cast-offs, to their bits of mothers and maidens and ladies-in-waiting. No, *chèrie*, we do not stoop to consider the sex of our parts.

SARAH BERNHARDT AND LOUISE ABBÉMA

Before Sarah Bernhardt became divine, she had been the illegitimate daughter of a Jewish courtesan. Very early she learned which parts were offered to women without means. As she rose through the ranks of the Comédie Française, the Count of K and the Prince of L vied for her affections; she earned her keep as best she could. In 1864, when she was twenty, she gave birth to an illegitimate son. In French this was called a *fils naturel*, and Sarah thought it natural to give the baby her own last name. In fact fathers were nothing to Sarah.

By then Sarah Bernhardt was fêted as a great actress and lived accordingly; in her household she kept a leopard on a jewelled leash, a parrot, a monkey, her *fils naturel*, and a pack of rare chameleons. Once Sarah was known to be divine, she chose the parts of mortal life she wanted and made them hers. She slept in a coffin and sailed in a hot-air balloon over Paris.

Moreover Sarah Bernhardt elected to be escorted everywhere by the painter Louise Abbéma, who wore dark trousers and smoked a scandalous lot of cigars. Louise was scorned in society as a *gousse d'ail*: not merely a clove of garlic, but rather a woman whose mouth had been in unspeakable places. When the French newspapers enquired of Sarah Bernhardt, how did she interpret the paintings of Louise Abbéma?, Sarah replied that all artists lived double or even triple lives, one scant meaning was not enough for them. Then Sarah Bernhardt smiled with all of her teeth showing.

EVA PALMER, *MÉLISANDE*, 1901

In the final scene of *Pelléas et Mélisande*, Mélisande sits on a bench tilting her chin up and closing her eyes as if in a dream, and Sarah Bernhardt bends down to kiss her. It is a rare moment when the divine touches the lips of a mortal woman. An actress, like an acolyte, might spend her life waiting for that luminous moment to descend upon her. One afternoon in her *loge* at the Comédie Française, Sarah said fondly to Eva, What a Mélisande you would be to my Pelléas! An emerald gown, the light on your face!

In ancient Greek, to utter a wish or a hope, there is the optative. The optative is a mood, almost a feeling. It hovers in the air just outside of time or subject, wistful in colour, its edges slightly tinged with foreboding. If only, if only, would that it were so, the optative pleads, Let it be so, may it somehow come to pass! We were well acquainted with the optative mood, in those days we used it often with each other. We wavered between invoking our desires aloud and shyly hoping that they would simply happen to us, like weather.

VIRGINIA STEPHEN, *POETICS*, 1905

Virgil's *Georgics* were full of technical terms for beekeeping, so in 1905 Virginia Stephen preferred translating the Greeks. The English word 'poet' was merely *ποιητής* trimmed at one edge, and at the same time the *Poetics* of Aristotle gave a clearer view of literature than any novel by Henry James.

In 1906, translating thought into action, Virginia Stephen sailed with her sister for Patras. Upon her arrival in Greece she remarked upon the light shattering into scintillations on the sea, the grapes swelling on their vines, the view of Olympia. Yet once at Olympia she was unsure how to proceed, there were so many words supplied already by guidebooks and with the glare it was hard to see which century it was. Ascending the slopes of Mount Pentelicus by donkey, Virginia paused at a spring plashing among the pines: this is no scene from Baedeker, Virginia said, but rather an idyll by Theocritus.

ELEONORA DUSE, 1897

Eleonora Duse sat overlooking the ruins of a seaside villa built for the summer pleasures of the emperor Tiberius. She was very tired. The Swedish physician who attended her had prescribed strychnine injections and lemon water. Eleonora harboured suspicions about the curative effects of the Swedish regime but found it preferable to the one prescribed by her Italian gynaecologist; in order to lessen the heavy flow of blood each month, he had ordered her womb cauterized.

Eleonora closed her eyes against the blue-green sea. The isle of Capri was beautiful, but it was too close to the world, the boats bearing doctors and newspapers from Napoli arrived every morning. If only an island were like an interlude, Eleonora Duse thought, she could rest for a time.

She had already been so many women in her life. But even in an intermission, an actress must change her costume and prepare to go on again.

SARAH BERNHARDT, *PHÈDRE*

In 1879 when Sarah Bernhardt travelled to London to perform *Phèdre*, Oscar Wilde spread out adoring sprays of white lilies on the quay for her. He wrote a sonnet in her honour and begged her to visit him at home in Chelsea. She was delayed at her lodging in Chester Square, however, because the English press wished to hear at once what, according to Mme Bernhardt, was the moral value of a scandalous play like *Phèdre*? Ah! said Sarah Bernhardt, *Phèdre* is a classical tragedy, who are we to judge the morality of the ancients? An artist must not be subject to the mores of the day! Then, evading further enquiries, Sarah Bernhardt went off to Liverpool to acquire a pair of small lions.

MRS PATRICK CAMPBELL, *PELLÉAS*, 1903

Eva Palmer came to London to meet the English actress Mrs Patrick Campbell. Mrs Pat was practical and did not believe in the divinity of actresses. An actress, Mrs Pat felt, had as short a lifespan as a daffodil, it was useless to pretend otherwise, you bloomed for your day and then if you had been clever, you retired comfortably to the South of France. In fact Mrs Pat in her day had been a beautiful Mélisande to Sarah Bernhardt's Pelléas, she had sat on that bench and tilted up her rosy little mouth, she knew how it went. Now Mrs Pat was rehearsing to be Pelléas herself.

Eyeing Eva over the edge of her teacup, Mrs Pat said, You are quite promising, my dear, you would make a ravishing Mélisande, but you must give up certain of your friends if you are to maintain your reputation. Eva shook her head so sharply a curl came loose. She would sooner play bit parts in Natalie's back garden than star on the London stage if it meant renouncing her friends. In fact, Eva declared hotly, as soon as Renée Vivien finished her translation, Natalie would make a play of it, Eva would have the leading role, they would be Sappho together in public!

Practical Mrs Pat decided that the audition of Eva had now come to its end. Really there were dozens of Mélisandes to be had, Mrs Pat said to herself, and not all of them rash Sapphists. Eva Palmer was a good-hearted girl to be sure, but Mrs Pat was saving her pennies for a cottage in the Pyrenees. Eva Palmer would have to make her own way in the world.

DIALOGUE AU SOLEIL COUCHANT, 1905

One afternoon in Neuilly, while the sun was still dappling the back garden of Natalie Barney, Eva Palmer put on a white linen shift and unbound her hair. She was going to be the mellifluous, maidenly half of the *Dialogue at Sunset*, while Colette would be the Arcadian shepherd who pursues her. Natalie clapped her hands for silence. Colette lay in the grass entreating Eva to abandon herself to the late afternoon, to recline in verdant light, to sink down like the sun as it rests upon a hill. The hill, we understood, was Colette. Watching the sky grow dusky over the garden, we too wished to stretch out our bodies on the grass, to murmur to each other some words that we had crossed centuries to find. Only in Natalie's garden did we feel that we were making our way in the world.

PENELOPE SIKELIANOS DUNCAN, 1906

The reason that Natalie Barney eventually left her garden in Neuilly was Sappho. In fact Natalie was fond of the house; Eva lived nearby, and in the summer the salon stayed cool and umbral. Its only flaw was that whenever Natalie staged Sappho on the lawn, the landlord threatened to call the *gendarmes*. In 1906 Natalie put on a play about Sappho watching the wedding of her beloved acolyte Timas. Circled by barefoot dancers, Eva Palmer was Timas in a nuptial reverie until the landlord arrived, incensed. He ordered them out, dancing girls, inverts, Amazons, Sapphists, actresses, the whole lunatic lot of them, inflicting their immoralities on the respectable residents of Neuilly!

Penelope Sikelianos Duncan, who had been playing the harp with ivy twined in her hair, asked Eva Palmer in an undertone what it meant, this word 'invert'? Born on the island of Lefkada, Penelope could play the flute and the harp, sing boundless Greek folk songs, recite demotic poems. But she had only recently married an American man; sometimes she did not understand foreign words. Fortunately Eva Palmer was by then very good in Greek and explained it to her. An invert is someone thought backwards, Eva said, the way that the British colonists had thought the people of Lefkada too barbaric to rule themselves.

SAPPHO, FRAGMENT 51

An invert is not exactly someone thought backwards. An invert is someone thought in a different order. A part that others might display on the outside, like a bronze breastplate, is instead kept chambered in the heart. Or inverts may have their warmest parts turned outwards, like orchids or octopuses.

In Fragment 51 Sappho writes of two states of mind in the same body. When two things are coupled together in one throat, in one belly, in one blush of feeling that runs up the spine, they orient the body in different directions at the same time. We were well acquainted with that warm disarray spreading through our nerves. Sometimes we wanted to be everything at once. An invert is someone who believes this is possible.

NATALIE BARNEY, *ÉQUIVOQUE*, 1906

For centuries the lexicographers had circulated the rumour that Sappho had killed herself for love of a man. They had heard it from Ovid: Sappho had thrown herself off a cliff for Phaon. Her body was smashed to bits by waves and rocks, then her eyes were eaten by gulls. Furthermore, some lexicographers added, before that Sappho had been a prostitute, she had slept with half the shepherds on the island. When she fell for young Phaon, all her pretty words were for naught, he scorned her, she was an older woman. Really she had no choice but to hurl her body from the white cliffs of Lefkada.

In 1906 Natalie Barney was thirty years old, she had heard all the rumours about Phaon. In response Natalie wrote her own Sappho, fierce and wise and keenly devoted to her acolytes, in the form of a play called *Équivoque*. The play was only thinly a story about Sappho watching a wedding. For Natalie *Équivoque* was not a plot but a scene: around Sappho is a radiant jostling of girls who wish to be near her, they beg her to string her lyre and sing to them, but it is not only her verses they praise, it is everything, Sappho is everything to them; one girl says, Your life is your poem/Most beautiful.

SAPPHO, FRAGMENT 149

In Natalie's *Équivoque*, Sappho quickly dismisses dull Phaon as unworthy of his bride Timas. In fact, Natalie declared, if ever Sappho were to throw herself off a cliff for love, it could only be for Timas, a woman whose hair flickered like a flame in the grass; a woman like Eva, barefoot in a silk tunic she had made herself, singing the verses of Sappho while the sunlight fell into her hair and tangled it red into the green lawn.

Natalie had loved many women since Eva, but still she cherished that poem of hair, that distant and mystical gaze. Precious Eva was almost an artefact, Natalie thought. Increasingly Eva put on her dresses like costumes; what Eva said at soirées were the lines she had memorized for the occasion. Even when Eva was not onstage, somehow she was still always at Delphi.

But Natalie had written *Équivoque* to tell us that we were possible in our own time. Whenever we gathered in her garden, it was a living consecration of those nights spent dancing on the slopes of Lesbos: *when all night long/it pulls them down*, Sappho writes, that longing and that memory. In the Temple à l'amitié we were a radiant jostling of girls, we were as close to Mytilene as mortals could come. Always, for Natalie, Sappho remained fervently in the present.

SARAH BERNHARDT, 1906

It was true, in those days we felt the blush of our inner parts turning out towards each other. We studied one another as intently as the books we had read as girls. We pored over the photographs of Natalie and Eva blurry in the woods behind the summer house. We had hopes of becoming artists, of writing lines that kept our lovers up all night or painting portraits of women serene in themselves. Except for Eva, we did not aspire to become actresses; the ancient rites seemed to us fearsome and strange. We had seen the faraway look in Eva's eyes, as if she were already at Delphi.

In the meantime Sarah Bernhardt had gone to America, bringing her own linens. All of her sheets as well as her revolver were embroidered with her motto '*Quand-même*': despite everything, the Divine Sarah. In America she was given an alligator, her own private train, an army of stagehands. The alligator died after drinking too much champagne, but Sarah Bernhardt was indomitable. She changed her costume and went on. Her train blazed across the continent, unconstrained by ancient ruins. We did not see how Eva could follow her.

NINE

ISADORA DUNCAN, 1899

At her debut in New York in 1899, Isadora Duncan danced the wedding night of Helen of Troy. She had fashioned a gauzy robe, following the illustrated plates of a book on Greek statuary, that left her arms free. While she danced, her brother declaimed verses from the *Idylls* of Theocritus. The programme explained that Miss Duncan wished to transport the public into a Noble Realm of Ancient Culture, if just for one evening.

Yards of gauze bandages, the newspapers reported, must be endured for one glimpse of a pretty leg. Amid much droning on about shepherds and woe, Miss Duncan was fetching but too fanciful for an audience accustomed to more substantial entertainment. The ladies of Paris or London might find her poses to their taste. But when a red-blooded New Yorker went to the theatre, he liked to see a real dancing girl, not a statue and an old poem.

SAPPHO, FRAGMENTS 82A AND 82B, 1902

Unhusking from sarcophagi their lining of papyrus, in 1896 the archaeologists came upon precious new shreds of a poem by Sappho. They passed the fragments to the philologists, who took them back to the Berlin Museum for further study. In 1902 the philologists announced the discovery of a line about Mnasidika, a young woman Sappho found even more lithe and shapely than her beloved Gyrinno. Mnasidika, the philologists hypothesized, might in another line be weaving together fronds of wild fennel, but further investigation was needed; meanwhile they insisted that Mnasidika be preserved in a glass case at the Museum. She smelled like dust, they said. To us she smelled like wet ferns and liquorice, and moreover, we wished to remind them, it was impossible to keep kletic time in a glass box.

ISADORA DUNCAN, 1900

Isadora Duncan made her way to London by cattle boat with her brother. She was bound for the British Museum, where she could study the gestures of marble statues from the temple of the Parthenon. Unlike the Parthenon, the British Museum was windless and orderly: Isadora could spend the morning sketching a caryatid straightening her shoulders under her stone burden, and then have tea.

The light in London was a sooty, sodden yellow-grey, yet the statues before Isadora were polished to a whiteness like teeth. She felt that they stretched out their ancient hands to her, bidding her to rise and dance. But the British Museum had strict rules: no touching, no dancing, no unruly Greek mobs who might demand the return of the marble statues to the temple of the Parthenon.

THEOCRITUS, *IDYLLS*, 3RD CENTURY BCE

In a little wicker cage the crickets were singing, Theocritus said, and the boy who had woven it for them was a sculptor of willow boughs. Theocritus, born in the cultured Greek city of Siracusa, wrote in perfect dactylic hexameter of shepherds in muddy fields, the braying of rams, rough tangles of ivy. He made the goatherds into gods and the oxherds into poets. Although he wrote one wedding song for Helen of Troy, most of his poems were idylls.

What is an idyll? It is a place in the country where everything is just as we have always imagined it. In fact 'idyll' comes from the Greek *eidullion*, which means a little picture, or a way of looking at something until it is perfect. In this sense it is a *tableau vivant*; it is like Eva Palmer, regal and naked, seen only by Natalie Barney and a silent crowd of trees.

ISADORA DUNCAN, *DANSES-IDYLLES*, 1900

In the front row sat Natalie Barney and Renée Vivien, close enough to rest their feet on the carpet where Isadora would dance. Isadora appeared in a silk chiffon tunic the colour of cold pearls. Her breasts were nestled in fabric and her legs were bare. She is almost Mnasidika from the poem, Renée murmured to Natalie.

Isadora Duncan gazed into the middle distance of the salon and raised her palms to the gilded ceiling. Renée watched the wisps of Isadora's tunic floating around her like clouds, like breaths, like the feathery moss that embraces a statue over the centuries. At the end of the performance, Renée thought that she might write a poem of clouds like cold pearls, to translate the *DansesIdylles* into verse.

Natalie thought it was absurd to see Isadora Duncan perform on a drawing room carpet. If only Isadora would consent to dance amid the Doric columns of the Temple à l'amitié in the back garden! Then it would be perfect, the very image of a Muse brought to life.

ISADORA DUNCAN, 1902

Isadora Duncan made her way to ancient Greece by caique with her brother. Actually first they had to go to Brindisi and take the ferry. But once they arrived on the island of Lefkada, they could hire a tiny caique, bright blue and white, to sail them to Kravasara, so that they could arrive at dawn, disembark in ecstasy, and kiss the soil of ancient Greece. They had been up all night singing to the Ionian sea.

Isadora and her brother journeyed to Agrinio, Missolonghi, Patras. There were bedbugs. Undeterred, staunch in their song, Isadora and her brother went on to Athens in leather sandals. From a hill outside the city, they beheld the Acropolis rising on its great rock to meet their gaze, shadowing the lowly sprawl of modern streets. From that picture Isadora felt that she could not move. She bought the hill. She dreamed of a house, copied from the palace of Agamemnon, where they might dwell in ancient Greece. Noble stone would be quarried from Mount Pentelicus; acres of thistles would shield them from neighbouring peasants. Imagine, Isadora bade her brother, every morning they would arise and don their tunics, fetch water from the spring, gaze upon the Acropolis, and dance rhapsodies.

The first thing they ordered built upon their land was a temple. But it was discovered that there were no ancient springs nearby, not even a well, and construction was halted due to lack of potable water.

OSCAR WILDE, *THEOCRITUS: A VILLANELLE*, 1890

Still by the light and laughing sea, Oscar Wilde wrote, the island went on with its lives: the ivy twining, the goatherds whistling, the crickets singing in their wicker cages. Oscar Wilde was writing across the centuries to Theocritus. His villanelle was a letter with a question: Did Theocritus remember? Was there hope of recovering that time, that island, those boys like willow saplings in the meadow?

A villanelle repeats its address many times, and Oscar Wilde asks Theocritus the same question again and again. But a villanelle is also a monologue. There is no line left for Theocritus to answer. Moreover the Siracusa we knew was a ramshackle town in Sicily with cholera outbreaks; the Greek ruins on its outskirts were hopeless and deserted. We read the poem again and still we wondered, Where is the idyll promised us?

PENELOPE SIKELIANOS, 1893

As a child, Penelope sang to the starfish. She would walk along the shore of Lefkada, waving to the fisherman as they cast off, until she found the tumbles of rocks pocketed with seawater where the starfish clustered. Then she would sing. Her voice was thin and darting, she was still learning the modes, but she could sing for hours. Often she went on until the crickets joined her at dusk, and into the evening while the sky settled darkly on the sea and the fishermen moored their boats. When the stars came out she sang to them too, they were like starfish turned inside out, empty and bright.

PENELOPE SIKELIANOS AND ISADORA DUNCAN, 1902

Penelope met Isadora Duncan and her brother while they were walking through Athens in their leather sandals. Politely Penelope avoided looking at their bare, dusty toes. She was an educated young woman of twenty-one with large dark eyes. In the house of her family, the ancient Greeks were like cousins who had come from a great distance to visit: their speech was stiff and strange, but their words were wise. Therefore, said Penelope's brother, a modern, educated family should take their ancient cousins by the hand and walk them into the present, into our demotic language, for all Greek people to hear.

By 1902 Penelope had mastered the demotic, the classical, the flute, the harp, French literature, and the Greek musical modes. In the street in Athens, Isadora Duncan clasped Penelope's hand and asked her to join them in reviving a play by Aeschylus. They wanted something Tragic and Pure and Ancient, Isadora said, and also a hundred Athenian orphans to audition as singers. Penelope looked at Isadora and her brother, their unsightly toes, their tunics lumped on their shoulders, their earnest American faces. She found their naïveté endearing, and they would pay her to sing.

AESCHYLUS, *THE SUPPLIANTS*, 1903

While Penelope was assembling the Athenian orphans and Isadora was shut in her room studying vase paintings, their brothers would sit in the rubble of the unfinished palace and discuss the future of the demotic. Penelope's brother maintained that the demotic was the lifeblood of the living Greek language, while Isadora's brother was firm in his belief that the ancient tongue was eternal in itself and needed no modern form. To settle their disagreement they hailed a shepherd passing over the hill with his flock and bade him judge. He was the voice of the Greek people, they told him, and then Penelope's brother cleared his throat to give a spontaneous translation of the third *stasimon* of Aeschylus' *Suppliants*. But the shepherd, whistling to his dog, told them he could not stay; he was taking the flock to pasture and Greek sheep did not care for any language but grass.

PENELOPE SIKELIANOS DUNCAN, 1903

Although the staging of the third *stasimon* was deemed largely unsuccessful, the brothers of Penelope and Isadora became fast friends. It did not matter that they had made of Aeschylus a muddle of Byzantine motifs and ecclesiastical melodies, or that the orphans, singing in ancient Greek, could not understand their own lines. Isadora felt that the essential element was her own triumph: as long as she had danced like a vase painting, the rest was scenery.

Penelope's brother proclaimed that this was only the beginning, they must go on with the project of bringing Greek culture alive to the Greek people. Isadora's brother agreed, next he would found an Akadémia, Isadora could teach movement. But then they must find someone to teach the pupils to sing, Isadora's brother said, frowning slightly, and who would be suitable for an Akadémia as illustrious and impoverished as theirs? Within a month Penelope was married to the brother of Isadora.

SAPPHO, FRAGMENT 22

There were not yet riots, but the press warned that Paris would be brought to its knees by labour strikes. Penelope had an infant in her arms and her large dark eyes were pinched with fatigue. In the half-finished house on the hill outside of Athens, her husband would allow no one to cross the threshold in modern dress. But here in Paris they were the only ones in sandals and tunics, everyone stared at them, yesterday a Frenchman had laid his hand on Penelope's bare arm.

Eva had first heard Penelope sing by chance. Immediately Eva felt something in herself awaken, an idea seeping through her like water from an underground spring. Who was Penelope?

Eva thought she might be the origin of music in the world. Eva invited Penelope to stay at her house in Neuilly, far from politics and uncivilized men. In her sunlit garden Eva said dreamily, *I bid you sing/of Gongyla, Abanthis, taking up/your lyre as (now again) longing/ floats around you.* Penelope smiled and replied, So Sappho bade Abanthis. But I have no lyre, and you, are you Sappho?

SAPPHO, FRAGMENT 156

First they were building a loom together, and then they were weaving on it, working the shuttle through the shed, draping the swathes across their shoulders to see if the cloth fell like the folds on ancient statues. The world was made of threads humming into place, of Penelope singing while she pinned Eva's new tunic. To keep Penelope close to her, Eva decided that Natalie Barney's play *Équivoque* should be set to flute music. Thus dark-eyed Penelope twined ivy into her hair and stood beside a Doric column in Natalie's garden. Eva thought she had never seen anything more beautiful. But Eva refrained from reciting Sappho, *far more sweetsounding than a lyre/golder than gold.* Penelope with her flute and her dark hair might misunderstand.

TIMAS, 1906

At the end of *Équivoque*, Sappho leaps from the cliffs into the Ionian sea, mourning the loss of her beloved Timas. In the garden at Neuilly we watched as Sappho chose death over the marriage of Timas to a man. Better to lull your body to death in the waves, Natalie Barney believed, than to witness that fate for your beloved.

In 1906, Eva was Timas, ever a faithful acolyte, and in the final scene of *Équivoque*, she duly follows Sappho from the cliffs of Lefkada into the roiling sea. Timas, too, chooses death over marriage to a man. Whatever her future might have been, it is foreclosed to her; she never again utters a desire in the optative. At the end of the play, the remaining acolytes mourn her death, twinned with Sappho's and yet somehow more inevitable. We imagined her red hair trailing behind her in the waves like a flame going out.

Of course Eva was an actress, she delivered the lines of Timas as they were written; in truth we all did as Natalie directed us in those days, even Colette would put out her cigarettes when Natalie coughed. But we wondered if Timas would stay forever in Sappho's garden, as still as a statue circled by barefoot dancers. Was that our sapphic idyll, a *tableau vivant* contained by four walls like a photograph bound square in its frame? 1906 was an uncertain time, perhaps that was why Natalie Barney had called her play *Equivocation.*

EVA PALMER, 1906

Three white silk tunics with fibulae to pin them, a pair of leather sandals, and a Greek grammar went into Eva Palmer's luggage. She and Penelope had made the costumes for *Équivoque* together, it seemed a shame to waste them on one afternoon in Natalie's garden. Eva would wear them in the streets of Athens. She would stroll through ancient Greece with her hair unbound; if it trailed in the dust, that was the soil once trod by sibyls, the earth exalted by divinity.

For this voyage was no fleeting return to Mytilene, Eva had said scornfully to Natalie the night before she left Paris. Becoming Sappho was not play-acting in a garden! It was living the rites among the people who had tended the ancient shrines. Natalie watched as Eva finished packing her bags, her possessions winnowed to almost nothing; not Natalie's letters tied with a ribbon, not the volume of Renée's poetry, not a proper hat or coat.

Eva arriving hatless in Athens was welcomed by Penelope, who took her up to the hill that Isadora had bought. In their leather sandals they gazed upon the Acropolis. It was 1906. Eva Palmer felt ancient Greece under her feet. She looked down and saw that the earth had been dug away in a circle, as if someone were excavating each layer of the past. Buried in the hillside must be scatterings of marble and bronze, Eva imagined. But Penelope said no, it was only a well gone dry.

EVA PALMER SIKELIANOS, 1907

In the winter of 1906 Eva Palmer and Penelope Sikelianos Duncan left Athens for the Ionian sea. They were bound for Lefkada, the island of Penelope's birth. It was very cold to be wearing leather sandals and Penelope's breath hung in the air when she sang. In the home of Penelope's family there were dinners long into the night with demotic poets and Greek revolutionaries and bottles of Vertzami. They sounded like sisters now, Penelope and Eva, their voices rising and falling in the Greek modes: Lydian, Ionian, Aeolian. In the new year Eva was invited by Penelope's brother to visit the white cliffs of Lefkada. For a week she stayed there with him, overlooking the edge.

In 1907 Eva Palmer was no longer Timas who recited the lines that Natalie Barney had written for her. Instead she was enchanted by the singing of dark-eyed Penelope, resounding like an aeon eternal in the air. Unlike Timas, Eva stood at a safe distance from the edge of the cliffs of Lefkada. Penelope's brother took her arm.

By the end of 1907 she was Eva Palmer Sikelianos. She set up a walnut-wood loom to weave her own tunics and asked her new husband why the great theatre of Delphi stood empty. Where was the chorus, dancing its tragedies, calling out its ancient harmonies? Who practised the genitive of remembering? Eva went walking along the shore of Lefkada, looking at the sea. When she thought of Natalie Barney, in rare and bitter moments, she pictured an object encased in glass.

TEN

BEATRICE ROMAINE GODDARD BROOKS, B. 1874

On the morning in 1902 when Romaine Brooks sailed for Capri there was a hard, dazzling light on the bay. Squinting she saw the outline of the island, a promising mass of untamed rock with its teeth in the sea. She had barely enough money for the ferry, nothing for lunch; her paintbrushes were bald and clotted. For twenty lire a month she could rent an abandoned chapel in a low part of town. There were fig trees in the cracked courtyard and if she could sell a painting, she could buy bread and turpentine.

Romaine Brooks believed that she could sell a painting, at least one, because she believed that the island was detached from all fates she had previously suffered. Capri was distant from the taunting of her classmates at the Scuola Nazionale d'Arte by scores of nautical miles. It was even farther from her mother, an heiress who had left Romaine with a laundress when she was seven years old and then conveniently forgotten her. The laundress could feed Romaine only black coffee and fried bread, but she let the girl draw on discarded wrapping paper.

Romaine? her mother would say vaguely in Nice or Monte Carlo. Do you mean little Beatrice Romaine? She's somewhere being looked after, I believe. Such a difficult girl.

An island, Romaine Brooks thought, had no memory. In fact an island rose out of the sea to meet you just as you arrived at the marina. Disembarking, you found only the immediate, mindless glare of midday sun on the harbour. No one greeted you and all summer you read nothing. You might starve to death on Capri, but no one would call you Beatrice.

THE ZANARDELLI CODE

When Italy was first unified, its laws were an incommensurable morass of various moralities. The Albertine Criminal Code, the Sardo-Piemontese, the Napoleonic Civil: whether you were to be thrown in jail or let live in peaceable sin was determined by the region where you found yourself. Thus the politicians, wishing to make criminality the same all over the country, set about combining the Codes into one. For thirty years they were very busy.

In the end, the rights we didn't have under the Zanardelli Code were the same rights we hadn't had for centuries and therefore not worth enumerating, but we gained through omission one significant freedom. The Zanardelli Code failed to mention sapphists, inverts, tribades, Amazons, viragos, actresses, delinquent women, or anything else we might be called, and therefore failed to find us punishable by law in Italy. Moreover it extended the silence that sheltered sapphists to men who, in the manner of the ancient Greeks, enjoyed a philosophy of reclining with other men. This was one reason why Oscar Wilde, immediately upon his release from an English prison in 1897, fled first to Napoli, and then with his lover over the blue-green sea to Capri.

THE LADIES WOLCOTT-PERRY, 1897

Originally perhaps one was Wolcott and the other Perry, but when they appeared on the island they were always conjoined, their elbows interlinked, as inseparable as Capri and Anacapri. The ladies Wolcott-Perry had a seaside villa built for themselves with domed turrets sprouting up from braces of Doric columns; in the garden was a temple to the Roman goddess Vesta, whose priestesses spent their lives together in one house. In the temple of the ladies Wolcott-Perry, the vestal flame never wavered. Everywhere the villa was marked with their monogram, two hearts united by their initials.

Many years later Natalie Barney and Romaine Brooks had a villa built for themselves in the South of France. Each had a wing of her own: all afternoon Natalie could write and Romaine could paint in perfect, solitary freedom. In the evenings they met in the centre of the villa to dine together, in the only room that connected one wing to the other. They called their villa *Trait d'union*, or *The Hyphen*: the mark of a union, the juncture between two individual subjects who do not obliterate each other but rather remain linked at a single, voluntary point. In their own way, we reflected fondly, Natalie and Romaine were together for almost fifty years.

MRS BROOKS, 1903

Romaine Brooks was married once. It took a morning in 1903 to marry and very few weeks thereafter to see that this had been an error. His name was John. He disapproved of her hair, cut short and smart now that her mother was dead, but he was keen on her new inheritance. To be rid of her brief husband, Romaine Brooks settled upon him three hundred pounds a year, with which John and his lover Edward rented a house on Capri. They had a fox terrier that they walked to the Piazzetta and back, and were otherwise at leisure for the rest of their lives. On Capri there were now many such couples, with many such dogs; the ladies Wolcott-Perry began to keep lists of which Johns to invite to what dinner party.

Therefore Romaine Brooks left Capri and began painting all in shades of fog and charred wood. It was all very well that the laws of Italy did not descend upon its islands to torment anyone perceived of deviance, she acknowledged, but might not John have left Capri to her? Now she would have to find another haven, another isle without memory. Already it seemed to her that too many islands were consumed by their pasts.

EILEEN GRAY, B. 1878

Eileen Gray regretted that her father insisted on painting hot parched landscapes in Italy instead of the cool grey things that were shiny and silky in the county of her birth. Her island was Ireland, not Capri; her colours were grassy hillocks slicked in dew and the River Slaney blooming with raindrops. While she was still a girl, her father left her mother and went to live in an Italian village somewhere. Thereafter Eileen had a series of governesses who did nothing to dissuade her from becoming an unmarriageable artist.

ROMAINE BROOKS, *MAGGIE*, 1904, AND SAPPHO, FRAGMENT 156

Golder than gold was grey, Romaine Brooks believed. Grey was a range of feeling from the cooing of doves to the pale, relentless lichen that fed upon the marble marrow of fallen columns. In London in 1904, Romaine wanted to paint the cool grey light in the eyes of a woman thinking before she has decided exactly what to think of you. That was Maggie. In her portrait Romaine muddied the features with a touch of uncertainty, making shadows of her mouth and brow, even though Maggie herself had bright blonde hair and a ready wit. There were moments when Romaine found Sappho too intemperate for 1904.

EILEEN GRAY, 1901

Sanguine was a sort of red chalk used by students at the Slade School of Art in London to capture the ruddy tones of flesh. A stick of sanguine looked like a compression of dried blood. In 1901, when Eileen Gray enrolled at the Slade, it was still prohibited for women to commingle with men who were drawing from life. The bodies of models, even partially draped, were presumed to suggest an immoral carnality, like dried blood on a white bed sheet.

Wandering through Soho, Eileen stopped at the window of a workshop where a gleaming Chinese screen was displayed. That sheen, shiny and silky, that cool depth of colour like the surface of a river at dawn: Eileen had never seen paint gloss the base material of the world that way before. The following year she left for Paris to attend an art school where the models for anatomy classes were cadavers dragged out of the Seine. To sketch their greenish opalescence required no sanguine.

SAPPHO, FRAGMENT 150

For it is not right in a house of the Muses/that there be lament, Sappho writes, *this would not become us*. Eva Palmer Sikelianos knew this and tried to keep plaintive thoughts from crossing the threshold of her home in Lefkada. If lament pervaded a room, if the Muses were troubled by your weeping, it was almost always easier to abandon the house than to clear it of those inauspicious echoes. In 1908 Eva moved to a new house in Athens. In 1910 she bought land in Sykia and paced the shore, restless even before the lintels were set.

Of course it was not right, Eva told herself as she looked out to sea, to expect all Greeks to revere the ancient verses. Some part of every populace would want cheap modern things, ragtime and motion pictures and mail-order stockings. But where, beyond Penelope and her family, were the Greeks who tended the shrines of Sappho? The women of Lesbos did not recite in dactylic pentameter and the girls were not nymphs tumbling in violets. As far as Eva could tell, these Lesbians were utterly ordinary, with no fragment of Sappho flickering anywhere in them. This was the lament that Eva tried to still in her heart before it poured out in her voice. But it is as difficult to invert a lament as it is to unbecome.

ALFRED DELVAU, *DICTIONNAIRE* ÉROTIQUE *MODERNE, PAR UN PROFESSEUR DE LANGUE VERTE*

A Lesbian, according to one entry in Delvau's modern erotic dictionary, is a woman who prefers Sappho to Phaon. At first we were amused by this epithet, which would in an instant convert so many women that the isle of Lesbos could hardly hold them all; for who would not prefer Sappho over Phaon? We had all known too many Phaons, with their paltry charms. We had to keep lists of which Phaons had been invited to what dinner parties.

A Lesbian, according to another entry in Delvau's modern erotic dictionary, is a woman born on Lesbos who presently resides in Paris. In 1904 Romaine Brooks was searching for a place where she could live in peaceable sin and paint. She was tired of the hot loud light of the south and its endless ruins. In 1905 she put on the top hat that shadowed her eyes, packed up her paintbrushes, and moved to Paris.

GERTRUDE STEIN, *RICH AND POOR IN ENGLISH*

To be rid of her irascible landlord, in 1909 Natalie Barney left Neuilly and moved to 20 rue Jacob in Paris. Thereafter from the Temple à l'amitié we could stroll arm-in-arm to the house of Gertrude Stein, although we were careful to respect the days on which she received. Natalie had Fridays and Gertrude had Saturdays, when there were also men and raspberry brandy.

Thus between Natalie and Gertrude a correspondence arose. They would send each other *petits bleus* like reigning princes in neighbouring kingdoms, and between their salons was established a path, like a river cutting a canyon for itself, that ran down the rue de l'Odéon. It was easy and natural to follow, we had only to take each other's arms to be carried along. On the rue de l'Odéon were the two bookshops we frequented so assiduously that Gertrude Stein would say, I have almost a country there!

That country was Odéonia, we learned from the proprietor of La Maison des Amis des Livres. It was a small but marvellous realm where we encountered books on every imaginable subject. Leather-bound volumes we could not afford to purchase from La Maison des Amis were lent to us, wrapped in glassine paper, for a fortnight. Further along the rue de l'Odéon, a tumult of Americans streamed through the door of Shakespeare and Company, looking for airmail and the future of modern literature. They expected their change in pennies and their national poets prominently displayed. But Sylvia Beach would set out lopsided armchairs for everyone: she took in all readers equitably, as Gertrude said, rich and poor in English.

Thus in Odéonia we read atlases and biographies, tragedies and manuals for building boats of very light wood. From one atlas we learned that a narrow tongue of land is an isthmus, whereas an enchaining of several islands is an archipelago. Strolling between Natalie and Gertrude, we debated whether we were on land or at sea.

VIRGINIA STEPHEN, *MELYMBROSIA*, 1907

Virginia, who had begun her earliest journal with an account of bicycling to Battersea Park, was always drawn to excursions. She liked to see a landscape unfurl freely as she traversed it, the push on her pedals sending streets and trees streaming past her. But the return, especially to the gloomy house of her childhood in Hyde Park Gate, was dispiriting: she preferred unfamiliar destinations.

By 1907 Virginia Stephen was living with her younger brother in Fitzroy Square, writing her first novel. She bicycled through London thinking of how to launch her book into the world. Omnibuses bore down, cab horses reared up, errand boys darted by: she swerved and swore and wondered how *Melymbrosia* would find its way. Who would want to read the story of a girl sailing away from the island of England and towards an unknowable future, especially if it were penned by an entirely unknown novelist?

In fact Virginia Stephen's *Melymbrosia* would not be published until they had both changed their names: thus eight years later, when the landscape of the world had been irrevocably altered by war, Virginia Woolf became the author of *The Voyage Out*.

ROMAINE BROOKS, *THE BLACK CAP*, 1907

If grey encompassed many feelings, then black was where they were buried. The order of black, its austere self-enclosure, gave Romaine Brooks a sense of serenity in her new flat in the 16ème arrondissement. She bordered the carpets and curtains with black, and then ordered for herself several pairs of charcoal-grey woollen trousers with black coats to button over them, a scarf like ash. In 1907 Romaine Brooks painted a young woman looking down, her hands half-clasped, pensive in an unknown room. She might be anyone, in any room in Paris, without a past to bind her. Whatever she is thinking shadows her face like a black cap.

EILEEN AND JACK, 1904

Eileen and Jack lived together in a set of small rooms behind the Jardin du Luxembourg. Eileen aspired to be a painter; in a draughty hall of the Académie Julian she studied the soft inner curves of wrists and ankles. Jack aspired to be Jack. At night Jack would paint on the shadow of a moustache, don a jacket and trousers, and escort Eileen to establishments that no young woman could frequent alone. Nonchalantly Jack drank *eau de vie*, played chess, and found it all quite splendid. Eileen, who believed above all in private interiors, found it all quite terrifying. What if someone could see beyond the flat surface of Jack?

It was then that Eileen Gray began studying the art of making screens, of hardening surfaces, of painting layers upon layers of gleaming brittle lacquer that betrayed nothing of a substrate. From a master of Japanese traditions she learned that lacquer was made from the dried sap of a poisonous tree, mixed with stone dust. After she had painted the first few coats, the soft inner skin of her wrists was consumed by a vicious rash. Nonetheless Eileen kept working. She wanted to make a lacquered screen for Jack, oblique and impermeable, something to protect the sensitive act of dressing.

DAMIA, 1911

In the music halls where Damia sang, a girl was expected to dress so that she would catch the eyes of sailors. But Damia sang her chanties and laments in a simple black sheath that left her strong shoulders bare. When a critic compared her to a fairground boxer in repose, Damia shrugged. She had been born in a cramped room in the 13ème arrondissement to a family of ten; she had been sent to reform school; by the age of fifteen she had already heard every curse that could be hurled at a girl.

Eileen and Jack met Damia in a nightclub that no young woman could frequent alone. Damia's voice was melancholy, low, roughened by cigarettes. Her black dress was wrinkled and, although she was only nineteen, her eyes were old. Eileen, trying not to stare at her beautiful shoulders, asked about her repertoire: she sang mainly *chansons vécues*? Yes, Damia said, sadly they were all songs that she had lived herself.

NATALIE BARNEY, *ACTES ET ENTR'ACTES*, 1910

The acts we undertook then had fewer interludes between them. There were acts suitable only for private rooms but there were also, at least in places like Paris and Capri, increasingly acts that could be done in public. It was not only that under the Napoleonic Civil and Zanardelli Criminal codes sapphists went unmentioned. It was also that we were becoming bolder and more numerous. We had ivory-handled knives and were no longer girls. In Odéonia we were acquiring manuals, atlases, translations of Greek tragedies with the choral parts printed on pages we cut open ourselves. Like Romaine Brooks, some of us now had means of our own, and in lieu of further schooling we had Natalie, who read Renée Vivien's *Retour à Mytilène* aloud to us in her salon. It was true, however, that we no longer had Eva Palmer. She was in an interlude, on an island, alone in ancient Greece.

ROMAINE BROOKS, *THE SCREEN*, 1910

The first time that Romaine Brooks showed her paintings in public she felt nakedly displayed on a wall of the Galeries Durand-Ruel. All of her paintings were of women. In the painting Romaine could no longer bear to look at, a young woman stands leaning against a folding screen next to a little black lacquered table. She is wearing only a slip of frail fabric over her shoulders. She is looking away, melancholy, sallow and shadowy in form, while the table is made of exemplary hard edges. When we saw this painting we understood why it cast Romaine into despair. She had painted a table and a screen that knew how to be in a room. They were at home in an interior, perfect and angular, while Romaine Brooks herself remained restless and vague, still taking form.

EILEEN GRAY, *LA VOIE LACTÉE*, 1912

At that time Eileen Gray was only making private samples of her work. She produced for her intimate friends some lacquered screens they might use while dressing, or undressing, in their rooms in Paris. *La Voie Lactée,* for example, never left the bedroom of the woman Eileen Gray had made it for. The surface of the screen is darkly enamelled in a moonlit blue, and the body of a woman glides across it, bathed in the pearly light of the stars. With her hair drifting behind her, milky and brilliant, she makes the whole cosmos luminous. She knows how to float softly over the hardest of surfaces, her body moves between the world and a dream.

SAPPHO, FRAGMENT 104A

Eventually the lacquered objects of Eileen Gray and the paintings of Romaine Brooks were gathered together in the house of Natalie Barney. Natalie had a way of assembling the interiors of disparate women that never ceased to astonish us. On Eileen's low black tables, Natalie would light candles for Renée and set out vases of the lilies Liane loved. We were struck by the image Natalie had created: how the flame, mirrored by the dark gleam of the tabletop, warmed the pale throats of the lilies.

Then Natalie settled herself under Romaine's portrait and we made our circle around her, like nymphs in the woods, to listen to *Retour à Mytilène*. As long as we stayed in the rooms of Natalie Barney, we felt, we would be lit from within by the images of what we could be. On Fridays at Natalie's we thought of Sappho: *Evening/you gather back/all that dazzling dawn has put asunder.* But Romaine Brooks, exasperated by our poetic and overheated rooms, demurred. Amazons, not nymphs, Romaine said brusquely. And no one is going back to those islands.

PENELOPE SIKELIANOS DUNCAN, *AKADÉMIA*, 1912

In 1912 Penelope returned to Paris. On the fifth floor of a cold building, in an Akadémia bearing the name of her husband, she began teaching Greek drama, music, and weaving. It was difficult to teach French schoolchildren the story of Elektra, Penelope found, but to impart to them the difference between the Lydian and Mixolydian modes, this was perhaps impossible. Instead Penelope felt that they should produce something of their own, a new staging of the ancient arts for the people of France. She would ask Eva, she told her husband, and Eva would come back to Paris for her, she was certain, they were like sisters.

ELEKTRA AND CHRYSOTHEMIS, 1912

Of course Eva came back to Paris for dark-eyed Penelope. She would have descended to the underworld to hear Penelope sing again. In Paris it was decided that Penelope would be Elektra and Eva would be her sister Chrysothemis. Together they would perform the Sophoclean chorus, dancing its tragedies, calling out its ancient harmonies. They were the daughters of Clytemnestra and Agamemnon, they knew what it was to act. And yet to belong to that family was a heavy gift.

In 1912 we did not tell Natalie Barney that Eva had returned to Paris. In February, on an evening that was not Friday, we went to the Théâtre du Châtelet to see the new *Elektra*. We sat in a dim row and held our breath, watching the light shine on Penelope. The play was less a series of events than a succession of images, like a moving picture seen frame by frame. We forgot Clytemnestra and Agamemnon. We forgot Cassandra. We watched only Penelope and Eva, in profile, an entablature passing before us. Half-kneeling in her anguish, Penelope implored the gods to take pity, while Eva followed her, stumbling, heedless, her arms outstretched.

VIRGINIA WOOLF, *ON NOT KNOWING GREEK*

Elektra stands before us like a figure so tightly bound, Virginia Woolf wrote, that she can only move an inch this way, an inch that. But each movement must tell to the utmost.

Elektra must tell through movement because no one understands the verbs she uses. Even the poets are mystified:

λυπειν, what kind of suffering is that, to wound yourself for some future already foretold? Flinging out her stiff-fingered hands, Elektra demands of the gods what dark cage they have made of her life, and why. She will not listen to reason, her brother says. But is it unreasonable to dance the bare inch you have been given, knowing how it will end?

Eva had departed for Athens before teaching us all of the moods of Greek verbs. It was only later that we discovered, for example, that two moods lack a future. One is the imperative, used for demands and orders. The other is the subjunctive, used for everything that is not reasoned fact. Perhaps Elektra suffered in verbs no one understood because there was not a future for the mood she lived in.

ROMAINE BROOKS, *NO PLEASANT MEMORIES*

It was in her first year of boarding school that Romaine Brooks met the Greek girl. She had insouciant red hair and could recite from the dictionary in alphabetical order, astonishing Romaine who had never memorized anything except how to make coffee in a tin pot. At night the Greek girl left her windows open for Romaine, who came in like a black wind and stayed until dawn. When they were caught together, Romaine had no explanation. Perhaps she was sleepwalking, perhaps she had lost her way to some other room where the furniture was arranged in a similar order. Romaine came from too wealthy a family to be punished, but the Greek girl was sent back in shame to the island where her parents still lived above their taverna. The Greek girl was a sign, Romaine thought, that there was no fate worse than returning to an island you had abandoned. Once you had set out for the future, there must only be the hard edge of the horizon before you.

The Greek girl was the subject of several paragraphs in Romaine Brooks' memoirs, which were never published. As Romaine said darkly to Natalie Barney, the only title her life merited was *No Pleasant Memories*, and what publisher would consent to doom a book before it was born?

ELEVEN

SARAH BERNHARDT, *ROMANCE OF AN ACTRESS*, 1912

In 1912 we had cinema and lacquered screens, we were content to sit in rooms with shadowy corners. Even those of us who earned our livings modestly could now treat ourselves to evenings of Beaujolais and the films of Sarah Bernhardt. We had lost some few of our company, it was true. After *Elektra*, Eva went back to Greece while Penelope went on to London. Then Penelope's husband took her to a tiny village where they piled up stones from the ruins to make houses. For three years Penelope breathed stone dust. She coughed more than she sang. In the house in Sykia, Eva wove long senseless skeins, waiting for Penelope.

But in 1912 Sarah Bernhardt made four films. She was Queen Elizabeth in *Les Amours de la Reine Elisabeth* and she was dashing Adrienne Lecouvreur in *Romance of an Actress*. She was sixty-eight years old, indefatigable, with a baby tiger she let walk down the dinner table. In the summer of 1912 she made a film in which she was merely the Divine Sarah. It was a film of her life at the summer house she shared with Louise Abbéma, on the island of Belle-Île-en-Mer in Bretagne. Enraptured, we watched every scene as if it had been made for us. We felt that at last we were seeing the true romance of an actress.

Thus we did not spare many thoughts for Penelope, for Eva, for any forlorn cries of prophecy or doom. We were watching Sarah and Louise on their island, picnicking on the cliff.

GIUSEPPE PISANELLI, *JUS SANGUINIS*

The law of blood ran hot in the veins of the Pisanelli Code. Anyone could get themselves born on Italian soil, Giuseppe Pisanelli argued, but true citizens must be made from the blood of their families. For indeed, he asserted to the Italian senators, the principal element of nationality is race. The senators nodded knowingly, their bloodlines flush with pride.

It was in the name of the Italian race that, in 1900, the nation began to conquer other lands and call them colonies. This led to unforeseen problems that nearly always ended in blood. For example Italian men, having taken Eritrea for themselves in 1900, also took many Eritrean women; thus by 1905 the colonial government was confronted with unprecedented numbers of illegitimate children. The politicians of Italy debated this dilemma: whether to call these children Italian by the blood of their fathers or colonial subjects like their conquered mothers.

In the meantime they ordered the construction of foundling houses in Asmara.

OSCAR WILDE, *SALOMÉ*, 1891

Sarah Bernhardt was a jewelled dagger among the dull wits of theatre, Oscar Wilde had always said, the Divine Sarah was the most ancient and cunning of goddesses. He would worship at her fur hem if she would allow it. He was quite willing to let her pair of lions devour him down to his bootlaces. In 1891, while Sarah was Cléopâtre, he imagined her entombed in a pyramid, an asp on her breast. Delicious shivers ran through him as he lay on the yellow velvet fainting couch of his hotel room in Paris. Oscar Wilde closed his eyes and let the vision palpitate under his eyelids: a new play, yellow shivers writhing like asps on velvet, the jewelled eyes of a murderous queen of the Orient. Sarah would be Salomé. Although in truth, Oscar Wilde mused, Sarah Bernhardt had always *been* Salomé, she was a daughter of Babylon.

PAOLO MANTEGAZZA, *FISOLOGIA DELLA DONNA*, 1893

The Italian senator Paolo Mantegazza had a theory about what lay inside women and Africans. First of all it was quite dark and underdeveloped. Secondly it was inferior to Italian men. Thirdly, Mantegazza professed, Italian women and all African peoples were little better than children, due to their innate physiology; for the good of the Italian race they should be patronized by those who knew better, namely the senators of Italy.

SALOMÉ, 1892

In 1892, Oscar Wilde set about ensuring that Sarah would be his Salomé. He had written the play in French, he had dressed his princess Salomé in the same golden veil that Sarah had worn as Cléopâtre. The stage would be filled with smoking incense to set off her sharp and sinuous form; out of that haze the Divine Sarah would gleam like a snake, a treacherous blade, a river scythed by moonlight. For indeed, Oscar Wilde said to himself, Sarah was a perfect serpent of the old Nile.

But when Sarah Bernhardt read the script of *Salomé*, she blanched. She had been born the illegitimate daughter of a Jewish courtesan. To make her way in the world she had taken the parts she wanted and ignored the remarks that accompanied them: that her hair was too curly, her body strangely skinny, her cheeks rouged in high colour; she was ill, she was contagious, she was deceitful, she was lavish, she was decadent; she was her mother's daughter, a daughter of Babylon.

When finally Sarah Bernhardt was known to be divine, she seized the right to be an actress instead of what she had been called since birth. Above all she gave herself life and more life: she titled her memoir *Ma double vie*. But the princess Salomé calls for death. She dances in her gold-fringed veils for the pleasure of betrayal, she bestows her murderous kiss in a murky cloud of incense. Thus in 1892 Sarah Bernhardt abjured the role assigned to her, she could see where that would lead.

PAOLO ORANO, *LA LUPA*, 1910

La Lupa was an Italian newspaper named after a she-wolf. With the grim precision of a grey shadow *La Lupa* began circulating on the peninsula in 1910. Paolo Orano, the editor, urged his shewolf on her ravenous hunt; her prey were the decadent, lavish, deceitful, melancholy, effeminate peoples of the Orient and the South who were diluting the pure blood of the Italian race. *La Lupa* harried the Jews with charges of socialism, deviance, and Semitic plots; there were imprecations against the lazy dark people of the South, little better than sly children; and of course women. Essentially women were primitive beings, Paolo Orano concluded, subject to bouts of emotional hysteria and irrational prejudice.

In her flat in Rome Lina Poletti tore *La Lupa* into scraps and cast them into the fireplace. After a minute the words of Paolo Orano were blazes of nothing. But when Lina leaned down to light her cigarette, her hand was trembling.

CASSANDRA, 1912

We went to the theatre, we went to the cinema. We sat in darkened rooms and watched bright lives pass before us. Untroubled by shadowy corners, we adored the romances of actresses and envied their beautiful islands. By that time we had forgotten Cassandra.

Yet Cassandra too could see after and towards at the same time. She ran along the walls of Troy seeing madly on all sides while men derided her: she was called a *commediante* and worse. But Cassandra could not hide her tongue from what she had to say. She raised her voice to a pitch like the screaming of wind. From her throat she poured out the darkest things. It was true that men never listened to her. But we should not have forgotten Cassandra and those like her, women who had already lived our futures.

SALOMÉ, 1897

Any role spurned by Sarah Bernhardt was summarily refused by Eleonora Duse. La Duse would not be cast as a second-choice Salomé! Yes, yes, she understood that Signor Wilde had come directly to Napoli to see her upon his release from that English prison. But he looked quite unwell. He should perhaps go away for some time before recommencing a public life, especially a life in the theatre. A rest cure, somewhere far from English laws and newspapers, Signor Wilde; yes, there were sailings every day for Capri, the island was not as far as it looked. And there were many of his compatriots there who had sought, how do you say, a refuge? An idyll. Only he should take care in his dealings with the local people, there had been some scandals with young boys asked to pose for foreign sculptors. *Attenzione*, Signor Wilde, do not mistake a bronzed boy of the islands for a statue to put in your garden.

ISADORA DUNCAN, 1904

Nature had endowed Isadora Duncan with Grace, she explained, and so it was her duty to embody the Beauty of

Nature on the stages of the world, to free the Art of Dance from crimped artifice and restore its honourable Heritage. Here in St Petersburg, had they seen some Greek friezes, some classical vase paintings? she enquired. Ah, they had, very good, they would understand then that her dance arose from the Noble Beauty of the Ancients, that her gestures were as Pure and Natural as the white marble statues in the British Museum.

We must save the Dance not only from the stilted frivolity of ballet where it has languished, Isadora Duncan went on, her voice rising, but also from the Primitive and Degenerate Races who would corrupt it! Our Art must not be debased by the sensual or tainted by the decadent: let us scorn the skirt dance, the foxtrot, the nautch girls, the belly dance, the black bottom! She extended her arm entreatingly, like a white marble statue that has lost its way. She cleared her throat. She hoped that her esteemed audience would understand what she meant.

Ida Rubinstein, sitting at the back of the theatre in St. Petersburg, understood perfectly well what Isadora Duncan meant. Ida Rubinstein had been born the daughter of a wealthy Jewish merchant in Tsarist Russia. She had studied French, Italian, German, singing, dancing, and Greek. She had staged her own *Antigone* and ignored the remarks that accompanied its premiere; that her hair was a snaky seething mass, her body strangely gaunt, her wealth of suspicious origins, her ideas deviant and cunning. It was rumoured that she was a Salomé, a lascivious daughter of Babylon; she should be cast out of the Country by its Citizens, banished beyond the Pale of Settlement.

Very well then, Ida Rubinstein said to herself, if that were the only part offered to her, she would take it. Or rather she would seize it with both hands before it strangled her.

SIBILLA ALERAMO, *L'ORA VIRILE*, 1912

In 1912 Italian politicians were lauding twin triumphs of the nation: they had invaded Tripoli and they had limited suffrage to men alone. So adroitly had the men of Italian government arranged 1912, in fact, that while an unknown number of people in Tripolitania and Cyrenaica would either be conquered or put to death, every woman in Italy would remain disenfranchised. The empire would swell while the citizenry would narrow.

On the general subject of Italy, Sibilla Aleramo was stingingly lucid: men had made it, they had excluded women from it, and now they were killing people in its name. That was the nation. A war between one country and another, between one race and another, Sibilla wrote, a war of iron and flames: this is no creation of women.

It was in this war, for the first time in the history of the world, that bombs were dropped from aeroplanes. Torpedoes ripped through the sea, civilians were massacred at the oasis of Mechiya, islands were occupied and ports blown up. Of course we agreed with Sibilla that the war was utterly barbarous.

But Sibilla's article was titled *L'ora virile*, the virile hour, and in 1912 she must have heard that hour striking. Some seductive, sonorous tone called to her, although we could not hear it.

Perhaps Sibilla was weary of being the primary object of Italian laws and theories, perhaps she was adrift on illusions of mutual interest. In any case *L'ora virile* concluded that, even though Italian women had not supported the war, Italy was after all home to both sexes; the country was still therefore a unity of hearts, palpitating in the hot unison of nationhood, coursing with the vaunted blood of the Italian race.

CASSANDRA, 458 BCE–1913 CE

Itys, itys, Cassandra cried out. What was Itys? A child, a birdsong, nonsense, a barbaric sound. The chorus did not understand what she was saying. Generally the citizens of great empires did not wish to understand Cassandra. She was a foreigner. She was always seeing serpents and flames, birds and blood. She was always saying that she had seen this future before. To Cassandra, the violence done before rendered inevitable what came after. Itys was a little bird with its throat slit, she said. Itys was the darkest of old things rising again. *Itys,* the nightingale was singing and singing, but no one would listen.

IDA RUBINSTEIN, *SALOMÉ*, 1908

Oscar Wilde did not live to see the premiere of his *Salomé.* He died in a hotel room in Paris in 1900, syphilitic and unrepentant. To the very end he remained unloved by his compatriots. Even on Capri, where bronzed boys were diving into the blue-green sea, Oscar Wilde had not found his idyll. Instead he had been met with the chilled stares of landed gentry in the dining room.

After three days the hotel staff were obliged to turn him out, he was tainted by English law.

Ida Rubinstein did not wait to be cast out of the Pale of Settlement by her compatriots. In 1908 she had already taken the role of Salomé, shedding her seven veils with voluptuous slowness. It was often said that Ida Rubinstein was not a gifted dancer. But she could make an exquisite pose and hold it forever. She could wait until an audience was feverish, slavering in their seats, before letting the last veil slide from her body. In other words Ida Rubinstein knew how to make of herself an image: a portrait framed by what everyone already thought of her. She could take the part offered her and dance it to death.

ROMAINE BROOKS, *THE CROSSING*, 1911

When Romaine Brooks left the theatre, she kept the image of Ida Rubinstein behind her eyes. Once Romaine had cleared away the haze of incense, the jangling of anklets and beads, the blue wig with golden braids twisting from it, she could see Ida in her own form: almost colourless, elegant in her contempt. Ida Rubinstein might be wilful and vain, but she was not Salomé, not Cléopâtre, not the treacherous sultana Zobeide. When Romaine looked at Ida, she saw the long blank angles of her body, the edges of her hard like a table.

Later, when Ida was looking at herself half-painted on the easel, she asked Romaine how to render an image flat and fixed, when in truth a model was always moving. A person was composed of so many sides, Ida said, was it possible to depict anyone in their fullness? Romaine studied the crest of Ida's bare hipbone rising to its point. A body is always a risk, Romaine replied slowly, it is difficult to work from life.

SAPPHO, FRAGMENT 151

We had grown drowsy in the garden of Natalie Barney. Amid the heady white perfume of the lilies, we lay down on the grass with our books half-read. The ivy grew steadily, wrapping the walls, and in the Temple the candles burnt down to their ends. Then, as Sappho writes, *on the eyes/black sleep of night.*

Perhaps we closed our eyes in order to linger in that dream of our idyll. Or perhaps we did not wish to see the dark stories sitting in the trees like screech owls, their talons buried in the bark of Natalie Barney's elms. We were still young, and sleepy with possibility. Dimly we knew that in other lives the darkest of old things had already descended: that people were dragged across the seas as slaves, cast out of their countries, delivered to fates of mute terror. The foundling houses of Asmara filled with children begotten in violence. Women were massacred at the oasis of Mechiya, bombs plummeted from aeroplanes and disgorged their deathly contents upon villages. But these stories were bundled, blurry masses to us. We kept them at a distance and turned our eyes to Sappho, to Lina Poletti, to the Divine Sarah. We wanted stories set about us like gleaming surfaces, reflecting and burnishing our hopes. Was it not at last our time to become?

In the garden it seemed that time hung in the air like incense, a burnt cloud. It obscured our intentions and the contours of our faces. We could hardly see to kiss each other goodnight.

OVID, *METAMORPHOSES, BOOK VI*, 8 CE

In the beginning, Ovid recounts, Itys was merely the son of sweet Procne. But the screech owl attended his birth; violence brooded over the house of the infant Itys. The husband of Procne looked down at his own brute hands and considered what throat to bruise.

In secret the husband of Procne dragged her sister Philomela to a house of stones in the forest. With his brute hands he forced her down under him. Afterwards, when she was nothing but bruises and rags, he cut out her tongue so that she could not tell. Yet Philomela, blood where her tongue should have been, told everything: she wove a tapestry for her sister Procne to read. And so Procne ran in horror to the stone house, and so the sisters ran together to find Itys, in vengeance for the man who had fathered him: innocent Itys, dead for his blood.

Thus Itys became a little bird with its throat slit, just as Cassandra had foretold. And Procne became a nightingale who flits forever bereft, doomed to sing, *Itys, Itys*. The death of a child makes a barbaric sound.

SAPPHO, FRAGMENT 154

Those were the stories we were given. When we were children, we learned what happened to girls in fables: eaten, married, lost. Then came our bouts of classical education, imparting to us the fates of women in ancient literature: betrayed, raped, cast out, driven mad in tongueless grief. It was not unusual, we discovered, for women to be dragged across the seas as slaves and then murdered on the threshold. Cassandra was merely one of many.

Was it any wonder that we read Sappho instead? The worst of Sappho's heartbreaks are bitter dawnings of envy, the keen emptiness in her arms where a beloved no longer sleeps, an exile from one beautiful island to another. Sappho has the luxury of growing old in her own bed. Her hair goes white on the pillow, her acolytes listen to her cracked voice singing the memories of those wild silver nights: *full appeared the moon/ and when they around the altar took their places*. Sappho had many years of long afternoons and celestial nights. Nothing happened to Sappho except her own life.

ISADORA DUNCAN, 1913

Isadora Duncan had two children. She did not say their names in public, perhaps because they were very young or perhaps because they were illegitimate. But in 1913 a car went off a bridge into the Seine, taking with it the lives of the children and their governess.

Immediately the newspapers were ravenous. The death of a child makes a barbaric sound, even in print. Isadora fled the words that had been the names of her children.

First Isadora fled to Penelope in the remote village of stone ruins. But Penelope and her child were coughing stone dust and specks of blood. Isadora could not bear to hear that little voice gasping, ragged of breath. She fled to the coast of Liguria, to the seaside villa where Eleonora Duse was convalescing.

Eleonora Duse had been so many women that she could understand any sorrow: an actress is someone who carries ghosts for a living. Even when she is tired and ill, she remains a prism of other selves. In 1913 Eleonora Duse was still Ellida who stands at the edge of the sea serene in her own life, a beacon for women everywhere. Isadora Duncan could see her at a great distance.

But there is no art to losing a child, Isadora said bleakly to Eleonora. I know, my sweet, Eleonora replied, stroking the head that rested on her shoulder. There is always this risk, in life, that we have our parts in a tragedy and we do not know it.

ISADORA AND ELEONORA, 1913

Ancient Greek has a singular and a plural, as in other languages. But there is also the dual, which is used for two things that naturally occur together: twins, a pair of turtle doves, breasts, the two halves of a walnut in one shell. Do you see? Eleonora asked Isadora, looking up from the Greek grammar that lay open between them. Only for two things that embrace each other. As when you sleep in my arms, my sweet.

Isadora buried her face in her hands and wept until the tears ran through her fingers. Eleonora closed the book softly. Of course, the dual would also be used for two children in the back seat of a car as it goes off the bridge.

Quietly Eleonora went out of the house and down to the sea. She would not say it aloud to Isadora, but there is always this risk, in life, that we see only our own parts as tragedies.

SIBILLA ALERAMO, *IL PASSAGGIO*

When Sibilla came to Paris in 1913, she told us stories of all of the women Eleonora Duse had been. In truth we only wanted to hear the romance of the actress: gossamer summers, shattered champagne glasses, love poems by Lina Poletti. But Sibilla was intent on recounting every woman, onstage and off, that Eleonora had poured herself into. Even Isadora Duncan, so lost in grief that she saw only her own pale ghosts, was embraced by Eleonora Duse.

We knew that Sibilla was writing a book called *Il passaggio*: the passage, the way through and beyond, the voyage to a destination we had dreamed of since our earliest days. We wondered if Sibilla would tell us how to gather our threads, how to set out for the idyll promised us. Was her very name not a sign that she should foretell our fates?

But Romaine Brooks, passing by late at night with Ida Rubinstein on her arm, was exasperated by our talk of sibyls and signs. The Temple was a hothouse of nostalgia, Romaine said, she was going to take Ida to walk in the snow. Ida wrapped herself in a long ermine coat, leaving her throat bare, and departed in cool white silence. At the threshold Romaine looked back at us and said in a low voice, It is more difficult than you think to work from life.

TWELVE

VIRGINIA WOOLF, *MR BENNETT AND MRS BROWN*, 1924

Virginia Woolf in a railway carriage destined for Waterloo was trying to decide when everything had changed. It was not as though one morning you went out into the year and saw it bursting into flower and song. Instead, over time the cooks left off boiling the leeks into a pallid, watery sop, and began to brightly poach eggs with chervil; the tomes of the criminologists were relegated to ever dustier shelves; gradually it became less scandalous that a woman could run a hand press or read Aeschylus in the original. Now a widow in mended gloves like Mrs Brown, perched on the edge of a second-class seat, might occupy an entire novel by herself.

Virginia Woolf, writing in 1924, tried to remember when all of this had happened; it was before the war, certainly, but was it the year when Tolstoy died? Or that spring when everyone went around in hobble skirts and hatpins? In the end she decided that it was in or about December, 1910, when human character changed irrevocably, and kitchens and books and fashion along with it. We believed Virginia Woolf was right about everything, she could run a hand press out of her dining room while translating from the Greek. Yet for all of us looking back after the war, there was a bad blur around those years. We could not tell the edges of 1914 from anything else.

NATALIE BARNEY, *GIRLS OF THE FUTURE SOCIETY*

At first 1914 seemed like a sleek, exuberant step forward. In fact we had cause for hope and delight. Sarah Bernhardt was made a Chevalier of the French Republic with a bright red ribbon. Sibilla Aleramo, bidding us farewell at the Gare de Lyon, confided that *Il passaggio* would be a paean to the love of Lina Poletti. In our own small realm of Odéonia, Gertrude Stein published a book of poems called *Objects, Food, Rooms*; Natalie of course held the reading in her salon, where the housekeeper set out cucumber sandwiches on lacquered tables. Our lives seemed gaily mirrored in the surfaces all around us.

Thus we strolled arm in arm down the rue de l'Odéon, contented. We had our own books and films, our intimacies were by now virtually unpunishable under European law. Finally free of the criminologists, we now rallied for a skirmish with the psychologists who had begun pontificating on our breasts, coughs, and fathers. Above all we had Natalie Barney, who promised us that the Girls of the Future Society would be legion and fierce. Amazons would ride rampant through the Bois de Boulogne, Natalie declared; temples to the Tenth

Muse would tower over the little bronze statues of great men in public squares. Woe betide any man who stood in the way of the sailing to Lesbos!

ELEONORA DUSE, *LIBRERIA DELLE ATTRICI*, 1914

The inauguration of the Library for Actresses was an intimate and auspicious occasion. Eleonora Duse wrote the invitations in her own hand. She had taken an ordinary house in Rome and made of it a sanctuary where any actress might find refuge; every wall was a bookshelf, every armchair was graced with a pool of lamplight. Furnished with Eleonora Duse's private collection, the library offered not only the scripts of Ibsen and Zola but also philosophy, poetry, political treatises, and an annotated copy of Ragon's *Grammaire grecque*. In the spring of 1914, Eleonora Duse turned the key in the lock with a sprightly click, and the door to the Libreria sprang open.

It was vital, Eleonora said to her guests as they filed into the hallway, that any woman who wished to act should be educated beyond the confines of the stage door. Ignorance might lead even the most intelligent woman of the theatre into unfounded prejudice and phantom fears, Eleonora concluded; she had seen it happen with her own eyes. But henceforth actresses would have a free, well-appointed place where they could learn to think for themselves, what the English would call a room of one's own.

CONGRESSO INTERNAZIONALE DELLA DONNA, 1914

In the same spring in Rome, many women were gathering on the Capitoline Hill for the International Congress of Women. They were amassing in hot rooms. They were wanting things of their own. Their voices were rising up together, phrases went flying round Sala degli Orazi e Curiazi like birds: emancipation, pacifism, libraries, workers' rights, gynaecology, juridical equality, divorce. Twenty-three countries of women, their pennants flying, rose to their feet and sang, O sisters! Anna Kuliscioff was there, exhorting everyone not to despair of the recent Italian parliamentary vote against women's suffrage. Eleonora Duse was there, on the arm of the Countess Gabriella Rasponi Spalletti, inviting all the young actresses to her Libreria.

Sibilla Aleramo was not there, because she was curled on a chaise longue in the Temple à l'amitié. According to Natalie, there was no need to journey to Rome; the Temple was its own international congress of women. As she said drolly while the sherry was served, O sisters! Is congress not a synonym for intercourse, coition, and other actions of coming together?

Meanwhile on the marble threshold of Sala stood Lina Poletti, shading her golden eyes with one hand, looking out across the sea of women.

SAPPHO, FRAGMENT 56

Eugenia Rasponi, half-sister to the Countess Gabriella, believed in solid carpentry and radical political action.

Despite the descendance of her family from various Napoleons, Eugenia had refused all noble suitors. What she wanted, she explained to her dismayed mother, was not one nice man, but rather the total emancipation of women from that tyranny of men known as the Italian government. This was taking longer than Eugenia would have liked, and kept her from woodworking. *Insomma,* Eugenia would sigh to her companions at the Lyceum, Well, when there is freedom for Italian women, then we too shall have our free time.

The Rasponi Spalletti Lyceum for women's intellectual collaboration was a grand name for a small room in the palazzo of the Countess Gabriella. But its windows directly confronted the Quirinale, the seat of Italian government, and Eugenia could often be found there late at night, reading volumes of legal history or repairing the rickety chairs of her companions. In the halls of the Quirinale, where men sat behind satinwood desks deciding the fate of the nation, rumours persisted about the Lyceum, that it was subversive, even sapphic.

And what if it were? Eugenia said aloud, shrugging off her scarf as she strode through one hot room of the Congresso after another, looking for her companions. Is not sapphism a modern practice? In 1914, in Italy, we are still jailing the publishers of books describing love? We are still denying to women the rights to their own bodies? It is as if the new century has changed nothing. If we could gather our forces, we would wreak such change on the world that the leaves on every tree in this country would be left trembling in our wake.

On the threshold Lina Poletti swung around to face Eugenia, saying in her low, ardent voice, No other woman *I think/who looks on the light of the sun/will ever/have wisdom/like this*; Sappho, Fragment 56.

VIRGINIA WOOLF, 1914

In 1914 we had such hopes. We were gathering in our circles: the Girls of the Future Society, the Lyceum, the Temple à l'amitié, the Congresso Internazionale delle Donne, Odéonia. We carried on as though together we would shortly wrench the world around.

Yet in patches of 1914 we could hear voices muttering, as if the year were a radio badly tuned. We heard shots, cries, whispered agreements at satinwood desks. We heard some material being ripped into shreds, a flag or perhaps a skirt. We heard an Englishman saying solemnly, The lamps are going out all over Europe, we shall not see them lit again in our lifetime.

Virginia Woolf wondered later if perhaps we should have asked the men of Europe why they went to war. Frankly it hadn't occurred to us that they might produce a coherent answer. We had tried reading the histories: there were the Italo-AustroHungarians in 1866, the Franco-Prussians in 1870, the violent scramble to colonize Ethiopia in 1887. During thirty-eight minutes in the summer of 1896, the entire Anglo-Zanzibar War began, raged, and concluded. By 1900 it was something else again, a jumble of revolts, slaughters, conquests, and insurrections; in 1911 the ruthless Italian invasion of Tripoli. And now, in 1914, still this mad hurling of bodies and bullets at each other, until everything was a raw torn mass of mud and shrapnel wounds turning rapidly to gangrene. Might we ask them to behave like rational persons for once? Why had they put out the lamps all over Europe just when we had hopes finally of becoming Sappho?

VIRGINIA WOOLF, *CASSANDRA*, 1914

In the autumn of 1914 Virginia Woolf opened the newspaper. On the third page she was instructed that there had been no female of first-rate literary ability since Sappho; on the fourth she was assured that the war was utterly necessary and right. She sighed. She closed her eyes and pressed her hands to her temples. Then she opened her eyes, threw the newspaper onto the andirons, and began to write about Cassandra.

In those years Virginia Woolf published her first novel, but she also began to try to kill herself. Like us, she was desperate for someone to light the way to a future where we might see our lives unlatched before us like windows. Virginia Woolf knew that the newspapers would always insist that there were no more Sapphos, only more wars. She invented a Cassandra for 1914. Cassandra was the one who saw everything and instead of sighing, screamed.

CASSANDRA, 458 BCE

In Aeschylus, Cassandra screams in translation. She is a noble Trojan, now enslaved by the Greeks, and the house she is dragged to is a horror. She stands in the doorway and screams the unspeakable future: the house is lit red with blood, she foresees it, she cries out her own death.

Actually we should say that Cassandra screams outside of language. The scream is to gash the fabric of normal life, to rend it into strange tatters. Then it is open to prophecy. Then Cassandra lives in her own future.

VIRGINIA WOOLF, A *SOCIETY*

By 1914, therefore, Cassandra had become modern, sharp, English, a little ironic. She lived in London and Virginia Woolf knew her well. With six or seven companions Cassandra assembled a Society of the Future: their quest was to determine, once and for all, whether men were actually a worthwhile endeavour. Should the men of Europe be discontinued, they wondered, or had they proved themselves sufficiently useful and good?

Promptly the Society began its enquiries into barristers, capitalists, scholars, earls, admirals. One member read every book in the London Library. A second was lectured at such length on the market value of colonial rule that she developed a terrible polite cough and had to be quarantined. Another toiled through seven hundred pages of claims about Sappho's chastity, written by a learned, doddering man at Oxford. Dutifully the Society visited the sites trumpeted as triumphs of modern civilization: prisons, coal mines, the dockyard of the Royal Navy, and hospitals where every year a certain percentage of women died from maladies incident to childbirth. It dawned on the members of the Society that the most powerful and educated men of Europe had not understood at all what a life should be.

MRS ETHEL ALEC-TWEEDIE, *WOMEN AND SOLDIERS*

As soon as the British declare war, Mrs Ethel Alec-Tweedie proclaimed, every man is a soldier and every woman is a man. In fact, any man bound for the front would find, travelling through Britain, a squadron of women smoothing the way for him with cheery efficiency. They would punch his ticket on the tram. They would direct him to the correct platform and wave him onto the train. He would go off to the front, and they would stay behind to run the country with their steady hands. Mrs Ethel Alec-Tweedie could see how this news might be discomforting to some British men who were used to driving the lorries and manufacturing the munitions themselves. They might well think, Ye Gods! The women have eliminated us. We shall soon be as extinct as the dodo.

In a lively meeting of the Society of the Future, Cassandra and her companions debated whether or not this was an outcome to be desired, albeit discreetly. Some objections were made to the comparison of men and dodos, as the peaceful dodo had done nothing to cause its own demise; it had been killed off by men.

THE SOCIETY OF THE FUTURE, 1914

Meetings of the Society of the Future were by turns despairing, arch, bewildered, and utopian. From Cassandra and her companions we gathered that, while further evidence might yet be heaped up, the question of men was at best rhetorical. There was no use waiting any longer. At last it was time for us to set forth, raise our sails, clear the shoals, and steer into the open sea, believing that beyond the blue abyss our island awaited us. We were devout and well-provisioned, the daughters of educated men. Thus the girls of the future society began preparing the voyage to Lesbos.

GLADYS DE HAVILLAND, *THE WOMAN'S MOTOR MANUAL*

It was reported that scads of young Amazons had recently taken up motoring. The Girton Girls of yesteryear, with their bicycle stockings and book bags, had now taken the wheel. Fast and modern, motoring allowed us to clamber into our seats side by side and set off for a destination barely visible on the horizon. We had khaki car coats and emergency rations. It was true that our motor cars often broke down unexpectedly; we kept a packet of books on hand, so that when stalled on the roadside we could read Renée Vivien. In fact we had learned how to motor by reading the manuals. It was not unlike tribadism or clitorism, if you studied the diagrams closely you could generally manage the manoeuvres once en route.

ARTICLE 14

Since 1882 the commercial codes of Italy had stipulated that a married woman working as a merchant was not, in fact, a merchant. She might manage a shop, run a lodging house, manufacture items of clothing, undertake all manner of enterprise: still, at best she would be classified as *uxor mercatrix,* the *wife* of a merchant. Article 14 was very clear on this point. Yet by 1911 it was determined by census that a surprising number of women, widowed or working with their daughters, had become merchants in all but name. What might Zaira Marchi, sole proprietress of a silver shop in the centre of Bologna, be called? What taxonomy accounted for Rosa Grandi the laundress, who deeded her *lavanderia* to the women who came after her? Reluctantly the Italian politicians recognized the emergence of *foemina mercatrix*, a female merchant, as if she were a new species of beetle.

NATALIE BARNEY, *PENSÉES D'UNE AMAZONE*

We discovered belatedly that the men of Europe had decided, in 1907, how their countries ought to declare war on each other. They had called this agreement a Peace Conference. We threw up our hands. It was as if we had called our international feminist congress a 'Rally to Continue the International Oppression of Women'. And now they were having their 'Great War': what a preposterous masculine fiction, Virginia Woolf exclaimed in despair; what a grand empty title for mangled bodies and mustard gas. Had they no respect for truth or logic? Frankly we did not see how we could go forward unless we left men entirely behind. In the Temple à l'amitié Natalie Barney declared, Let us march to love as men march to war!

We watched as the men donned their uniforms and filed away to the front. Where now should we march to love? If necessary we could motor away from the war, we had atlases and manuals. But Natalie Barney urged us not to leave. In cities emptied of men, she said, we could at last occupy our own realm: Odéonia and Mytilene, Amazons and pages yet uncut! We were always asking how to find our way to some isle we had not yet glimpsed, but why not establish our sapphic idyll here, now, by ourselves?

Yet we felt that Lina Poletti would bid us venture onwards and outwards, to fight in public for what we wanted. The Divine Sarah would not cloister herself in a garden of endless ivy. Even Natalie dreamed of a society of the future, not merely a temple to the past. It was 1914: sapphism was a modern practice. Could we not ask at last for the rights to our own lives? Moreover we had vowed to seek the passage to a future where girls like us, even from their earliest days, could be free. We needed only a sibyl, a sign, to orient ourselves. To our dismay *Il passaggio* was still an unfinished manuscript, and Sibilla Aleramo had gone away to Capri.

THIRTEEN

SAPPHO, FRAGMENT 42

Thus we gathered, the future girls of the Society of the Future, to divine our own way forward. In a bar near the Gare du Nord, we were talking all at the same time: those who thought we should seek the passage to our own separate island, shaded by olive groves, and make our idyll there; others who thought we should rush to fill the seats of government, to change everything while the men were caught up in their war. There were some few who maintained that we might now return to our various cities of origin, to seed Sappho everywhere we could. So earnest and impassioned were our voices rising all together, amid the glasses clinking on the tables, and Colette who came late banging the door open and whistling for another bottle, that we did not hear the first bomb go off.

But we heard the second bomb, and then the third. There was a shattered sort of scream in the street. Thus the war came upon us.

Until that night we had believed that we would choose for ourselves how our story would go. We held all of the threads in our hands, it remained only to decide together which one to unspool. We had always admired those women who knew what it was to act. But it was Eleonora Duse, after all, who said that we might have our parts in a tragedy and not know it. Perhaps she had meant to warn us of this risk, in life, that we see only our own parts? Amid the rubble we could hardly tell the edges of our lives from anything else.

Were those the voices of the chorus we heard, flying around in our heads like birds in a room? Were those our voices echoing in the bar, in the moment after the bomb went off? They made a ragged sound, the saddest fragment of Sappho: *Their heart grew cold/they let their wings down.*

RADCLYFFE HALL, 1914

In our hearts a snow of feathers came down. We shivered and glanced fearfully at the sky. We had disdained the bellicose idiocy of men, we had intended to remain aloof from the war, and yet it had come upon us unbidden. It had flown over our houses like a screech owl: whistling, then eerily silent before the blast. The third bomb had killed an old woman in the *quartier.*

You see how the modern world is perishing under a flood of ugliness, Natalie Barney said vehemently to Radclyffe Hall. They were walking through the Jardin du Luxembourg in a wind that scoured the horse-chestnut trees of their last leaves. The war is a great peril, Radclyffe replied. But some of us have always seen the modern world as a sea meant to drown us.

SAPPHO, FRAGMENT 168B

After the blast of the first bombs, the war crept into our houses like smoke. Solemn letters from distant families were slipped under the door, informing us of the deaths of brothers and nephews. The keening of aeroplanes woke us in our beds. We heard over the radio that Lesbos had been occupied by the Hellenic Royal Navy. Was there any land that persisted out of time, as drowsy and Arcadian as ever?

By then the oracles of our early days were unreachable. Renée Vivien was entombed under withered violets and snow, Sibilla Aleramo had gone away to Capri. Virginia Woolf was as prescient as anyone, but each day was now for her a delicate question, as fragile as blown glass with grains of veronal strewn through it. We dared not ask.

The war had come within thirty kilometres of Paris. We lay awake at night in our rooms, wondering who would light our way forward. The city, besieged, was the only wall around our Odéonia. *Moon has set,* Sappho writes, *and Pleiades: middle/ night, the hour goes by,/alone I lie.* Our nights were like the hard lacquered screens of Eileen Gray, except that all the stars had been scratched out.

EILEEN GRAY, 1914

Eileen Gray did not wait for the war to come upon her. She went to meet the war at the front where it flamed. Out of those flames staggered mutilated figures, barely men, in dire need of tourniquets, iodine, morphine. Any one of them might have been her brother or two nephews. With great care she washed the ash from their eyes and loaded them into her ambulance. She drove them back through the night. She sent word to us in Paris that there was an urgent need for women with steady hands; anyone who could tie a knot or drive a motor car might have her part in history. If there were ever a time for Amazons, Eileen Gray wrote to Natalie Barney, it is 1914.

ROMAINE BROOKS, *LA FRANCE CROISÉE*, 1914

Romaine Brooks had come back to Paris when the war broke out and brought Ida Rubinstein with her. Ida drew a hard line in the air wherever she went; Romaine kept her charcoals sharp, tracing the slash that Ida made in the muddled grey light of Paris. Ida was like a falcon, like the wing of an aeroplane shrieking across the sky. She might dive through a cloud of flame unsinged. Thus in 1914 Romaine and Ida went to the front as ambulance drivers.

At Ypres for the first time there had been chlorine gas released in the trenches. The French soldiers watched wondrous as a yellowish cloud rose from the enemy line and crept towards them on the evening breeze. Then they were dead, or dying horribly. After that sight Romaine and Ida gave up driving their ambulance. Instead Romaine began painting Ida, with her sunken eyes turned to the horizon, standing before the smoky ruins of Ypres with the cross marked red on her shoulder. What does she see in the distance? we asked Romaine. Ash upon ash, said Romaine, and no way back.

ELEONORA DUSE, *LIBRERIA DELLE ATTRICI*, 1915

When the war came to Italy, one of the first casualties was the Libreria delle Attrici. The books were boxed up, the lamps were put out. Eleonora Duse sat on a lone footstool with her old *Grammaire grecque* in her lap, the green leather spine flaking. What would become of actresses, now that the Libreria was nothing but an ordinary house on the outskirts of Rome? Was there any beacon still shining amid this mustering of violent fears, this herding of people into common hatred? Eleonora Duse could not see what was to come. She felt herself flickering, loose and uncertain, like a film run to the end of its reel.

Evening was coming on, the swallows were diving and swooping over the trees. The library sat dark and hollow. A chain coiled around the handles of the front door would rust before anyone unwound it. Despite Eleonora Duse's many invitations, Isadora Duncan had never taken a room at the Library for Actresses; now she never would.

VIRGINIA WOOLF, *EFFIE*, 1915

Effie was going to be a novel, but she did not survive the war. Amid the air-raid sirens and spatterings of gunfire, Virginia Woolf could not make a haven for her. There were black cloths tacked over all the windows in London, people lived half in their cellars. Effie believed in keeping a dispassionate distance from the war. But the war pressed in upon her, wailing at her, plaguing her nights, conscripting her for its own purposes. Effie became impossible to imagine, much less to write, and Virginia Woolf fell violently ill.

In 1915 the world was like the night nursery. Virginia lay in bed while the firelight flared into hellish fingers. There were shadows on the wall shattering into shells, a screeching sound came in through the windows. In a fever dream she saw the impenetrable black mass of a yew tree, a stalking silhouette at the end of a garden, out of which exploded a sudden shrieking of rooks, rending the evening sky into black fragments that splintered the air and lodged themselves in everything.

LINA POLETTI AND EUGENIA RASPONI, 1916

Lina at breakfast with Eugenia flung down the newspaper and exclaimed, Do you know what the German and Austrian soldiers are doing to our sisters in the Veneto? And rape is not even a crime under the laws of war. We must fight, on every front, there is no question, tell your sister Gabriella, the Lyceum must rise in their defence!

But in 1916 the son of the Countess Gabriella Rasponi Spalletti was grievously wounded in battle, and she withdrew from the world. The room in her palazzo where the Lyceum had flourished was requisitioned for the sickbed, the curtains always drawn.

LINA POLETTI, *IL POEMA DELLA GUERRA*

Trucidatori di donne/sono, Lina Poletti began the stanza: they are the slaughterers of women. In the courtyard of the prison, she continued, lay the nurse Edith Cavell, against whom were turned the guns of twelve men; they shot her through the temple, when she had sought only to heal them. *Per voi, per voi tutte, cadute*, Lina vowed, pressing her pen bitterly into the page, For you, for all of you, women leached of your lives and lying now bloody and stilled, we will vindicate you, we will say: beyond her they cannot pass, we will stop them at this death, this body, this woman left like a scrap in the prison-yard mud: there shall not be one more.

All through the war Lina wrote her poem, there were so many women slaughtered and no time to despair. Eugenia in the evenings sometimes sighed. Lina was burning and burning, her mind was aflame with flares and bombardments, with screams, she heard them in her sleep, before dawn she rose from the bed where Eugenia slept and wrote yet another stanza. Eugenia awakening called out, Lina? Lina said, low and urgent, Do you know of the sacking of the city of Ypres, what they have done? And Eugenia replied, Lina my love, I know that after the burning and burning there is nothing left but ash.

LINA POLETTI, *COMITATO FEMMINILE*, 1916

Lina Poletti said that she would lead the Committee of Women herself. Her eyes molten, she urged her companions, Let us rise and resist, let us strive for justice! A hundred years from now, said Lina in her low ardent voice, our sisters will remember us. No monument will mark our battle, but our song will echo in their mouths, the streets of the future will ring with our words, *Siamo il grido, altissimo e feroce, di tutte quelle donne che più non hanno voce:* We are the piercing fierce cry of all the women who no longer have voices. They cannot bury us under stones, they shall not entomb us in despair, our voices will live on even after our deaths. The chorus of us will never be silenced.

Lina was like that, she had her own ways of escaping the century. From the earliest days she had been drawn to the outer reaches of any space meant to bind her. Now it seemed that she could see into a future after ours, as if we were all at sea in a great turbulent wash of time, and Lina, only Lina, had swum to the crest of a wave to sight land.

CASSANDRA, 1918

The final meeting of the Society of the Future was held in the autumn of 1918, when the last leaves were clinging brittle to their branches. Evening clattered by outside the window, a brisk stream of motor cars and men selling newspapers. The companion who had suffered through the monograph on Sappho's chastity was the last to speak. She burst out, Oh, Cassandra, why do you torment me?

Yet by then we understood: Cassandra torments us because she already knows the answer. More terribly, Cassandra tells us that we too already know. Even before the war, we sensed that we could not simply invert every story around ourselves. It was true that Eva and Natalie had turned Phaon out of the centre of the *Heroides* so that we could dance there, glorious and barefoot in our vengeance, for love of Sappho. We could take back from Ovid the tongues of women.

But with the modern world it was infinitely more difficult. Stories were now tangled skeins that seemed to have no centre, no heroine. The threads unravelled in our hands. For example, in Paris in 1917 the midinettes were striking, they were women working in the factories who wanted a fair wage and safe conditions. Of course we supported them. But they were working in the very factories that produced uniforms for soldiers. Clad in the uniforms the midinettes made, soldiers went on killing people, and then soldiers clad in other uniforms retaliated; thus not only brothers and nephews died, but also old women in the *quartier*. Thus girls were raped in the Veneto. Thus the nurse Edith Cavell was shot in the prison yard. How could you drive an ambulance in a war like that? we asked Eileen Gray and Romaine Brooks, and of course they answered, How could you not?

Itys, itys, Cassandra cried out. What does it mean? we demanded. You who have already lived our futures, Cassandra, tell us! All at once the air trembled, the leaves of the tree against the window were shivering, there was a light too bright for an autumn evening, voices went flying around like birds in a room. Romaine Brooks was saying, It is more difficult than you think to work from life. Eleonora Duse was saying, There is always this risk, in life, that we have our parts in a tragedy and we do not know it.

Then Cassandra said, It is not true that nothing happened to Sappho except her own life. Have you forgotten that a poet lies down in the shade of the future? She is calling out, she is waiting. Our lives are the lines missing from the fragments. There is the hope of becoming in all our forms and genres. The future of Sappho shall be us.

FOURTEEN

CASSANDRA, 1919

After the war we were left with ash in our eyes, in our mouths. We set about clearing the rubble and dust from our vision; we were free to buy butter and petrol, we could walk in the streets without fear. Almost all of us had stayed, except Eileen Gray who had left after her nephew was killed in battle at Ypres. From London she told us that Virginia Woolf was writing short pieces from life now.

For so long we had said to ourselves that we were going to be Sappho that Cassandra's words were strange on our tongues. We pronounced them in a halting litany, as if we were reciting the tenses of foreign verbs:

> We who had come after Sappho would now go onwards.
> From her fragments would emerge our new and modern forms.
> There would be a future for the mood we lived in.
> No longer would we follow in the style of, wistful and optative.
> Now Sappho was going to become us.

We were going to happen to Sappho,
and Sappho would never be the same.

We discarded our classical grammars, our drapings of silk and ivy, the volumes of Renée Vivien. Henceforth, we told Natalie Barney, Sappho would wear our clothes with buttons and collars. Sappho would drive our motor cars and write our novels.

We imagined Sappho watching us, expectant or even impatient, waiting for her future to arrive in the form of us. We thought of Virginia Woolf: short pieces from life now. Yes, said Romaine Brooks, Enough lyric poetry. Not another still life with flowers. More portraits of us.

VITA, *JULIAN*, 1918

Julian was striding through the wintry streets of Paris with his wife Violet on his arm. Amid the many soldiers who could only crutch themselves along the boulevards, he cut a jovial figure, hale and handsome. It was rare to see such a lucky one, all limbs intact and a lovely young wife like Violet. In fact Julian was writing the story of his own extraordinary life. Whether it would be a novel or a memoir was as yet undetermined: the life of Julian was comprised of episodes that strained the most heroic imagination. Even Julian, scribbling the first draft, was astonished by the fates that befell him in each chapter.

Julian! Natalie Barney cried gaily as he came in the door. And Violet, what a delightful surprise. There are cucumber sandwiches, *faites comme chez vous*! Romaine Brooks gave Julian a queer look and said, Haven't we met before? But before Julian could explain, Natalie cut in with a wry smile, My dear, allow me to present Julian David Mitya Victoria Mary Orlando Vita Sackville-West Nicolson of Knole. I see, Romaine said, scrutinizing the figure before her. And might I paint you?

VITA SACKVILLE-WEST, *PORTRAIT OF A MARRIAGE*, c. 1920

A marriage might be for the purpose of laying out a garden symmetrically. It might be useful to have at dinner parties, to explain to foreign diplomats what you were doing there. If a heavy object needed to be carried four-handed from one room to another, that was a good marriage; also in the case of sailing a small craft in high winds. The best sorts of marriage were companionable and involved a shared taste in novels and furniture. In extreme cases, such as Lina Poletti's, a marriage could be wielded like a pistol with a silencer.

We did not need to read *Portrait of a Marriage* in order to understand the marriage of Julian and Violet. As soon as they came through Natalie's door, we could tell that if one of them had her hand on the tiller, the other would stand ready to trim the sail. We would have watched an entire film of Julian and Violet picnicking on the cliffs of an isle in Bretagne.

At the same time, in a different key, we could see why Vita Sackville-West had married Sir Nicolson. The front garden of the castle where Vita and her husband lived was laid out very clearly, with immaculate hedges framing roses that blushed in the sun. It was orderly and English until you went round to the back, where the bower had been savaged by blackberry vines and a shed, blowsy with ivy, sheltered the trysts of feral cats. For Vita and Sir Nicolson, Natalie intimated to us, had agreed to preserve on the grounds of their marriage some discreet, wild idylls.

What we did learn from reading *Portrait of a Marriage* was that Sir Nicolson, while married to Vita, was also married to a man named Raymond. It appeared that they shared a taste in novels and furniture.

ÉLISABETH AND NATALIE, 1918

To the consternation of her mother, a French princess, the tastes of Élisabeth de Gramont ran less to claret than to communism, feminism, and sapphism. Tender with her lovers, gracious with her friends, implacably utopian in her politics, Élisabeth married Natalie Barney in 1918. They were both writers and Élisabeth was the most delightful person Natalie had ever met. They wrote their own marriage vows, they wrote each other affectionate deluges of love letters; when they summered in the countryside, Élisabeth wrote a warm invitation to Romaine Brooks importuning her to join them, it would be lovely, Romaine could have any room she liked and paint all morning in perfect solitude. In their own way, we reflected fondly, Élisabeth and Natalie and Romaine were together for almost forty years.

JACK, 1919

When Eileen Gray came back to Paris after the war, Jack had disappeared from the rooms they once had shared. His jacket still hung in the closet, his cigarette case still glinted on the desk, but Jack was gone.

Had Eileen not heard, Natalie asked, that Jessie Gavin had got married to a wealthy French industrialist during the war? There was no reason for the marriage really, no one was in love or needed money. But Jessie Gavin had always been a queer one, gallivanting about Paris, dressing up, frequenting establishments unsuitable for young women. Jessie was so nonchalant that she might very well marry a man in order to borrow a pair of trousers from him.

In fact, Natalie told Eileen, the eternally eccentric Jessie Gavin had refused on her wedding day to take the surname of the groom. Instead, mystifying the entire wedding party, she had changed her first name to Jackie. That way, Jessie said as she raised her glass of *eau de vie*, her old friends could still call her Jack.

EILEEN GRAY, *SIREN CHAIR*, 1919

Damia had spent the war singing for soldiers at the French front; she returned to Paris with a deeper note of weariness in her rich, rough voice. She was known by now as a *tragedienne lyrique,* as if she were an actress or a sibyl. Eileen looked at the hollows under Damia's eyes and decided that she should rest.

Thus in 1919 Eileen sketched and carved and polished and upholstered until her idea took form. It was an elegant, sultry armchair, with lacquered black limbs and a velvet cushion in burnt orange. The back featured a golden siren caressing her own tail, against which Damia settled her beautiful shoulders. And now that I have made you this Siren Chair, Eileen said to Damia, I hope that you will not cast me upon the rocks.

EILEEN GRAY, *JEAN DÉSERT*, 1922

In 1922 Eileen Gray opened a gallery of her own. It was meant to show all of her ideas about light, surface, and self-enclosure. She lacquered the front doors in gleaming black and laid panes of blue glass into the floor to make the cellar workshop transparent. Inside the gallery the objects were both hard and soft, each standing alone. An ebony desk was edged sweetly in silver, a rug was like moss under a stone.

At first only women came, and only because they had been sent by Natalie Barney. But gradually Eileen Gray became known outside the circle of the Temple à l'amitié; some men came and bought armchairs. Eventually even wealthy French industrialists could be found peering through the blue plates of glass into the workshop. One of them asked Eileen Gray curiously, why call the gallery Jean Désert, who was he, a master craftsman? No, Eileen replied, it is a name I made myself, in part for the solitude of the desert, and in part because Jean is the most common man's name in French, as in English we have John, you know, or Jack.

VIRGINIA YARDLEY, 1922

Since her birth Virginia Yardley had been told that she was a daughter of the American Revolution, descended from a lieutenant of sterling pedigree. But Virginia intended to be a modern girl; she went to Bryn Mawr, stayed up late, painted wildly. She fell in love with Eva Palmer. She attended art school in New York, scraping by on coffee and stubs of charcoal. Like Eileen Gray she went on to Paris, to the Académie Julian, where life drawing classes for women were separated by preference: nude model, draped model, or the back stairs avoiding any rooms in which life disrobed and stood bare in its cold glory. Virginia Yardley soon became adept at nude models. Her family sent her no money and considered her pedigree wasted, but Eileen would buy her a drink now and then at the Chat Blanc. And, Eileen asked, what will a modern girl like you do next? Stay up late painting wildly, Virginia answered, until I become a modernist.

ROMAINE BROOKS,
RENATA BORGATTI AU PIANO, 1920

Lowering her fingers to the keys, Renata Borgatti gave a rapid nod, an almost involuntary gesture of beginning. The first sheet of music was spread out translucently behind her closed eyelids and the first notes were held, still silent, in the air cupped under her palms. That was the moment of Renata Borgatti.

After that instant Renata opened her eyes and pressed her

fingertips into the keys, the first notes went out from under her hands and resounded in the room, a slight swaying took her shoulders, she bit the inside of one cheek and grimaced. No, Romaine interrupted her, it's only the first instant, before you begin.

Thus Romaine Brooks did not paint a portrait of Renata Borgatti playing the piano. How Renata appeared to her public at concerts, severe and impassioned, was merely the image an audience paid her to play. Their desires refracting around her were noisy with colour, memory, loud chords, opinions. Neither did Romaine paint Renata languorous in bed with a strand of sunlight on her short dark hair: that was the image Romaine kept for herself from their summer together on Capri. Thus in 1920 Romaine painted the moment that belonged to Renata alone, before sound takes form: Renata as she sees her own music, Renata replete unto herself.

VIRGINIA WOOLF, *NIGHT AND DAY*, 1919

In 1919 Virginia Woolf had the dream that the night might not entirely drown the day. She called it a novel, for lack of a better word. She might have said it was a portrait of an evening. She might just as well have called it a chapter in a painting or a way of seeing birdsong, there was not yet a word for the forms she dreamed in.

It was a June evening, Virginia Woolf wrote, when the unfinished, the unfulfilled, the unwritten, the unreturned came together in their ghostly way and wore the semblance of the complete. Someone had lit the lamps in the house. Each window gave out its light, some full and golden and others dim, glancing, cloistered by curtains. She was seeing the house in her own way, as one moment unriven.

It was only 1919; there were still ordinary birds singing; yet the birds sang across the garden and down to the river where she stood, bearing in their voices the wavering light. How kind the birds were, to carry to her on the brink of the river, on the edge of evening, this rippling, fluted sound of light poured out of a window in welcome! They were nightingales, she saw now, and in the house it was Cassandra who had lit all the lamps. Cassandra would know the verb she was seeking. There must be a verb in some language that means, to leave the lamps burning for someone who has not yet arrived.

RADCLYFFE HALL, *THE UNLIT LAMP*, 1924

To expect a lamp to be lit for you, in the view of Radclyffe Hall, was frankly to invite despair. Perhaps there had been an interlude, during the war, when women could finally become Englishmen, as Mrs Ethel Alec-Tweedie had proposed. There had, Radclyffe would concede, been ambulance drivers; yes, she knew about Gertrude and Alice rattling round France in their Ford, by now everyone knew that story.

But the rest of us, in ordinary times, for what could we hold out hope? We could stubbornly hack off our hair with a penknife and refuse to knit. But that was not the same as a future where every window blazed with love. At best that was a fleeting glimpse of some other creature like you, blunt and shorn, mournful and wracked, with whom you might find a companionable sympathy. And if that hope cast any light, Radclyffe felt obliged to note, it was whatever meagre flicker you could get from a stiff wick, stewed for centuries in cold oil, to which you touched a match that burned your fingers.

ROMAINE BROOKS, *PETER (A YOUNG ENGLISH GIRL)*, 1923

Nonetheless in the evenings we stood at our windows, hoping. Twilight made the glass flat and silvery; a dim interior widened the very centre of our eyes. Through the faint reflection of our own faces we watched the scuttling of figures along the streets, the slivers of doors opening and closing. From our vantage point the world occurred in fragments and shadows, a silhouette, a gesture, a figure stepping out of the background. The outer surfaces seemed mottled, brittle, temporary. To piece the fragments into portraits: that was why in 1923 so many of us were aspiring painters and novelists.

At that time Romaine Brooks had her eye on Peter, a young English girl. Peter insisted on having only one name, without prefix or further explanation. In a starched collar and a half-buttoned black jacket, Peter sat upright and hooked a thumb into a black belt. In profile Peter appeared thoughtful and resolute: a slight narrowing of the brow, dark eyes fixed on some distant object. Peter was the kind of person who simply donned a jacket and went out into the evening, regardless of lamplight.

We could see in Romaine's portraits how the surface of an image, the page or the canvas, would stand flat by itself: that was Peter, that was Renata. The moment it took was a quick, glancing slice across the thickness of time. Like flash powder, the illumination was brief and total: it touched all of the surfaces at once and was done. It was a modern way of seeing someone.

ÉLISABETH DE GRAMONT, *LES LACQUES D'EILEEN GRAY*, 1922

Mme Eileen Gray wants to create the room as a whole, Élisabeth de Gramont wrote admiringly in *Feuillets d'art*, Mme Gray wants to create interiors in keeping with our lives. At that time, the shape of our lives indicated one inner compartment punctuated by many possible windows.

Often we dwelt alone in our interiors, the way an orchid or an octopus might shelter its soft parts in a rocky crevice. That was the room as a whole, wrought entirely around us. There were lacquered desks for writing, rugs we sank into, divans like the seed pods of foreign fruits. Once inside we might lock the door and think for days at a time. Thus we began to consider whether a flat image might be merely the front of an interior. A novel or a painting was in the end a square packet of ideas. But without a room to harbour its tender, tentative beginnings, how could a portrait come forth in finished form? We thought of the blue glass panels that split Jean Désert into gallery and workshop: a floor to present the scene of a salon, undergirded by the space of its making. Perhaps Eileen Gray was furnishing our rooms with the possibility of thinking behind the surfaces we produced.

So few poets, Natalie Barney sighed to Élisabeth de Gramont, and no one plays the lyre any more. Élisabeth smiled indulgently and settled her head between Natalie's breasts. They were lying on a rug softer than the cress at a river's edge, in a room Eileen Gray had wrought around them. You miss Sappho, Élisabeth said, but this is an age of chapters and portraits, *ma très chère Amazone*. Even the paintings now are set each in their frame, not running round the sides of a vase. You do see why Eileen wants to create modern interiors for all of us? It is like Virginia in London, writing short pieces from life now.

ROMAINE BROOKS, ÉLISABETH *DE GRAMONT, DUCHESSE DE CLERMONT-TONNERE*, c. 1924

At first each portrait had seemed to Romaine solitary in its frame. An image of Ida Rubinstein had only to do with falcons, ash, and wind. Renata Borgatti in a shapeless cloak was far from Peter, whose every hem was cut sharp, tailored to the angles of shoulder and jawbone. But gradually the portraits became like a line of windows at night, each showing a different silhouette pinned by lamplight. Thus Peter without prefixes was followed by Élisabeth de Gramont, poised at the foot of the stairs in a white silk scarf. In her studio Romaine arranged them in a row, like a lineage or a line of sight. In the centre was *L'Amazone* herself, Natalie Barney, grey before a window, wintry, wrapped in a fur, flanked by the small jade statue of a horse. Eventually, Romaine told us, there would be enough portraits to fill a room.

ROMAINE BROOKS, *UNA, LADY TROUBRIDGE*, 1924

Una, Lady Troubridge, was the first to return the gaze that fell upon her. We had not seen this before: a portrait that looked back. Una seemed to be eyeing us and every other painting in the room at the same time. She did not need a portrait to reflect herself, she told Romaine. Una already knew quite well how she looked. She squinted; one eyebrow arched quizzically; her thin mouth twisted at the edge. Instead Una wanted a portrait to depict how she *saw*.

The way that Una looked at someone could build a nest, a name, a scandal, a fashion. In fact every glance of Una carried in it a fragment of her lover John, like a bird ferrying in its beak the countless twigs that will construct its home. In the fastness of Una's adoring gaze, John let her former name fall away. Thus everyone except Natalie, who initially insisted that she had known Radclyffe far too long to change now, began to call the two of them John and Una, or Una and John. In this way Radclyffe Hall became merely two words that appeared on the outside of books shortly to be banned, whereas John was daily called to dinner. It was for John alone that baths were run and slippers laid out. Addressed tenderly by Una at bedtime, John gained a comfortable solidity usually reserved for patriarchs in their middle age.

To be painted by Romaine Brooks, Una wore her monocle. Her right eye seemed thus unusually engorged by pride and scepticism, and with her right hand she held the collar of a fat little dog who worshipped her with trembling eyes. Una knew that the dog would rather be trotting through the park with John.

But Romaine Brooks had persuaded Una by promising her a portrait that, under the title *Una, Lady Troubridge*, would show the world how to see John.

ROMAINE BROOKS, *SELF-PORTRAIT*, 1923

At midsummer the air in Paris was cramped and sultry. Romaine had gone away to the countryside with Natalie and Élisabeth. Those of us who had stayed in the city meandered by the canals with our stockings rolled down. We were the ones without summer houses: we were loose, a little lonely.

Romaine had offered us the use of her roof garden. We were welcome, she said, as long as we watered the pear tree and didn't fall drunkenly to our deaths. Thus one humid evening we trooped up the stairs like bedraggled sparrows, passing through her dimmed rooms. It was Colette who ordered us into the studio to gather some old sheets, she wanted to lie on the grass.

As soon as we pulled the sheet away from the canvas, there was Romaine, gazing evenly back at us from under the brim of her top-hat. She was wearing grey gloves and a cool, distant expression. From the crisp arch of Romaine's collar to the crook of her elbow, all of her edges were hard and clear.

Finally Romaine had found her moment, her way of being in a room. In the midst of creating portraits of everyone else, she had made her piece from life. At last she had taken the risk of her own body.

FIFTEEN

NOEL PEMBERTON BILLING, *THE BLACK BOOK*, 1918

One great risk of our bodies, and thus of our portraits and novels, was that someone like Noel Pemberton Billing might attempt to read them. The principal aim of Noel Pemberton Billing's existence was to catch the wives of men in Parliament entangled in lesbian ecstasy. Not that he could have recognized lesbian ecstasy if it had bit him on the foot; this was a man who, reading Sappho, had thought her the headmistress of a finishing school for ancient young ladies. Still, he went trundling through galleries and bookshops, snuffling suspiciously at certain paintings and poking the spines of modern novels.

Noel Pemberton Billing was such a deplorable reader that he could only comprehend books he had invented himself. These books, though inextant, were allegedly filled with descriptions of Sodom and Lesbia, written in the most appalling prose. In 1918 he invented *The Black Book*, which he never bothered to write, supposedly containing the name of every lesbian in Britain. We imagined him poring greedily over each imaginary page. If he hadn't been such a dreadfully bad reader, we thought, he might simply have perused Léo Taxil's *La Corruption fin-de-siècle* from 1894, from which he would have learned that by law lesbians did not exist.

MAUD ALLAN, *SALOMÉ*, 1918

Oscar Wilde had been dead eighteen years when the dancer Maud Allan became Salomé. She was giving private performances in London, we had heard, when Noel Pemberton Billing got wind of it. Scenting lesbian ecstasy, he became hysterically excited; immediately he denounced her in the papers as a high priestess of the Cult of the Clitoris.

What is a clitoris? the papers wished to know. Is it an unsteadiness in the hand? Is it a trembling in the mouth? Is it an organ unduly excited or overdeveloped? A certain Lord was overheard remarking to a fellow at his club, I've never heard of this Greek chap Clitoris they are all talking of nowadays!

Thus Noel Pemberton Billing set about teaching all of England what was a clitoris. A clitoris was a kind of lesbian, he maintained; that is, Salomé of Sodom and Lesbia, being the Oriental regions of Germany, had indecently penetrated our noble land, thereby making of Miss Maud Allan a Lesbianist; he could vouch that her name was listed in *The Black Book* under sadism or sapphism, perhaps both. Clearly, this was the case of a clitoris.

REX V. PEMBERTON BILLING, 1918

Indignantly Maud Allan brought charges of defamatory libel. Privately we thought, in a country where a man elected to the House of Commons could not find a clitoris in the history of literature, Maud Allan had a slim chance at justice. But we followed the dispatches from London closely. The papers reported that Maud Allan was cross-examined on veils, anatomy, Germany, lewd vices, dancing, decadence, Oscar Wilde, Oriental Philosophies of Love, sadism or sapphism, Jews, art, and where were Sodom and Lesbia on a map. Noel Pemberton Billing testified that he had read *The Black Book* and Maud Allan's name was everywhere in it. The jury barely deliberated before pronouncing their verdict: Maud Allan knew what a clitoris was. Therefore nothing worse could be said about her. She lost the case.

VIRGINIA WOOLF, *THESE ARE THE PLANS*, 1919

We feared that Noel Pemberton Billing and his ilk had destroyed half a century of our careful becoming. We had not foreseen that a hysterical mob might drag us back to the years when X was imprisoned in an asylum and Rina Faccio sentenced to marriage under Article 554. We were plunged back into a history we had barely survived the first time.

In England there was a chilled, cautious withdrawal from public life. Julian and Violet set off abroad; Virginia Woolf began to spend weeks in her house at Rodmell, writing. In Paris we were scathingly angry; Colette dashed off a cruel sketch of those venomous toads of Parliament, as she called them, squashed under the thundering hooves of a hundred Amazons riding to hunt. Even Élisabeth de Gramont vowed vengeance by near-strangulation with her white silk scarf. But Natalie Barney, ever the pacifist, rebuked us: we had never won our lives by law, she said, only by literature. If we were no longer reading Sappho, whose lines would we follow?

LINA POLETTI, *IL CIPRASSETTO DELLA ROCCA A SANT'ARCANGELO DI ROMAGNA*, 1919

The last of our poets was Lina Poletti. After the war, we heard that she had gone with Eugenia to live in the countryside near Sant'Arcangelo di Romagna, where the provincial papers chronicled harvests instead of battles. Just after the threshing in 1919 Lina wrote her last poem, an ode to an ancient cypress on an outcropping of rock. Gnarled by its centuries, the tree stood tranquilly as the birds settled on its branches; to Lina it seemed to upturn its limbs to receive them.

Do you see, Lina asked Eugenia as they sat among its roots, how this cypress turns away from us, as if it has seen enough of humankind? The trees have an art unto themselves, it is only that we are too ignorant to understand their poems.

LINA POLETTI, *ANCORA UN CERO CHE SI SPEGNE*, 1921

Perhaps Lina turned away from poetry because she had seen enough, even in the year before the Fascists marched on Rome; perhaps she foresaw, perhaps she listened to the trees instead of the politicians. In 1921 the Fascists began to torch the offices of newspapers and trade unions; all over Italy the ominous murmuring of armed men could be heard in the *piazze*. Yet there was much talk of pacification and the necessity of restoring order; Giolitti assured the nation that the Fascists were all reasonable men, did we not see the value of compromise?

Lina did not. In 1921 she wrote a manifesto, blunt in its despair and unsparing in its prophecy. When the Fascist squads began raising their brute hands and shouting, This is the hour of virile glory, seized in the fist and beaten half to death, all hail the era of *impadronirsi!,* we knew that Lina would spit in their faces and stride away in her high buttoned boots. She would always go onwards, she was forever buoyed by the far face of the wave. Lina was the one who had promised us that the chorus would never be silenced. But she was always swimming inexplicably away from the shore, only to arrive at an island of her own invention.

The manifesto of Lina Poletti was titled *Yet Another Candle is Extinguished*. Almost as soon as it was published, the Fascists marched on Rome.

AMENDMENT TO THE LABOUCHÈRE AMENDMENT, 1921

In the same year it was proposed by the House of Commons to criminalize female homosexuality. It was a beastly subject, the men of Parliament agreed, and they were terribly sorry to raise the grossest spectre of gross indecency, but after the affair of Maud Allan there had been a great deal of talk about the clitoris. Otherwise upstanding women were enquiring about it. Wives were curious. Orders of French novels and other seditious materials had shot up. It was high time for England to stem its bulging tide of lesbians.

The House of Lords concurred, but countered that the creeping ranks of lesbians were only swelled by any mention of their shocking practices. Better to muffle discussion entirely, the House of Lords argued, than to unduly incite any innocent woman to experiment with, as it were, in a manner of speaking, anything. Therefore the Amendment to the Labouchère Amendment was never ratified in Parliament. Thus Lesbians were not outlawed in England: the very word froze hoarily in the mouth of a Lord.

Radclyffe Hall had no patience with the House of Commons, but she thought the House of Lords could be made to understand: a lesbian was a gentleman of the highest order. She herself exemplified the finest qualities of an Englishman: she was decent, reasonable, and an excellent shot. Her wife, the Lady Una Troubridge, was a noblewoman who kept small dogs. In other words, there was no difference between Radclyffe Hall and the most upstanding citizen of the British Empire, she was as good a fellow as any other John.

JOHN, 1921

From her country estate, John undertook a campaign to convince the men of Parliament of the many merits of lesbians like herself. She wore sensible tweed skirts, she was charitable and well-mannered, she paid her taxes and rode to hounds. Did they require more evidence? Many of her kind had gone heroically to the front to drive ambulances and nurse the wounded; chivalrous inverts had saved the lives of English soldiers from shrapnel and ash. Had they not read the stories? John could see that they had not. Thus Radclyffe Hall began writing some instructional parables for the most deplorable of readers, men who could not tell Sappho from an umbrella stand.

COLETTE, *MITSOU OU COMMENT L'ESPRIT VIENT AUX FILLES*, 1919

Colette objected to John's claims on many counts. What use was a life of itchy, decorous skirts and pot roast on Sundays? But principally Colette maintained that there were quite enough authors among us already. She herself had written a score of novels and been thrown off the music hall stage by the Prefect of Police on account of one particularly piquant play script. What we needed now, Colette declared, were *readers*. Witness the havoc wreaked by those idiots who couldn't tell Sappho from Salomé!

Readers according to Colette were like lovers. The best were attentive, intelligent, exigent, and promiscuous. She urged us to read widely and well, to seek out precisely the novels prohibited to us and lie down for hours in bed with them. We should read to gorge and sate ourselves, Colette enjoined us; after a good book we should lick our fingers. We should especially read the lives of women, for example she had just published the story of Mitsou, whose alternate title was *How Girls Learn Things.*

ADA BEATRICE QUEEN VICTORIA LOUISE VIRGINIA SMITH, c. 1922

Born in West-by-God-Virginia, as she called it, Ada Smith had been named by every neighbour who wanted to get a word in. Her mother ran a rooming house in Chicago where everyone passed through, immigrants and working girls and families going west. Down the street was a theatre where as a girl Ada learned things.

Thus by sixteen Ada was a lesser princess of the vaudeville circuit that carried black troupes to mostly white towns. She could dance a little, she could sing a little, she knew things. She had burnished auburn hair and a white dress with flounces at the elbows. By 1922 she had made it as far as a nightclub in Harlem. In two years she would embark for Paris on board a Cunard ship called *America.*

ADA BRICKTOP SMITH, 1924

Ada like Colette knew when to burst open a bottle of champagne for everyone at the bar and when to smile tightly and walk away. Like Colette she lived in Paris, understood the intimate workings of music halls, and eventually wrote her own life. But Ada Bricktop Smith had also learned things we would never know: what it was like to black up your face when you were already a black girl, for example, in order to earn your living singing minstrel songs to white Southerners.

In Paris Ada worked late and gave dancing lessons until she could become the empress of her own nightclub in Montmartre. There she presided over the bookkeeping with her cigar and glass of champagne, singing whatever she liked and dancing a little. She took in other girls when they came from America with their cardboard suitcases and mournful songs about love. We invited her to Natalie Barney's for cucumber sandwiches, but she smiled tightly and said she was too busy. It was true that one of the middle names of Ada Bricktop Smith was Queen.

BRICKY AND JOSIE, 1925

Josie was one of the girls from America whom Ada Bricktop Smith kindly took in at the Music Box. A chorine from Missouri, Josie too knew about minstrel shows and leg shows and how to keep her spit curls slick all evening. But she had almost no formal schooling, Bricky discovered, and now that everyone was clamouring for the autograph of Miss Josephine Baker it was a shame that she could scarcely sign her name. Bricky poured herself a glass of whisky and told Josie what to do. The thing was, Bricky said, that no one cared about Josie really, they just wanted a piece of her. Just a token. Thus Bricky helped Josie get a rubber stamp made of her signature, and when the stage door was crazed with fans of the *Danse Sauvage*, Josie could stamp a score of photo portraits and slip away unscathed. Bricky was right, they would tear you to pieces if you let them.

VITA SACKVILLE-WEST, *KNOLE AND THE SACKVILLES*, 1922

When it seemed that hysterical mobs of men threatened to drag us by our hair back into the last century, Vita Sackville-West was tempted to burrow herself into the gallery of portraits that lined the walls of Knole. Each long white face gave way to the next at the seemly pace of oil-painting; each gilded frame held the ponderous assurance of orderly succession. The vulgar frenzies of the men of Parliament would never intrude into the great house. At Knole it was never quite the right time for the excitable events of the twentieth century.

But one could not stay forever cloistered in a gallery of one's own face, infinitely refracted. Briskly Vita put on her trousers. She whistled for her trunks, which were packed just in time for Julian to meet Violet on the quay; that very afternoon they would sail for France. Julian, darling! exclaimed Violet, you are – but a bright wind blew her words away, slapping the water into little waves. What was Julian, according to Violet? Moreover who was Julian, when Vita eyed him in the mirror? Idly Vita wondered if it were possible to write biographies of everyone she had ever been. And if she did, who would read them?

RADCLYFFE HALL, *THE FORGE*, 1924

Leaving the comforts of their country estate, Radclyffe Hall's fictitious lesbian couple journeyed to Paris. They were the nicest sort of English inverts: Hilary was a novelist and Susan was a wife. In fact you could hardly tell that Hilary was a woman at all, he had a fine sense of moral virtue. A decent fellow if there ever was one, Hilary found himself ill at ease in Paris, with its eccentric artists and feverish dance halls where bodies rubbed themselves together at all hours. Paris offered tins of cocaine, rouged cheeks, back rooms with brocade wallpaper, the *Danse Sauvage*. Swiftly Hilary took Susan back to England. They were not, Radclyffe Hall said, *those* kind of people.

Colette, who had spent the better part of a month in 1923 taking John & Una dancing at the Bal Bullier, asked Natalie Barney about *The Forge*. Was it fond, was it charming? Did you want to lie down in bed and read it for hours? Would Natalie translate the best bits into French for her? Natalie Barney sighed. John was always seeing the modern world as a sea meant to drown us, she said. Unfortunately *The Forge* was just another sad inlet.

VIRGINIA WOOLF, *INDISCRETIONS IN LITERATURE*, 1925

On the subject of John, Virginia Woolf tried to say as little as possible. To be sure, Virginia Woolf would defend to the death Radclyffe Hall's right to compose grim moral tales about sexology. Virginia Woolf would box the metaphorical ears of any critic who censored a woman's writing. But it was an open secret that Virginia preferred, as she wrote in *Indiscretions in Literature*, those poets who dwelt in the upper reaches, where time is a garden and love runs coolly through it: Sappho, for instance.

We had not heard Virginia Woolf speak of Sappho since the war. Little flames of hope licked brightly at our hearts. In Italian the love of girls for each other is called a *fiamma*, a fervent flickering of yearning. We had not felt it for many years, but we all remembered the rosy uncertainty of our back gardens. It was true that Virginia Woolf struck a match to our spirits and left us in a state of blue flame. Since the very beginning we had been incorrigible readers; our veins were forever swelled with cassia and myrrh. We could not help but hope that Virginia Woolf would be the first to write Sappho into becoming us.

SIXTEEN

VIRGINIA WOOLF, *MODERN FICTION*, 1919

Someone had got modern fiction terribly wrong. Or rather a number of men, writing their copious novels, had so persistently hammered it into wrongness over the course of thousands of pages that English literature was now concentrated into one dull flat mass. No character rose in relief against the conventions that stamped her life, no giddy edges of feeling or thought were to be discerned. Buttons were buttoned. Marriages were conducted every weekend in June, in fine weather. Here and there a spinster aunt died, leaving a solid inheritance to the young hero. Everything proceeded as expected.

But life *itself* was in constant variance, Virginia Woolf protested, a novel ought to run alongside it the way the shadow of a railway carriage travels over the landscape. Now rising fleetingly along a low wall, now falling away into a riverbed, passing its silhouette unevenly over grass and gravel: *that* was a novel, *that* was the spirit of a life moving on a page. Is it not the task of the novelist, Virginia Woolf demanded, to convey this varying, this unknown and uncircumscribed spirit, whatever aberration or complexity it may display?

In our rooms we read those beautiful words aloud: varying, unknown, uncircumscribed, aberration, complexity. Even if we had to turn our forms inside out, we told Natalie Barney, this was the line we would follow. A life would unfold across uneven interiors; a face would be the surface of several thoughts at once. Every chapter would run alongside its characters like the shadow of a train thrown in split-second, scattershot relief against a landscape. Everything would not proceed as expected.

SARAH BERNHARDT, *DANIEL*, 1920

We immediately recognized Daniel, an excitable young man who would not lie back on the sickbed. He fidgeted under the coverlet, his forehead feverish, his eyes ringed with blueblack shadows. Despite the ravages of morphine, the doctor found Daniel animated and voluble, refusing any medicament beyond brandy. I want none of these vials and poultices, Daniel exclaimed, straining forward. Give me my coat, let me rise from this deathbed, I want my life, more life!

Daniel was the only film that Sarah Bernhardt finished after the war. She was seventy-seven years old, indefatigable. One of her legs had been amputated above the knee; still she was the Divine Sarah. She painted her face an enamelled, ghostly white, and peered out at the camera from under heavy drugged eyelids. It is incredible, the director said, peering back at her through the camera, Madame Sarah, despite everything, you are Daniel! Sarah Bernhardt shook her head.

No, she said, I have many lives, but *quand-même*, I am not him; it is Daniel who becomes the Divine Sarah.

VITA, 1922

Julian? the host enquired when she entered. Vita, actually, said Vita Sackville-West, I've been Vita all week, very kind of you to ask. It was the winter of 1922 in London, an evening for candles and roast fowl. Around the table were ranged faces flickering in the dimness, some eyeing Vita quizzically, some discoursing with great feeling on the rise of fractured narrative or the decline of *plein-air* painting, others bestowing upon her a brief, charitable nod, as if she were of no great interest.

Vita Sackville-West was unaccustomed to being found of no great interest, especially when she had dressed for the occasion. Leaning into the candlelight, she broke in, What a pleasure to meet you at last, Virginia! I must confess that I admire you terribly, really, I think you the Sappho of our time. Virginia Woolf looked up sharply. Have I met you somewhere before? she asked, her gaze fixed on Vita's face. Oh, I doubt that, Vita replied with a carefree laugh, I have many lives, but nonetheless I remember most of them.

COLETTE, *EN PAYS CONNU*, 1923

In 1923 Sarah Bernhardt began to make another film. She was too weak to travel; discreetly the director arranged to film in her salon. Refusing crutches or pity, Sarah had herself carried downstairs in great style for each of her scenes. She was to play *La Voyante*: the seer, the sibyl, she who foretells what is to come.

One day between scenes Colette, who had swooned like a schoolgirl over Sarah's Hamlet, was invited to dine. At the end of a long hall hung with portraits and dried roses sat the Divine Sarah: imperial, eternal, pouring out the coffee herself. Sarah Bernhardt's hands were like wilted flowers, Colette said, but her eyes were as insolent and piercing as ever. She seemed an excitable young man who would at any moment rise from her chair, clattering the cups. At her foot were curled two wolf cubs with attentive grey ears. The Divine Sarah fed the wolf cubs cream from her saucer and gave Colette a smile that showed all of her teeth; an irreducible smile, Colette told us, even at eighty Sarah Bernhardt went straight up to the gates of death and demanded her life, more life.

SARAH BERNHARDT, *LA VOYANTE*, 1923

What Sarah Bernhardt foresaw as *La Voyante* was never known. Colette suspected that Sarah saw a vast untamed menagerie milling about her and smiled that irreducible smile. The director guessed that she was remembering her Hamlet, her Pelléas, her Duc d'Aiglon; onstage Madame Sarah had been a prince among men, the director said admiringly. But Sarah shook her head wearily on the pillow of her sickbed. Marguerite and Joan of Arc were as much hers as Hamlet; moreover actresses did not stoop to consider the sex of their parts.

We of course imagined that Sarah saw herself rising over the crowds of Paris in a hot-air balloon, never descending until she reached the picnic on the cliff of her island. We hoped that Sarah pictured all of her lives at once, a throng of characters clamouring to become her, her linens and revolver faithfully inscribed with her motto. *Quand-même*! we exclaimed all together, raising our glasses to the Divine Sarah.

VITA SACKVILLE-WEST, *CHALLENGE*, 1923

Brandishing, rousing, and storming were suitable verbs for Vita writing. As Julian roamed a Greek isle, suffused with revolutionary spirit and hoarse with love, he seized the verbs with one sure hand; the other clasped a pistol of some model Vita would look up later. Now bareback by pale steed, now limping heroically, Julian traversed the chapters of *Challenge* with a manly grace Vita began to envy; for what was a man's life but the inalienable right to verbs of action? What might Vita have become, given the transitive and a pair of sturdy boots? With a frown she roused herself, rose from her writing desk, and brandished a candelabra at her reflection in the darkened window. In a fortnight her novel would go to the printers, and directly thereafter storm the bookshops.

VIRGINIA, 1923

I want to make life fuller and fuller, Virginia Woolf wrote. She was writing four new pieces at once, she was seeing Vita whenever she could, she had decided that her next book would entirely exceed the category of 'novel' and demand some description as yet unthought by English literature.

In her mind there were parentheses enclosing an expansive possibility that had until now escaped notice. Some rare spirit had gone unbuttoned, unwed, uncowed: Virginia could almost make out its silhouette. Was there a personage who, spurning a timely death, had lived merrily for another century, enjoying her own good fortune? Was there an ellipsis, a slip of time, a back garden where some inexplicable form of life had taken root and was even now twining its delightful branches into the air?

(I want to begin to describe my own sex.), Virginia Woolf wrote late one evening in London. Thus she was going to Paris.

LINA POLETTI, 1923

As soon as Eugenia had built the bookshelves for their new house in Rome, Lina had filled them with books on epigraphy. A light shone late in her study while she deciphered Dorian and Eteocretan inscriptions. From diagrams she learned how to brush the dust from potsherds with a horsehair brush; from a young archaeologist she learned that the excavation of the ancient Cretan city of Gortyn had already yielded fragments of a code of civil law, rumoured to grant unusual rights to women.

Thus Lina packed up the necessary books and embarked for the island of Crete.

RACHEL FOOTMAN, 1924

No one at Oxford had explained to Rachel Footman how to evaporate the sulphate from ether. She wanted to be a chemist, she was taking her first laboratory course. She had carefully prepared a water bath and propped open her notebook on the table. But no tutor had told her what an ungodly long time a water bath takes; at this rate she would miss tennis practice and quite possibly supper. An inventive undergraduate, she lit a Bunsen burner under the bath. There was a strange sound like air collapsing, a sudden smell of something burning: her hair, her overalls, her notebook.

Rachel awoke in the hospital; from the white walls and the morphine haze, she deduced that she had died. No, dearie, the nurses assured her, and her pretty hair would grow back by next term. Her tutor bluntly recommended that thereafter she pursue art history or abstract maths. But Rachel Footman had gone to Oxford to study chemistry, and by Degree Day in 1926, she knew how to evaporate sulphates from anything.

EILEEN GRAY, *HOUSE AT SAMOIS-SUR-SEINE*, 1923

With an unsparing eye Eileen Gray went at the house on the Seine. Its windows looked out over the willows lining the river, but its balconies were stubby and its stairwell was a blight. There was only one studio, as if the architect could not conceive of two artists working in rooms of their own under a single roof. But Eileen believed that eventually any house could be converted from an ordinary domestic appurtenance into a space of living feeling. She punched a skylight into the stairwell and unleashed the balconies.

By 1923 the house at Samois-sur-Seine was inviting, private, cool, and luminous. In its interior unfolded a series of places for thinking and working. Eileen had arranged rugs of knotty undyed wool near the great hearth, carved chairs by the bookshelves. Each guest room gave off its own colour. Damia, who had become a frequent guest in Eileen's bed, found the house so alluring that she called it Siren-upon-Seine. One afternoon, as the breeze from the river drifted in through the windows, Natalie Barney arrived with a bouquet of lilies to congratulate Eileen on having turned an entire house inside out.

VIRGINIA WOOLF, *MRS D*, 1923

Who was Mrs D? One question of that depth might absorb an entire novel. But almost immediately the interior of that question unfolded itself and others swam into the light: who might Mrs D have been? If she had not been so slight as a girl, for example, so easily swayed by the importuning of young men who were inevitably presented to her as 'promising'. If she had laughed at their promising. If she had looked up from their insistent faces and seen instead a cloud sailing straight out to sea. If she had herself sailed away from familiar shores, mastless and unmanned. Might there have been no Mrs D at all? Could she instead have become a venerable figure, hatless with dark serious eyes, interested in politics like a man? Who in fact was Clarissa, before a prefix had been hung on her like a jewelled chain?

Virginia Woolf paced the bank of the Seine, each step making a word in the question: who was Mrs D? who might have been? who in fact was? A cigarette dangled and burnt away in her fingers. She crossed the Pont Marie, she crossed the Pont Saint-Louis. A man hawking newspapers on the bridge was calling out the headlines, garbling the wind. In a street on the Île de la Cité a flower seller was nestling irises into a bed of ferns and wild fennel. Wrapped in newspaper, the flowers would soak through the words.

SEVENTEEN

VITA SACKVILLE-WEST, *SEDUCERS IN ECUADOR*, 1924

Seducers in Ecuador was a trifle really, Vita said modestly to Virginia, but still quite a handsome thing when inked and bound. It was a novella, a birthday present, and an alchemical experiment all at once. Vita had written it for Virginia out of thin air, and then Virginia had transmuted it letter by letter into lead; finally its spine was stitched neatly into the edition that lay now on both of their writing desks.

In public Mrs V. Woolf said that Hogarth Press was very pleased to have brought Mrs V. Sackville-West's latest novella into the world. Privately Virginia remarked with a wry smile that certainly Vita was a seducer, but rarely went to such great lengths as Ecuador to conceal it.

EILEEN GRAY, *LACQUE BLEU DE MINUIT*

In the history of Japanese lacquer there existed the most striking hues of ebony, pearl, and carnelian, but there was not a midnight blue until Eileen Gray invented one. She did it by staying up all night, watching the stars illume around themselves the tiniest margin of sky. Each star silver in its firmament bled a bit of light into the darkness; thus black became almost imperceptibly a deep blue. Thus the starlight that would not reach the eyes of Eileen Gray in her own lifetime bestowed upon her an infinitely distant gift: *bleu de minuit.*

In the novella *Seducers in Ecuador,* the main character is a man who embarks on a voyage from which he never returns. From the familiar quays of England he sails across strange seas, arriving at last in a land where, squinting, he puts on blue-tinted spectacles. His eyes no longer perceive common morals and mundane objects. He leaves the orbit of ordinary colour. Like Eileen Gray, Vita stayed up late at night to achieve the necessary state for this alchemy. She too ground lustrous oyster shells with a powder of lapis lazuli and silver leaf. In the end Vita wrote for Virginia the story of seeing the world change colour forever, which is one way to say that you are in love.

VIRGINIA AND VITA, 1925

If you'll make me up, Virginia wrote one morning to Vita, I'll make you. By the evening post Vita replied: *man camelo tuti*, as we say in Romani; I cannot live without you.

Bit by bit they laid out their lives for each other as if they were swaths of coloured fabric on a table. Here was Vita's face in the gallery at Knole, ancestral and slightly dusty. Here was Rosina Pepita dancing so merrily that she was no one's grandmother. Here was Julian waving his pistol on a Greek isle; here was Vita, weeping at the foot of the great oak tree never to be deeded to her, for she was not a Lord.

Then there was Virginia as a girl sorrowful in the deep recesses of a window seat, the stub of a candle clutched in her hands. If she blew out the flame it snuffed a memory, Virginia explained, at least for the night. Thus she slept. Her dreams were otherworldly birds. They flew out of a stunted yew tree in the garden of her childhood and circled the roof of her house, cawing, years of their hoarse cries and black wings. For Virginia this too was a life, the life of nestless birds in her mind.

VIRGINIA WOOLF, *AGAMEMNON*, 1925

Originally *Agamemnon* was a story about Cassandra, but she was exiled from it by the history of literature. She was made a foreigner in her own story. On the border she stands waiting, century after century, while all of the other characters come home.

Everyone, including Agamemnon, was always telling Cassandra not to speak about this. Her mouth was full of madness and birds, the chorus was dismayed by all the blood and small bones.

By 1925 Virginia Woolf had rewritten the story of Agamemnon by hand. Now the margins were half of what was happening.

Cassandra could never go home again, but Virginia's notebook gave her many more pages to live in. Cassandra filled the new space with her words: her madness, her birds. When the chorus told her that she sounded like a nightingale,

Cassandra retorted, If I were a nightingale, would I be writing this? The chorus did not know what to think of her. Even Vita who loved Virginia did not understand the madness and birds, the nestless parts of her mind.

VIRGINIA WOOLF, *HOGARTH PRESS*

The hand press was intended for afternoons, a distraction from overthought mornings. It was solid, dirty, and took up most of the dining room. At first Virginia Woolf had set each letter in its place herself; added the flourish of titles and frontispieces; blown the ink dry with her own breath. For the first book she had also stitched the spine in red yarn, so that when the pages lay open it was like a bright day in winter: the snowy margins, the black stick-legs of birds hopping towards the red berries in the rowan tree.

We opened those books with reverent hands. We did not know what kinds of birds would fly out of them.

LINA POLETTI, 1925

In the ruins at Gortyn were magpies and mysteries. Lina brushed the dust from each scratch in the stone, slowly uncovering each line of the civil code. In Dorian and Ionian dialects were set out the ancient rights of women to own property, divorce their husbands, and inherit from their mothers. In fact rape was punished more severely in the fifth century BC on Crete, Lina noted, than it had been in Italy when Sibilla was young.

That night, in her letter to Eugenia, Lina described the sole mystery remaining to her in the ruins of Gortyn. She could decipher the inscriptions, certainly she could comprehend why the rights of women would be fundamental to any civilized society. But Crete had been a crossroads since the Minoans, inhabited by Byzantines, Arabs, Greeks, Romans, Ottomans, Venetians, all overlapped and intermixed. Why then this insistence by Italian archaeologists that Gortyn represented only the greatness of classical Greece? It was as if the archaeologists fantasized some pure lineage, handed down from father to father since Zeus. But in truth, Lina concluded, Crete is as much an island of Asia, an island of Africa, as it is an island of Europe. And if we do not see that, we shall be no better than the Fascists.

EUGENIA RASPONI, 1925

Lina, my love, Eugenia wrote back, the police have been here again to pay us a visit. You remember last time they were very interested in your archaeology notebooks? Well this time they have borrowed some of your books on Eastern philosophy. They wanted to see your poems as well, but for some reason I couldn't find any copies. By the way, that American poet who was writing his *Cantos*, you remember, has become very popular here. The police and the government like him very much. Really you should not write any more letters about how to see islands.

NANCY CUNARD, *PARALLAX*, 1925

In 1924 the hand press moved from Richmond to London with Virginia Woolf, groaning as it went down the stairs. In a basement in Bloomsbury it resumed its grubby, satisfying labours. Virginia looked at the inky blotches on her palms and the yellowed tips of her fingers: what would Freud say? It all meant something to him, the way one held a cigarette, the dim shapes of dreams from childhood. There was always something rustling behind the curtain of one's waking thoughts, Virginia allowed; but it was more often parallax than phallus.

Parallax is a phenomenon of viewing the same thing from different angles. From the perspective of a man concerned with civilization and its discontents, for example, a woman unresponsive to the sexual attentions of men is a source of great mystery. The curtain rustles; such a man sees himself behind it, furtive and important. Volumes of poetry and analysis thereby issue forth from him. From the perspective of the woman in question, this is tiresome. Why must we always talk of the dreams of great men?

In 1925 Hogarth Press published a long poem called *Parallax,* by Nancy Cunard. When it was said by several critics that Nancy Cunard's poem was merely an imitation of the work of a great man, she shrugged. Parallax can be used to measure the distance between two perspectives, especially when the distance between them is vast.

NANCY CUNARD, *THE HOURS PRESS*

A hand press is a querulous sort of empress in one's house, Virginia Woolf cautioned Nancy Cunard. Whenever Milady summons, you abandon your afternoon of leisure! There is the drudgery of it day after day, then the ink spots eternal on one's hands.

Nonetheless Nancy Cunard bought her own hand press. It was nearly two hundred years old and its ink had to be scoured off her skin with petrol. But to feel the click of words under one's fingers! Besides, Nancy knew from Hogarth what it meant to see your poem find its little nest. With a press of one's own, literature became less a wasteland of critics and more a moment glistening like pigment, red or black on the page.

Nancy gave up sixteen hours a day to the empress of books. It was her idea to print only the writing of others, and to encourage above all flights of poetic risk. If there was some elegy too outlandish, some conceit too queer to be published elsewhere, it might find its home at The Hours. But Nancy Cunard did not entirely ignore the warnings of Virginia Woolf: she kept the hand press in her stable.

GERTRUDE STEIN,
THE MAKING OF AMERICANS, 1925

You would think the Americans four parts water to one part bluff. Boiled or diluted, they never reduced to more than half a cup at forty proof. The delicate operations of whisking were unknown to them. But by God if they got into a motor car they gunned it! The clouds were vaporized by the speed of Americans in the making.

Starting in 1902 Gertrude Stein began making Americans every day and calling it a novel. In 1911 the first batch of them was done but as Americans they pushed on into overtime. At last in 1925 they came out blaring in a fanfare of nine hundred and twenty-five pages with a cover declaring *The Making of Americans*. Her publisher in New York City despaired of selling them even at Christmas. What a meat pie in an icebox those Americans were.

NATALIE BARNEY, *AMANTS FÉMININS OU LA TROISIÈME*, 1926

The book of Natalie Barney's triangle of lovers never found its home. It went unpublished into the darkness in 1926 and stayed there. It was an autobiographical novel called *Feminine Lovers or the Third Woman*: an elegy too outlandish, a conceit too queer for any press in France. There were too many women in it. Moreover the women were all in bed together, at least until N's latest beloved ran off with her old flame L de P in chapter fifteen. How vividly N remembered the *idylle saphique* of L de P from 1899! The lilies! The cancan! Natalie Barney finished the manuscript fondly and put it away in a drawer, where it remained until she died.

RADCLYFFE HALL, *MISS OGILVY FINDS HERSELF*, 1926

Finding herself, Miss Ogilvy, an ambulance driver in the war, she found many another of her kind. Miss Ogilvy had cropped hair and no idea how to be a girl, or why. She was entirely literal: she shouted at her sisters, If only I had been born a man! In short Miss Ogilvy had *always* been a *queer* sort of person, Radclyffe Hall said meaningfully.

Miss Ogilvy was written in 1926 but remained unpublished until many years later. Upon finishing the manuscript John considered where to seclude her: a drawer, a war, a well, a cave? In the end, Radclyffe Hall insisted in a tone of mournful pride, she must blaze a lone trail through the difficulties of her nature.

Sentences like that were why we avoided the books of Radclyffe Hall. We all wished for Miss Ogilvy to find herself, and many another of their kind, but reading her was like being hammered one word at a time into a tinny symbolic order. Our ears hurt. Secretly we did not regret that Miss Ogilvy was secluded in a cave, where she remained until she died.

EILEEN GRAY, *E.1027*, 1926

Eileen Gray would only say cryptically that a house was like a body. At last she intended to build her own, beginning from the very bedrock. Each joist would reveal a subtle ligature; each wall would occlude a room. She made drawings of alcoves, bookshelves, sunken entryways. To those who protested that she had never properly trained as a draughtsman, Eileen Gray replied that she had read all the books, it was no more technical than binding a tourniquet. Furthermore, Eileen added, furniture *is* architecture. It is all the small bones that make a room.

On a rocky stretch of shore between Roquebrune and Cap-Martin where only a footpath ran to the road, Eileen Gray began the house she called E.1027. It had cool white walls and above all, as Eileen wrote later, it considered the problem of windows. A window without shutters, Eileen felt, was an eye without eyelids. No one should be made to live in a space peeled naked, but especially not women and artists. There must always be a way to withdraw into the innermost chamber, just as there must be the choice to throw open the windows and see a great swathe of the world before you. Clad in its shutters, the house of Eileen Gray showed us the shape of an interior both public and protected. It was a house with the hollows of a body built into it.

GERTRUDE STEIN, *COMPOSITION AS EXPLANATION*, 1926

The composition is the thing seen by every one living in the living they are doing, Gertrude Stein explained to the members of the Cambridge Literary Club. Some twitching of lips and glazing of eyes had already ensued, but Gertrude Stein pressed on, This makes the thing we are looking at very different and this makes what those who describe it make of it, it makes a composition, it confuses, it shows, it is, it looks, it likes it as it is, and this makes what is seen as it is seen.

Gertrude Stein took a breath and examined the faces of her audience. Their mouths were confusions and their eyebrows were askance. She had been engaged to give a series of lectures explaining *The Making of Americans*, but she doubted that the Cambridge Literary Club had understood the book any more than her American publisher. Perhaps they were daunted by the thousand pages? Perhaps they still believed that portraits should be paintings, rather than books or houses or lives in themselves?

Three days later at Oxford Gertrude Stein tried again. She tried to find them where they were, in their strange stone halls barely encroached upon by modern thought. For the four centuries preceding 1920 no woman had been admitted to a degree at the university. 1926 seemed to have sputtered out before it could illume the lead-paned windows. Nonetheless Gertrude Stein spoke to them of the present continuous, of writing a life in all its before and afterwards. It is *that* that makes living a thing they are doing, Gertrude Stein concluded. After a long pause, the Oxford literary society made its scant and hesitant show of clapping. Gertrude Stein left the stone hall and did not attempt to further elucidate her ideas to English readers until *Composition as Explanation* had safely been published by Hogarth Press.

NATALIE BARNEY, *LE MAKING OF AMERICANS PAR GERTRUDE STEIN*, 1927

The Making of Americans began its second life when Natalie Barney, by birth an American, translated bits of the book into French. Natalie found *Le Making*, as she called it, refreshingly lucid. It was a portrait of its time, if only time could catch up to how women composed themselves. Indeed, Natalie explained in her preface to the translation, Gertrude Stein is not a writer in any sense of the word as it is understood at present.

Who was an American any more? Was a translator the fabricator of foreign Americans? What is a writer, in any sense? We had pages upon pages of questions about these words as they were understood at present. In fact we could have written a book composed entirely of what we still did not know about writing a portrait in the present continuous.

VIRGINIA WOOLF, *HOW SHOULD ONE READ A BOOK?*, 1926

Sixty girls were sitting attentively on the floor of the drawing room when Virginia Woolf arrived. It was a wintry afternoon in 1926, and girls' schools were perpetually cold; she was wearing a blue sweater and looked distantly amused. Her talk was titled *How Should One Read a Book?*, a phrase in which the essence was the question mark, she said. For indeed it was an open question: how are we to bring order into this multitudinous chaos and so get the deepest and widest pleasure from what we read?

First, Virginia Woolf counselled the girls of Hayes Court Common School, you might try writing a chapter or two yourself. Do not be alarmed if a scene snaps into splinters under your hands, or if your characters manage only to croak out clichés. Half of writing a novel is looking out of the window in gentle despair and idleness. The other half is hauling in from the world yard upon yard of its finest stuff, great hanks and skeins of scenes and stories; little by little you lay out the lives of your characters upon the writing table. If you go hand over hand, slowly at first, you shall either find you have written your chapter or that you have become no writer at all, but a wonderful reader.

But which books should we read? asked one girl very seriously, twisting the ends of her plaits. Virginia Woolf replied, If a novel bores you, leave it. Try something else. Poetry is too like fiction to be a change. But biography is a very different thing. Go to the bookcase & take out a life of anybody.

EIGHTEEN

BERTHE CLEYRERGUE, B. 1904

Berthe Cleyrergue was not merely anybody. It was often said that Berthe began her life with Natalie Barney in 1927. But Berthe was born in 1904. She was first called Philiberthe, a heavy name to pull like a wagon. Shortly thereafter she changed to Bébert, a lithe little tomboy in the fields of Bourgogne. At ten she ran the farm, at fourteen she left for Paris. It was not yet 1927 and she had lived several lives already. But then Berthe Cleyrergue was always one to do things herself.

BERTHE CLEYRERGUE, *CARNET DE BAL*, *PALAIS D'ORSAY*, 1923

Berthe wanted to dance, Berthe wanted to travel. Like her father she loved a glass of Gamay and the songs that young people sang. When Philiberthe had fallen ill as an infant, they kept her alive with spoonfuls of wine, watered down to be sure, but still strong as beef blood. In 1923 Berthe went dancing every weekend at the Palais d'Orsay. Her *carnet de bal* was an object of worship. A dance card in those days was an archive of flattering glances and hard-knuckled hands pressed to her back. Berthe in 1923 worked all week for what she wanted: dresses for dancing, and more dancing.

BERTHE CLEYRERGUE, *DJUNA BARNES*, 1925

Djuna Barnes lived in the 15ème and shopped in the 16ème. It was there that she met Berthe Cleyrergue, her arms full of the tins of cocoa powder you could find nowhere else in Paris. Djuna was a smart girl, Berthe said, but with careless hands: an American. It wasn't long before Djuna burnt a hole in her rug and Berthe had to go round to pacify the landlord. After that, Djuna told Berthe, they would be friends forever.

BERTHE CLEYRERGUE, *MISS BARNEY*, 1927

It turned out that Djuna knew an astounding number of other women like her: Americans, writers, women like that. Almost none of them could cook. Some few of them could speak French. Djuna, who could not really speak French, made a meagre wage and cooked for herself; Miss Natalie Barney, an heiress who spoke French like Louis XIV, had never entered the kitchen of her house. Berthe was willing to work all week, and Miss Natalie Barney would give her 450F and a little room on the mezzanine. Thus in 1927 Berthe came to live with Miss Barney at 20 rue Jacob. She could cook, she could sew, she had intelligent green eyes that observed everything.

BERTHE CLEYRERGUE, *ROMAINE BROOKS*, 1927

Berthe met Romaine Brooks in a crowd of a hundred people and sandwiches in the salon of Miss Barney. Romaine detested crowds and sandwiches, she liked solitude and cakes that were half-chocolate and half-vanilla. Romaine wore black clothes that made a room colder, more elegant. In her house she wore black outfits in black rooms and painted all day without eating. She brooded like a crow, Romaine Brooks did, but she loved Miss Barney until the end of her life.

BERTHE CLEYRERGUE, *VILLA TRAIT D'UNION*, 1928

Romaine had the left side of the house to herself. Miss Barney, on the right, filled her rooms with bronze lamps and bearskin rugs, with gay posies of marguerites from the fields. Or more truly it was Berthe who filled the rooms of Miss Barney with wondrous comforts and bright objects; once the villa was bought and named, Berthe was sent down to clean and furnish it. After two months of work Berthe regarded it as a masterpiece. Then at last Miss Barney and Romaine met in the dining room that joined the two separate wings of *Trait d'union*, and made a toast to the indelible Hyphen that linked their lives. Berthe made a cake, half-chocolate and half-vanilla.

BERTHE CLEYRERGUE, *LA DUCHESSE, ÉLISABETH DE GRAMONT*, 1928

The sojourn of Élisabeth de Gramont at the villa *Trait d'union* was delightful, like everything else undertaken by the Duchess. She amused Miss Barney, she soothed Romaine, they all went swimming in the sea and Colette came from St-Tropez for supper afterwards. The Duchess was like a *coquelicot*, a red poppy, she was as noble in blood as they come but hardy as a wildflower, and a communist to boot. She used to speak on the radio so eloquently about the revolution. Every year on May Day there was the anniversary celebration of Miss Barney and the Duchess: a lunch of white wine and lapwing eggs, six each.

BERTHE CLEYRERGUE, *ALICE AND GERTRUDE*, 1927

Alice was one of the few Americans who could both cook and speak French. When Berthe brought a partridge back from Bourgogne, Alice would pluck it herself. Gertrude on the other hand was always writing, brusque, impatient with any interruption. Gertrude got on well with artistic men and dogs, she always had a poodle at her feet. In 1927 there was no telephone at Miss Barney's, it was Berthe who dashed down the street to deliver an invitation or a packet of books to Alice and Gertrude.

BERTHE CLEYRERGUE, *AVENTURES DE L'ESPRIT PAR MISS BARNEY*, 1927

Of all of the books written by Miss Barney, Berthe considered *Aventures de l'esprit* her best. In 1927 Miss Barney had just begun writing it and she was nervous, excitable, when she rang for something she had forgotten what it was by the time Berthe came upstairs. She changed dresses four times a day. *Adventures of the Spirit* was to be a book of portraits, Miss Barney told Berthe; each poet would have her pedestal.

Miss Barney was thinking of Renée Vivien, Berthe could tell. Once a long time ago Miss Barney and Renée Vivien had travelled to an island where they believed every poet would be honoured as she deserved. It was an island in Greece, very ancient, where they dreamed of building a villa called *Sapho* and holding splendid receptions. That was the same year Berthe was born.

BERTHE CLEYRERGUE, *COLETTE*, 1927

Berthe preferred the books of Colette above all others. Colette too was from Bourgogne, she was lively and warm-hearted and trilled her *rrr*. Colette had an untameable mass of curls that flared every which way in the rains of Paris. She wore simple sandals with rope soles. She was not one of those stern barking writers like Gertrude Stein who could not be disturbed for anything less than Art. As a girl Colette had worked in the music halls, she knew what it was to sit lightly in the lap of power and smile. Even her staff was *sympathique*:

from the villa *Trait d'union* it was a short trip by boat to St-Tropez, where Berthe would meet the governess of Colette and dance until five in the morning.

BERTHE CLEYRERGUE, *THE ACADÉMIE DES FEMMES*, 1927

At that time there was not a single woman admitted to the Académie Française. Miss Barney rightly found that ridiculous, all you had to do was look round her salon to find a dozen who deserved the honour more than Paul Valèry. Frankly Berthe could scarcely make enough eclairs to feed all the women writers of merit! Thus the Academy of Women was founded at 20 rue Jacob. On a series of Fridays in 1927 Berthe poured out tea and cream, and then with wickedly pompous ceremony a woman artist would be inducted into the Académie des Femmes. As Miss Barney proclaimed upon the day of Colette, her work was so greatly superior to that of male novelists that she ought to tread carefully among them in her rope sandals, so as not to step on their heads.

BERTHE, 1928

In 1927 Colette told us that at last Natalie Barney had found someone steady. It had been several vagabond years of maids, cooks, and chauffeurs coming and going at 20 rue Jacob. Some of them were too scandalized to stay, what with the homosexuals on every floor of the house, and others found Miss Barney too vexing a mistress. When we first saw Berthe in her neat white blouse with her lips tucked together we thought she might last a week. At the first reception she clung to the curtains like a frightened cat.

But by 1928 we learned that Berthe was merely observing everything with her intelligent green eyes. She knew that Djuna, too poor to buy the extravagant clothes she desired, wore the cast-off capes of other ladies. She saw Romaine in her moods of burnt ash, she saw Natalie nervous in a new dress with puffed sleeves. Berthe not only had all of her own lives to herself; she also saw straight through a dozen others. In short Berthe Cleyrergue was the one who taught us that we had been wrong about housekeepers.

BERTHE CLEYRERGUE, *BERTHE, OU UNE DEMI-SIÈCLE AUPRÈS DE L'AMAZONE*, 1980

After almost everyone else had gone, Berthe Cleyrergue remembered. She had written some things down and other things just remained hanging in her mind like dishcloths on their hooks. She remembered how dusty the house was at 20 rue Jacob, how you had to go out into the garden to beat the carpets. She remembered her first Friday reception, the sheer quantity of sandwiches, everyone talking of books she had never heard of. There was Colette, at least someone else from Bourgogne, laughing and giving her the first novel about Claudine, was it *Claudine à Paris*? There was Berthe herself freshly arrived in Paris, her *carnet de bal* scrawled all over with gallant yearnings; then in no time at all Berthe was pouring flutes of Kir for Miss Barney and Romaine lounging salty under the trees after their swim. When they had all gone away, Berthe wrote a portrait of everyone she remembered and called it by her own name: *Berthe, A half-century of life around the Amazon.* That was Miss Barney, who liked her *pain au raisin* toasted with butter and cinnamon.

NINETEEN

COLETTE, *LA NAISSANCE DU JOUR*, 1928

Reading the letters of her mother who had died in 1912, Colette decided to write an autobiography. In it she painted the achingly blue sea at St-Tropez, various romantic affairs, a bucolic view of Bourgogne with mist blurring the canals like breath on a mirror. It was going to be a poem, Colette told us one day in 1927. The next day she said no, it was a collection of her mother's private papers. The day after that, it was an intimate journal of one summer, so salty it would sting the tongue. Whose summer, whose journal? Colette, her mother, and her daughter were all named the same thing, so it was difficult to know.

In 1928 *The Birth of the Day* was published with this epigraph: Do you imagine, reading me, that I am painting my own portrait? But it is only my model. What, we demanded plaintively of Colette, what genre of thing was this? Smiling mischievously, Colette replied that its *genre* was feminine: *la naissance, la vie, la morte; voilà!* Colette could be insufferable when she was being clever; her daughter, now fifteen, was equally exasperating. Trying to pin an autobiography to a Colette was as impossible as separating one life from another.

SIBILLA ALERAMO, *AMO DUNQUE SONO*, 1927

You may have sensed in this novel that the novel does not exist? Colette remarked to one baffled critic of *La Naissance du Jour*. It was a time of autobiographical paradox. Sibilla Aleramo after a long silence had published a book called *I Love Therefore I Am;* from the title alone we discerned that Sibilla had never recovered from her sojourn on Capri in 1918. Even when she returned to Rome, the island had kept her in its narrows: that was the peril of an idyll. For the subsequent years Sibilla Aleramo had remained in that interlude, vague and amorous, drifting about in her dressing gown. She took lovers and languorously discarded them; she wrote poems about the flights of her own wingéd soul.

In the meantime, the Fascists had swarmed Rome. In 1922 they had declared themselves the patriarchs and patrons of the nation, in 1925 the overmasters of the empire. That winter the funeral procession of Anna Kuliscioff was attacked by squads of men in black shirts. With their heavy boots they trampled down the flowers of her funeral wreaths. Anna Kuliscioff had not lived long enough to see the day when women could vote in Italy, only long enough to die under the dictatorship.

After the funeral Lina Poletti was interrogated by the police in her study while Eugenia bundled the remaining manifestos into the false bottoms of every chair in their kitchen. Homosexuals were sent into confinement at the sulphurous edges of the country. Immediately it was proclaimed that there not was a single homosexual in all of Italy, the Italian race would not permit it. There were only Italian men in this virile hour, and supine at their feet the Italian women destined to love them: *amo dunque sono.*

LINA POLETTI, c. 1927

We never knew exactly when Lina Poletti disappeared. All we heard was that the Italian nation no longer permitted certain things. The police were ever more insistent in their interrogations. The bottoms fell out of chairs, the solid ground of cities like Rome swayed under the feet of their citizens. It seemed that the Italian race was coagulating in the veins, expelling foreign bodies. Ancient monuments cracked and crumbled into a marble dust that thickened the sky. The chorus began to cough uncontrollably. There was an urgent rising of birds, black as slits in the sky. We feared for the life of Lina Poletti.

EVA PALMER SIKELIANOS, *FESTIVAL OF DELPHI*, 1927

At last Eva was kneeling in the hot white dust of the great theatre at Delphi. She had finally gathered all of the threads in her hands, the money borrowed and the costumes woven, the singers and the stonemasons: she brought them together amid the circles of limestone seats hewn into the hillside. Of course Eva herself had always been at Delphi, the temple of Apollo rising at her back.

In 1927 Eva Palmer Sikelianos held the first Festival of Delphi since the time of Aeschylus. Before a throng of thousands, Eva directed the dance of the chorus. In double rings they moved towards the tragedy; in solemn lines they bent to fate.

An actress unlike a sibyl cannot lose herself in the steam of prophetic madness. She may see the very stones fissure before her, the pitiless maw of the world gape open: still the actress says her lines, she sings her part. She has practised all her life the genitive of remembering. Thus she goes on forever as if it were still the fourth century before the new gods, flecks of dust in her long grey hair.

CASSANDRA, 1927

Biographies without births, elegies without deaths: we could hardly tell what bounded a life any more. Moreover in French *genre* means both gender and the form of a book. Some autobiographies were disintegrating into solipsism while others were turning their warmest parts outwards, opening at the centre into a dizzying constellation of moving parts. Lina Poletti had disappeared before revealing the orientation of our futures. We remembered Cassandra telling us that we would invert the order of things: time would turn inside out around us like a portrait swallowing its own frame.

We thought of the house of Eileen Gray, looking out from under its eyelids. A hinge swinging made the difference between seeing and being scrutinized. An alcove was a secret, curved around the forms of reading or embracing.

In the interior of E.1027 might be secluded one of us, or a multitude, or everyone we had ever been. We considered how to write a life with all of its rooms.

NATALIE BARNEY, *LE TEMPLE DE L'AMITIÉ ET SES FAMILIERS*, 1928

The drawing that Natalie Barney made of us in 1928 was a map shaped like a house. Wending through its rooms was a river called the Amazon; at the centre, tea was served in the salon. Outside was the garden of the dead, their spirits hovering in Elysian repose around the Temple à l'amitié. The uppermost of the spirits was of course Renée Vivien, who crowned the Doric columns with the wisp of her name. But even the living were slight scrawls. In order to contain so many intimacies in the flatness of cartography, Natalie had written only our names. We could thus be seen from above, as if from an aeroplane, but we were each reduced to a word or two. Looking at the map you had to imagine for yourself all of the bodies and verbs, who was pouring out the tea and who was reading aloud from her book. And as it was most often Berthe who was serving the tea, we wondered if we might be the last ones to see these rooms animated by bodies, to know the interior of a life like Natalie Barney's.

DJUNA BARNES, *LADIES ALMANACK*, 1928

Ladies Almanack was a book that slammed all of the shutters and laughed to itself. If you were not already inside of the novel, it was useless to try to discern what was happening behind its cover: all you could hear was that private, mocking, maenadic amusement. Djuna Barnes had changed the names, but everything else was brazenly true. In one chapter the thin-lipped Lady Buck-and-Balk with her monocle, accompanied by two small fat dogs and her spouse, the exceedingly English novelist Tilly Tweed-in-Blood, visit a friendly Temple belonging to a certain valiant Amazon. While the couple goes on complaining about Parliamentary laws forbidding the highest sorts of Passions, the Amazon smiles and nods. She laughs to herself.

Ladies Almanack was written only for those of us who had already seen the portraits, Djuna said. She would not even put her own name on the cover. But in fact *Ladies Almanack* was written only for Natalie Barney; it was a heroically private joke, published in 1928.

VIRGINIA WOOLF, *TO THE LIGHTHOUSE*, FIRST EDITION, 1927

Gaily Virginia inscribed the flyleaf of the first edition for Vita, In my opinion the best novel I have ever written! It was the day of publication: a bright-blooming day in May, heralded by beribboned hats and baskets of strawberries. Virginia sent the book off in high spirits and rang for Nellie to set tea out in the garden.

Two days later, there was still no response from Vita. The clouds plummeted out of the sky. Every sparrow swooping was an arrow through the heart, the strawberries rotted to death in their baskets. Perhaps Vita did not understand, had never understood. Virginia held her breath.

At last a note came from Vita. Of course Vita had got the joke, she had laughed like a jackdaw upon opening the dummy copy of *To the Lighthouse*, every page blank, the best novel anyone could write! If only Virginia had sent one round to every critic in England!

And then Vita had read the novel with all its words intact, she had plunged into its marvellous depths for two breathless days. Reading that book was like lying in the arms of your lover; the only difference was whether the covers were silk or paper.

VIRGINIA WOOLF, *POETRY, FICTION AND THE FUTURE*, 1927

The undergraduates of Oxford sat on the floor with an expectant air, for that very afternoon they were going to be told the secret of fiction. The notable writer Mrs Virginia Woolf would explain it to them herself.

Virginia Woolf arrived by motor car looking slightly ill at ease. She took her place before the undergraduates and explained, for an hour or so, the secrets of poetry, fiction, and the future. But the undergraduates heard scarcely a word. They were riveted entirely by a presence near the doorway. Dutifully their faces remained fixed on the notable writer as she spoke, but all the while their eyes were inching sideways, craning, insatiable, for at the back of the room was Vita Sackville-West, the famous author of *Challenge* and an infamous Sapphist.

VIRGINIA WOOLF, *SLATER'S PINS HAVE NO POINTS*, 1927

At the end of the story, Julia kissed Fanny. Or Fanny wished with such absolute breathlessness for Julia to kiss her that it must in fact have happened, right there in the drawing room. Or it would not have happened, Miss Julia Craye being a reasonable if enigmatic woman unlikely to burst into passionate kisses with her piano pupil, but Fanny by sheer force of herself made it. She made it up, her life, her Julia, the image of her own face glowing and dazed with that kiss. She made up the story that Virginia Woolf called *Slater's Pins Have No Points.*

Sixty pounds just received from America for my little Sapphist story of which the Editor has not seen the point! Virginia crowed in a letter to Vita. The way that Americans were made, in 1927, meant that they were generally unpricked by suggestions of Sapphism. The story was published in 1928 in New York and taken to be a daydream.

Perhaps the only point of Slater's dull pins, for Virginia Woolf, was to fasten a scrap of imagination to an otherwise ordinary afternoon. Or perhaps those pins kept in place our hope, like a carnation blooming on the lapel of Lina Poletti, that women might someday kiss openly in literature.

ISADORA DUNCAN, *MY LIFE*, 1927

Isadora Duncan published her autobiography in 1927, which was also the year she died. Isadora called it *My Life*, as if life were her domain alone, her birthright. The pages were heaving with her triumphs in Art and tragedies in Love; she remembered how she had disdained the ordinary citizens of Athens in order to dance in the moonlight upon her hill. She implied that other women artists with looser morals might caress each other in hotel rooms in Berlin, but never Isadora Duncan.

In her later years Isadora was often trembling with drink; she would fling out her arms like a caryatid falling, she would slur some aphorisms about Art and Love and the Nobility of Pure Form. The story of her death was its own melodrama. It was everywhere in the papers, taking a tragic form, and we did not wish to repeat it.

NATALIE BARNEY, *AVENTURES DE L'ESPRIT*

Beyond Isadora, many other women we knew would take the genre into their own hands, from the double life of Sarah Bernhardt to the memoirs of Berthe Cleyrergue. There was Colette writing the autobiography of her mother, or perhaps her daughter, and Natalie Barney who had just begun the first of three volumes of her life, largely given over to letters and portraits of the Académie des Femmes. In fact Natalie in her salon would exclaim, *Epistolary* autobiography! and shout with laughter.

This volume was to be called *Adventures of the Spirit*, Natalie told us. The spirit we felt hovering about us, in 1927, was more than a private joke, broader in ambit than the Académie des Femmes. We wished not only that women could kiss openly in literature but that literature would open itself for women as never before. We were slowly gaining the volumes of our lives; Ada Bricktop Smith had begun penning notes for her *Bricktop by Bricktop*.

Yet amidst all of these adventures of the spirit, we did not have an autobiography of Lina Poletti. Perhaps we never would.

VIRGINIA WOOLF, *THE NEW BIOGRAPHY*, 1927

In the old lives, someone was born a boy, grew expeditiously into the proportions of a man, and set out to conquer his share of noteworthy deeds. In the middle chapters he might compose a treatise or announce the discovery of modern thought. When he had become eminent enough, he died.

We had all read those old lives; they were as dull and weighty as pewter tea platters. They were the stalwarts of all twenty-six volumes in Leslie Stephen's *Dictionary of National Biography*. Moreover those lives were invariable in shape, bowed taut from portentous birth to the elegiac mode employed at the funerals of great men. Of course they were all great men: that was the only life, in the old lives.

Thus in her essay *The New Biography* Virginia Woolf expressed our desire for other lives. These new lives might be fuller, freer, by turns more rakish and more tender, taking now the shape of taproots burrowing blind under the soil of conscious thought, now the form of waves that went crashing over and under themselves on a pebbled shore, the foam caught in the undertow, the lightest parts an almost translucent green and the dark ones full of the dread sound of scree being dragged down to salty depths, stones scratching stones.

In these new lives, Virginia Woolf wrote, there would be that queer amalgamation of dream and reality we knew so intimately: it was the alchemy of our own existence. These biographies would bring forth moments of becoming that lasted for centuries; there would be more than one life unfurling in every life. The lines would not break off on the page just when we had fallen in love, and in each chapter Sappho might become a different one of us.

TWENTY

VIRGINIA WOOLF, *THE JESSAMY BRIDES*, 1927

Lucubrare is the verb that means to think by lamplight. Late one night in 1927, illumed by a low-wicked brass lamp, Virginia Woolf conceived a new book: a whole fantasy, she wrote in her notebook, to be called *The Jessamy Brides*. Into the lamplight emerged the silhouettes of two women, solitary at the top of a house. She sketched them out: legs, dreams, ages.

Sapphism is to be suggested, Virginia Woolf said to herself, & wildness.

Together the two women went to the window; their gaze fell upon the trees swaying in the night wind, the glimmer of distant seas, the stars wheeling in their ancient patterns. From that vantage they might have glimpsed Mytilene or Constantinople. Their future was as limpid and unlatched as a window opened quietly at midnight in 1927. All around their bodies was incandescence.

VITA SACKVILLE-WEST, *A NOTE OF EXPLANATION*, 1922

Before any story might be told, Vita Sackville-West wrote in 1922, it must be explained what has happened in the house. Why are the lights blazing, the windows banging open, the beds mussed? What unsettled inhabitant or stray spirit has wracked its orderly rooms?

One answer might be the two women at the top of the house. Two women together can eternally be used to explain suggestions of Sapphism & wildness. But the answer that Vita Sackville-West proposed instead was that the shade of one woman, living for several centuries, had turned the house inside out by herself. Thus *A Note of Explanation* foresaw a future for someone whose life could not be contained within ordinary walls or decades. After ranging freely across epochs, the protagonist was discomfited by modern life: querulously she snapped the electric lights on and off, ran the baths until the taps rattled. Therefore the house, and the usual span of a lifetime along with it, were left in utter disarray the next morning.

VIRGINIA WOOLF, *SUGGESTIONS FOR SHORT PIECES: A POEM*, 1927

Something about an island, Virginia mused: that was a poem. It was a landscape, it was a dream. On that island was the craft of not drowning, presumably there were manuals for building boats of very light wood. There were trees.

We wished to enquire of Virginia where the poem was to be found, in what atlas or biography: how might we arrive on the shores of that dream? Was it to this island that Lina had disappeared? Perhaps Lina had evaded interrogations and repaired to some isle only she could discern; perhaps at this very moment she was writing for us a manifesto in the form of an autobiography.

But Virginia's notes on *A poem* remained vague. It was a landscape, it was a dream, it was the merest slip of a life sketched out in two or three lines not blurred by water. Still we held in our hearts a hope of Lina: at least there were trees. In the meantime Virginia had turned to the second possibility in her Suggestions for short pieces: *A Biography*.

VIRGINIA WOOLF, *SUGGESTIONS FOR SHORT PIECES: A BIOGRAPHY*, 1927

A biography: This is to tell a person's life, Virginia Woolf explained. A genre telling people as if they were stories also tells other people how to read them. It is a book that slyly goes both ways. A biography attending to the subject herself is also, with a slight bow, turning to face her readers, like a quadrille in narrative form.

These were the notes of Virginia Woolf as she began to conceive a new biography. We understood the openness of orientations; certainly we had all felt something of dancing in the books we loved. But then Virginia Woolf, writing in handsome purple ink on the verso of what would later become her title page, imagined a life we had not yet seen:

Suggestions for short pieces.
A Biography
This is to tell a person's life from the year 1500 to 1928.
Changing its sex.
taking different aspects of the character in different Centuries. The theory being that character goes on underground before we are born; & ~~leave~~ leaves something afterwords also.

Afterwords: was this what Cassandra had prophesied for us? We were open to suggestions for short pieces, we admired a decisive change in genre and form. We thought of Lina, who had her own ways of escaping the century.

We had begun so long ago with our poems after Sappho, carefully styled in fragments, our paintings and blushes all done in likeness. Perhaps at last the future of Sappho would be delivered into our hands like a packet of books knotted up with string. For example we might open a seemingly ordinary biography, its chapters neatly partitioned, and find that it was webbed throughout with the most extraordinary filaments of a life. A life after all did not happen by itself, in discrete units. Thus this biography would be bound together with all of our lives, twined through from preface to index: curling, animate, verdant. In the end we might become the readers of our own afterwords.

VIRGINIA AND VITA, 1927

It sprung upon me how I could revolutionise biography in a night, Virginia wrote to Vita, and all it needs is you; shall you mind? Daringly Vita replied that Virginia might have every crevice of her, every shadow and string of pearlescent thought, her very sinews to braid.

In that case, Virginia told Vita, she would begin the book immediately. But of course the biography had already begun months ago, years ago, perhaps even centuries earlier. The theory being that character goes on underground before we are born, like the winding mass of roots that weave down through the soil, anchoring an oak tree to this madly spinning planet.

RADCLYFFE HALL, *STEPHEN*, 1927

Meanwhile, in an English manor house that was not Knole, in a room of genteel overstuffed furnishings, a child named Stephen was being well-bred. It was the first draft. Yet it was clear from the opening sentence, even before Stephen had been conceived, that this would be an infelicitous life. The trappings of empire and chivalry were dear to Stephen, who would inevitably ride to hounds and court the housemaids like Sir Phillip and all of the fathers before him. In short Stephen Gordon was not merely a queer sort of person but also a *gentleman*, Radclyffe Hall said to Natalie Barney, who sighed into her teacup.

REGIO DECRETO, 1927

It was declared in 1927 that Italy was charging into battle, a new battle, all of the warm hearts of women and all of the virile hands of men were solicited in the name of the nation. For although, the government hastened to add, no one was to be killed under the *regio decreto* of 1927, there was a solemn, martial air to the undertaking. It was to be a battle of demography. On one side, the government explained, were the *brava gente*, the good people of Italy who should now gird their loins, and on the other side were all of the lesser peoples of foreign lands. The government advised all Italians except priests to think of themselves as bayonets in this battle, they ought to thrust and gash with great vigour. Only thereby could the Italian race expand to fill its empire.

Under the Royal Decree beribboned medals would be awarded to the Italian women who bore the most children, and those who remained stubbornly celibate would pay a tax for it. Poets would receive prizes for long hymns to large families. In fact Sibilla Aleramo had recently requested a government stipend, she was writing an article called *The Italian Woman* that was, as she put it, an ode of gratitude to the Fascists who had awakened the female masses to their precise and sacred function as reproducers of the species.

We heard in these words the grave tolling of the virile hour as it struck. It struck us like a bayonet. It gashed our hearts. For as soon as Sibilla received her stipend, she joined the Associazione Nazionale Fascista Donne Artiste e Laureate. Thereafter Sibilla Aleramo was officially a woman artist associated with a nation of Fascists.

1927 was as unsettling as the raw entrails of birds spelling out fate; we longed for Lina Poletti to issue a new manifesto. But Eugenia had no word of her, only that the police had ravaged the house from study to kitchen. They had confiscated Lina's notebooks, though they could not have distinguished an ancient Dorian dialect from the scratching of magpies on stone. Thus instead of reading Sibilla Aleramo's new ode of gratitude to the Fascists, we returned to Lina's manifesto from 1921, titled *Yet Another Candle is Extinguished.*

VIRGINIA WOOLF, *PHASES IN FICTION*, 1927

In 1927 Virginia Woolf had dutifully pledged to write a book on the phases of fiction. There was the phase when all was Romance; then an intriguing inward turn to reading every book as if one had written it oneself; and finally the phase of authorial despair, for what could be said nowadays about novels except that the world was in various tatters and Virginia was in love with Vita?

In the eclipse of the phases of fiction, Virginia glimpsed the silhouette of a new form emerging: it was not a novel, it was not a shade. It was the colour of a woman or two thinking in the lamplight at the top of a house. Before the incandescence was dispelled, Virginia wrote herself a note of explanation: a biography called Orlando: Vita; only with a change about from one sex to another.

VIRGINIA WOOLF, *ORLANDO AS A BOY*, 1927

Orlando began with a wild blow at the grotesque trappings of empire and chivalry. He was not yet seventeen, and thus swayed this way and that by the wind that came through the open windows in the top of the great house. But when he saw his own face appearing in the line of lugubrious white faces, the portraits of all the fathers before him, he shuddered and drew back. Their crusades and their colonies, the people they had slaughtered or dragged across the seas as slaves: Orlando would not live in that virile hour, Virginia Woolf decided. He might well be vain, naïve, spoiled, romantic, and arrogant; many of us were. But even in his worst moods he did not have the brute hands of his forefathers. Thus after the first chapter Orlando shut the door to his room, and began to write.

RADCLYFFE HALL, *TRUE REALISM IN FICTION*, 1927

Half of what passed as literature these days was not true, Radclyffe Hall objected. She was lecturing the students of a London college as they drowsed towards the dim hope of a reception with rum cake. *True* realism in fiction, according to Radclyffe Hall, was a steadfast devotion to revealing the bare, literal, and tragic. An English writer ought to stick to the form without wild-goose flights of fancy. There were proportions to respect, schema to follow. Fiction was as precise an art as changing francs to pounds sterling; only thereby might a treatise on sexology correctly be converted into a novel.

VITA AND VIRGINIA, 1927

Jour de ma vie! was the motto of the Sackvilles. It meant 'day of my life', but was often used as a term of endearment. A beloved could be apostrophized as the day dawning in the life of some Sackville or other, awakening naked in a bed at Knole strewn with tasselled cushions, Vita explained to Virginia. Or, Vita added cheekily, slipping her hand into Virginia's pocket, she might already have been up all night.

They had motored to Yorkshire together to see the eclipse of the sun. Will you translate into French for me? Virginia asked Vita in the strange hush after the shadow had passed. Will you give me your likeness? May I borrow your grandmother, your poem, this velvet jacket in which you appear so divinely lovely and tousled? *Jour de ma vie!* Vita replied, you may have all of my lives as your playthings.

VIRGINIA WOOLF, *ORLANDO ON HER RETURN TO ENGLAND*, 1928

The year 1928 began with a new chapter of Orlando. On the eve itself, after the fireworks and some scandalous talk, going to bed everyone said that 1927 had been a year to remember. Virginia Woolf had finally got a motor car and they had seen the sun eclipsed in England for the first time in two centuries.

Meanwhile Orlando had grown into a fine youth with shapely legs and a habit of writing rubbish. In back gardens he had read and blushed; in half a bed sheet he had stretched out an arm to declaim fragments of sapphic verse. He had courted a boyish aristocrat who spoke the most perfect French; he had consorted with actresses and written far too many letters. After the necessary heartbreaks that drive literature forward, he had departed for Constantinople. By

Christmas it was rumoured that Orlando had married Rosina Pepita, his own grandmother. In the bleakest winter days of 1927 it was bruited about that Orlando was dead.

But Orlando was only in the fourth chapter and quite vivacious. On the eve of chapter five, after the fireworks and some scandalous talk, going to bed everyone in Constantinople said how divinely lovely and tousled Orlando looked in a velvet jacket. *Jour de ma vie!* Orlando murmured, reclining on a bed strewn with tasselled cushions. When she awoke, she had many more lives. It was 1928, and still the seventeenth century.

STEPHEN GORDON, *THE FURROW*

Zut alors! exclaimed Natalie Barney, reading the draft of *Stephen* as the bathwater grew cold around her. Frankly Radclyffe Hall had gone too far this time. Irritable and damp, Natalie ordered Berthe to bring her sheaf of pale blue writing paper at once. My dear John, Natalie scrawled, must you *really* have your sapphic heroine write a novel called *The FURROW*? Every halfwit in Parliament will read it, and we will never hear the end of *that*. Do have some care for the rest of us.

REPRESENTATION OF THE PEOPLE ACT 1928

In 1928, at last, Parliament granted the women of England, Wales, and Scotland the right to vote on those who governed them. That is, after some tens of thousands of years inhabiting these lands, men had recognized that half of the People were us.

In Italy, in France, in Greece, in Switzerland, this idea had not yet arrived. The men of various European governments resisted a future of indocile enfranchised women on the various grounds that we were too flighty, too simple, too angelic, too ignorant, too cunning, too hysterical, too impure, too modern, too housebound, not propertied enough, not married enough, not old enough, not educated enough, and not dependably inclined to vote for the same men who had been voting against us for most of our lives. Despite all of this, in 1928 we were gladdened by the idea that henceforth Virginia Woolf could vote.

VIRGINIA WOOLF, *ORLANDO AT THE PRESENT TIME*, 1928

(Here another self came in), Virginia Woolf wrote. It was the spring of 1928. The characters going on underground pricked their green tips through the soil. Across large bodies of water we listened for that tiny sound. The afternoon was slanting through the branches while we lay looking up at the dappled green light of leaves against the sky. In the sixth chapter Orlando too lay down in the shade of the future and drowsed among its roots. Her case was the genitive of remembering, until it is now.

Orlando at the present time was an illustrated plate of Vita in a velvet jacket, framed by the overhanging branches of trees and wild grass. It came near the end of the book, when

Orlando began to become everything at once. We could sense when the first draft of Orlando was finished, because the very air rang with the trembling of leaves. As Lina Poletti could have told us, *aithussomenon* is the weather of afterwords.

RADCLYFFE HALL, *STEPHEN GORDON*, 1928

All through 1928 Radclyffe Hall doggedly composed her novel. The general plot followed Stephen Gordon as she wrote *The Furrow*, examined her body in the mirror, wept, and lost everyone she loved. Unhappily in the middle chapters Stephen Gordon went to Paris, where she encountered a charismatic Amazon who offered sapphic poetry and cucumber sandwiches to lost souls; a hostess so placid and self-assured, as Radclyffe Hall was always saying, that everyone felt very normal and brave just to gather around her.

It had been impressed upon us at several interminable dinner parties that John believed in the British Empire, the sexological theories of Krafft-Ebing, and the sanctity of matrimony. Therefore Stephen Gordon prayed to God that she might settle down with a girl called Mary in a country manor principally decorated with the heads of dead boar.

But we ourselves did not see why the lodestar of a life should be to feel very normal. Moreover, while we would admit to being vain, naïve, spoiled, romantic, and arrogant, we were not lost souls. We had been fighting for decades, sometimes desperately, for the rights to our own lives. We had risked, we had renounced; there were those who had been punished for daring to earn a living in the trousers of their brothers and those who had barely survived the criminologists. Lina Poletti had roused us, Anna Kuliscioff had left us to carry on her revolution. Who among us wished now to be blessed by men or conscripted into their armies? We believed in the Divine Sarah: life, more life! It was 1928, we insisted to Natalie, it was time for books where we could poetically be everyone at once. Despite the diagnosis of Radclyffe Hall, an invert is someone who believes this is possible.

RADCLYFFE HALL, *THE WELL OF LONELINESS*, 1928

It was high summer when Radclyffe Hall's novel was published. Everyone with a villa was reclining bare-legged on its terrace, lulled by the warm hum of cicadas in the pines. On the wilted lawn of Romaine's roof garden we sat glumly reading aloud. Colette, fanning herself in the humid grey air, demanded occasional translations; gamely someone endeavoured to explain Anglican marriage. But it was to no avail. In the unhappy middle chapters, when Stephen Gordon was horrified by the perversity of dancing in our favourite bars in Paris, Colette rose abruptly.

These *terrible* ones? Colette repeated in disdain. These *terrible ones* started *pointing* at her with their shaking, white-skinned, effeminate fingers? *Celle-ci n'est pas une vie!* Colette called back to us as she stalked down the stairs, *Ce n'est pas notre vie!* Wearily we finished the book and watered the pear tree. This is not a life, it is not our life.

JAMES DOUGLAS, REVIEW OF *THE WELL OF LONELINESS* IN THE LONDON *SUNDAY EXPRESS*, 1928

I am well aware that sexual inversion and perversion are horrors which exist among us today. They flaunt themselves in public places with increasing effrontery and more insolently provocative bravado. They take a delight in their flamboyant notoriety. I have seen the plague stalking shamelessly through great public assemblies. I have heard it whispered about by young men and women who do not and cannot grasp its unutterable putrefaction. The contagion cannot be escaped.

Let me warn novelists and our men of letters that literature as well as morality is in peril. Literature has not yet recovered from the harm done to it by the Oscar Wilde scandal. In order to prevent the contamination and corruption of English fiction it is the duty of the critic to make it impossible for any other novelist to repeat this outrage. I would rather give a healthy boy or a healthy girl a phial of prussic acid than this novel.

OBSCENE PUBLICATIONS ACT 1857

Like Oscar Wilde before her, Radclyffe Hall was summoned before an English court to explain the scandalous spectacle she had so wantonly created. Or rather Radclyffe Hall was not summoned. She sat fuming three rows back while the lawyer of her publisher stammered to the Magistrate that in *The Well of Loneliness* all relations between women were purely of an intellectual character. The character Stephen Gordon was not, as it were, in a manner of speaking, like that. After all there were no Lesbians in England: the very word froze hoarily in the mouth of a Magistrate.

A livid shout of outrage came from the third row. By God it was 1928, Radclyffe Hall protested, in the most civilized country on earth! An invert, a lesbian, a person as queer as Stephen Gordon might seem: all of them, as eminent sexologists had argued in their treatises, were unwitting tragic creatures who deserved British benevolence. They might well be gentlemen like herself. Or they might be lost souls. In any case, without the magnanimity of the Magistrate they would all drown in a *well* of *loneliness*. That, Radclyffe Hall pointed out with great emphasis, was why she had called her novel *The Well of Loneliness*.

Virginia Woolf at the back of the courtroom had to bury her face in her hands to prevent a large number of exclamations from flying out of her mouth. She scribbled in her notebook: pale tepid vapid book which lay damp & slab all about the court. At her side wild-eyed Cassandra could hardly contain herself. It was not for this that she had already lived our futures.

VIRGINIA WOOLF, *THE NEW CENSORSHIP*, 1928

Of course Virginia Woolf rose eloquently to the defence of Radclyffe Hall in verb and body. If modern novels were banned, she wrote in *The New Censorship*, readers would merely turn back to the classics of Greek and Latin literature, which were a thousand times more salacious. Let us not begin to dissect Ovid or Aristotle, those staples of English schooling! Called to testify as an expert witness of the modern novel, Virginia Woolf prepared her notes: Would it please the Magistrate to consider, just for a moment, that the judgement of Radclyffe Hall's book as perniciously obscene relied upon the opinion of a critic who had recently advocated giving phials of prussic acid to children?

Privately however Virginia thought *The Well of Loneliness* a puddle of dank, self-righteous sentimentalism that leaked its morals in every sodden direction. Even worse than trying to read the book, she wrote to Vita, was trying to discuss it with John herself, who would countenance no defence except that her novel was a work of unimpeachable tragic genius. To the great relief of Virginia Woolf, the Magistrate decided that writers of modern novels could not be considered experts in obscenity. Thus Virginia spent the rest of the afternoon looking at the wan, treacly light seeping murkily through high windows in the courtroom, as if she were sitting at the bottom of a pond.

VIRGINIA WOOLF, *ORLANDO: A BIOGRAPHY*, 1928

But when can I finally read *Orlando*? Vita enjoined Virginia in every letter. I need hardly say that I can hardly exist till I get it.

Yet fiction could not be rushed into the future. Orlando was published on the very day that *Orlando* proclaimed in the last line of the novel: And the twelfth stroke of midnight sounded; the twelfth stroke of midnight, Thursday, the eleventh of October, Nineteen Hundred and Twenty-eight. Thus as *Orlando* came freshly into being, the type nearly still smelting on the page, midnight struck the eve of Orlando at the present time. Virginia Woolf had the manuscript bound in calfskin and sent as a gift to Vita, although it was not her birthday. It was merely the day when the *vita* of Vita came into the world.

This was a biography, the title announced. But it was also a novel, a whole fantasy, a view of two women at the top of a house, a talk on fiction and the future, a new biography, fragments of a sapphic poem, a composition as explanation, a heroically private joke, a series of portraits, a manifesto, an alcove in the history of literature, an alchemical experiment, an autobiography, and a long piece from life now. In fact no one could tell what was its genre, it was as mercurial in mood and ample in form as Orlando themselves. Every time Orlando awoke, there were many more lives.

VIRGINIA WOOLF, *WOMEN AND FICTION*, 1928

Having skirted the impeccable lawns of Cambridge, Virginia Woolf went at errant angles towards her subject. Imagine reading a novel, she said to the students eyeing her curiously as they opened their notebooks, in which you arrive at this line: Chloe liked Olivia. You may well say to yourself, Yes I remember, for hundreds of years Chloe has liked Olivia, they lay together shadowy in the ferns by the water's edge on an island we have never forgotten. Or instead you may fear for the lives of Chloe and Olivia, or for the novel itself, which is sure to be banned shortly by some Magistrate in a courtroom where the light is like ditchwater. Indeed the truths of women in fiction have meant trouble since the time of Cassandra.

Yet if you can lock the door to your room, you might try writing the story of Chloe and Olivia yourselves. The first thing is to change their names, so that the story will feel like your own.

AFTERWORDS

LINA POLETTI, N.D.

Thus at last the moment came for us to write the biography of Lina Poletti. We had feared for her life; but in truth she had many lives, all of her own and ours tangled in among them.

After *Orlando*, when we looked out of the window, we saw the exuberance of foliage twining green from every branch. A windless, deathless, bright morning air dappled the leaves until they fluttered on their stems. *Jour de ma vie!* we said to each other. We began to haul in through the window the great hanks and skeins of stories the world had yielded us.

In our hands Lina Poletti changed names. She fled in the middle of the night without setting fire to the back rooms. In a village called Pizzoli she wrote her way through the winter, through the nights when the stars receded infinitely from any human feeling. For a time she brought food to the huts and barns where people were hiding, bicycling along rutted lanes in her high buttoned boots. The people with hungry grateful eyes said they were surprised to see her, there weren't many like her. On the night when they bombed the libraries she passed through enemy lines; in the morning her ardent voice was heard crackling over the radio of a liberated city: We are the chorus, Lina Poletti called out through the static, the voices of us shall never be silenced.

After the war she travelled to the dustiest ruins in Greece, where she patiently scraped the bare earth until she found an eyeless statue flaking bright green and gold paint. It was surrounded by small bones and not what she had expected. Thus she changed her mind about the colour of gods and citizens. The magpies settled in the trees of the ruins while Lina wrote in her notebook, *perdere la propria vita*, which means to lose the propriety, the property, the boundedness and the ownership, the proprietary *impadronirsi* of a life.

Some years later Lina sat in a circle on the floor with other women talking about the rights they should have. She touched their cheeks when they cried. Together they decided they would open a library, to lend forbidden books freely. They would call it the library of women. Eventually Lina was scolded for smoking in that library; then a woman chided her as she went into the WC. *Non sai che cos'è una donna?* the woman snapped. Do you not know what is a woman? In fact Lina Poletti had read *Una donna* in 1906, when it was first published.

The modern world was sometimes bewildering, but Lina Poletti had lived for a century without setting fire to it. She learned the new words. She helped to wrench the old statues from their pedestals. She fought against the law of blood, she fought against the virile hour, she fought for the rights that Anna Kuliscioff had not lived to see. Every time the Fascists came, Lina wrote a manifesto; there is always some candle that will not be extinguished. She joined hands with people she had been told were unspeakable, savage, backwards, lesser, criminal, and foreign. They marched through the streets singing, *Insieme siamo partitə, insieme torneremo:* together we have set out, together we shall return; a fragment is yet unfinished, we shall only go forward together. Her voice grew hoarse with years. She changed names. She changed genres. She watched with molten eyes as we arrived at the present time.

We wrote the lives of Lina Poletti, but we did not always understand them. In some way Lina was always beyond us. She would crest a wave that left us thrashing for breath. She could sight land when we were becalmed, sheltering in our interludes. In other words Lina knew how to turn the interior of herself outwards and elsewhere. She was always beckoning us onwards into a future we did not yet know how to live. We are the chorus, Lina Poletti would urge her companions, taking different aspects of the character in different Centuries. Thus in the end we followed her beyond ourselves. Or we told her for others, as best we could: *These things now for my companions/I shall sing beautifully*. Sappho, Fragment 160.

BIBLIOGRAPHIC NOTE

This is a work of fiction. Or possibly it is such a hybrid of imaginaries and intimate non-fictions, of speculative biographies and 'suggestions for short pieces' (as Virginia Woolf called them while she was drafting *Orlando*), as to have no recourse to a category at all. There is, for example, no historical record of Lina Poletti kicking out of her swaddling in any church in Ravenna. Alessandra Cenni, who has worked tirelessly to recover the historical traces of Lina [Cordula] Poletti, wonders in the conclusion to her book *Gli occhi eroici: Sibilla Aleramo, Eleonora Duse, Cordula Poletti: una storia d'amore nell'Italia della Belle Époque* whether in fact Lina might have wanted to lose herself ['« *perdersi* »'] in obscurity, in order to make her future reincarnations possible.

Moreover, men like Gabriele d'Annunzio – who swaggers prepotently through every account ever written of Eleonora Duse and Romaine Brooks – do not merit here even a footnote about who they married or how they died. It has been surprisingly easy to leave out these sorts of men: a simple swift cut, and history is sutured without them. I think of Vita Sackville-West, who said in a letter in 1919 that the only revenge one could take on certain men was to brazenly rewrite them. At that time, all she had at hand was an unfinished chapter of her novel *Challenge*. Therefore, Vita recounted, 'last night I went to Aphros and imprisoned all the Greek officials, which gave me a certain ferocious satisfaction'. The fact that my claim here about gender and fiction rests upon a quote from a real letter – which I have gleaned from a reputable scholarly source, Georgia Johnston's *The Formation of 20th-Century Queer Autobiography: Reading Vita Sackville-West, Virginia Woolf, Hilda Doolittle, and Gertrude Stein* – in which the author explains that she has, in some fictional yet satisfying sense, gone to Greece for a night, in order to exact narrative retribution for the wrongs done to her protagonist (under whose name she sometimes went around in the world): this, I think, illustrates the genre of the present work.

As Saidiya Hartman explains in her 'Cast of Characters' for *Wayward Lives, Beautiful Experiments: Intimate Histories of Riotous Black Girls, Troublesome Women, and Queer Radicals*, a Chorus might well be 'all the unnamed young women of the city trying to find a way to live and in search of beauty'. And yet, for the most part, the figures who have become my characters lived real lives; many of them left material traces of how they felt about the world and their places in it. Therefore I have included indications of both primary sources (the copies of letters, paintings, novels, memoirs, photographs, speeches, etc., that Melanie Micir, in *The Passion Projects: Modernist Women, Intimate Archives, Unfinished Lives,* calls 'a diverse archive of biographical acts'), and the scholarship I have consulted while writing. When I have quoted, closely paraphrased, or translated directly from a source, I have noted it below; sources used synthetically or consulted for background are listed in a bibliography, available online at www.galleybeggar.co.uk/after-sappho-references. Any errors are my own, and of course no source can be held responsible for my imagination.

All translations of Sappho are taken from Anne Carson's *If Not, Winter: Fragments of Sappho*, to which my book is deeply indebted.

Excerpts of Sibilla Aleramo's published writings come from her books *Una donna* and *Il passaggio*, and from her articles (reprinted in Alessandra Cenni's *Gli occhi eroici* and in Sibilla Aleramo's anthology *La donna e il femminismo: Scritti 1897–1910*, edited by Bruna Conti.); all translations and transmutations, however, are my own. Material from the letters of Sibilla Aleramo, Lina Poletti, Eleonora Duse, and Santi Muratori is drawn from Cenni's *Gli occhi eroici,* as well as from Laura Mariani's *Il tempo delle attrici: Emancipazionismo e teatro in Italia fra Otto e Novecento*; all translations are mine. The paraphrase of Guglielmo Cantarano's 'Contribuzione alla casuistica della inversione dell'istinto sessuale' is based on Chiara Beccalossi's 'The Origin of Italian Sexological Studies: Female Sexual Inversion, ca. 1870–1900' and Daniela Danna's *Amiche, compagne, amanti: Storia dell'amore tra donne*; the paraphrase of Cesare Lombroso's *La donna delinquente: La prostituta e la donna normale* is derived from Mary Gibson's 'Labelling Women Deviant: Heterosexual Women, Prostitutes and Lesbians in Early Criminological Discourse'. Elements from Dr. T. Laycock's *A Treatise on the Nervous Disorders of Women* are taken from *The Lesbian History Sourcebook: Love and Sex Between Women in Britain from 1870 to 1970* (ed. Alison Oram and Annmarie Turnbull), including the phrase 'hysterical paroxysm' and a slightly altered version of the quote, 'Young females of the same age, he cautioned, cannot associate together in public schools without serious risk of exciting the passions, and being led to indulge in practices injurious to both body and mind.' The words of Anna Kuliscioff draw on Rosalia Colombo Ascari's 'Feminism and Socialism in Anna Kuliscioff's Writings'. Some details about the 1908 National Congress of Italian Women are drawn from Claudia Frattini's *Il primo Congresso delle donne italiane, Roma, 1908: Opinione pubblica e femminismo.*

Nora's line in Ibsen's *A Doll's House* is quoted from Toril Moi's '"First and Foremost a Human Being": Idealism, Theatre, and Gender in *A Doll's House*'. The description of Aleramo's unfinished play *L'Assurdo* is based on Charlotte Ross' *Eccentricity and sameness: discourses on lesbianism and desire between women in Italy, 1860s–1930s.* The case of William Seymour the cabman is paraphrased from Oram and Turnbull's *The Lesbian History Sourcebook.*

The episode of the lantern bearer is closely paraphrased from the collection of Virginia [Stephen] Woolf's early journals, *A Passionate Apprentice: The Early Journals, 1882–1941* (edited by Mitchell Alexander Leaska); the phrase 'the lantern bearer was none other than the present writer' is a slight variation on Woolf's own line. The account of Leslie Stephen's editorial work, including the phrases 'article in the first twenty-six volumes' and 'ammoniated tincture of quinine drops', are from Hermione Lee's biography *Virginia Woolf*. The poet whose characterization of Cassandra I quote – that 'when she stood up to prophesy she shone like a lamp in a bomb shelter' – is Anne Carson, from 'Cassandra Float Can' in *Float*. The line, 'is that Virginia Stephen was not born on the 25th January 1882, but was born many thousands of years ago; and had from the very first to encounter instincts already acquired by thousands of ancestresses in the past', is quoted from Woolf's 'A Sketch of the Past', reprinted in *Moments of Being*. The description of Laura Stephen draws on Hermione Lee's *Virginia Woolf*, including (with slight alterations) the phrases, 'fiendish, wicked, perverse, dreadfully passionate, extremely disturbing and extremely pathetic', 'vacanteyed girl… who could hardly read' (Lee is quoting Woolf's 'Old Bloomsbury' here, reprinted in *Moments of Being*), and Laura's line, 'I told him to go away.' The title *LOGICK: OR, THE Right Use of REASON WITH A Variety of RULES to Guard Against ERROR in the AFFAIRS of RELIGION and HUMAN LIFE as well as in the Sciences,* and the episode of desecrating it, come from *A Passionate Apprentice* (edited by Leaska), as does a version of Miss Janet Case's statement, 'let us note a very rare sort of genitive in the third line'. 'The Serpentine' was written into Virginia [Stephen] Woolf's journal in 1903; the quoted suicide note and some details come from that entry, reprinted in *A Passionate Apprentice*. 'Review of the Feminine Note in Fiction', by Virginia [Stephen] Woolf, originally appeared in *The Guardian* on 25 January 1905 (her birthday), and is reprinted in *The Essays of Virginia Woolf, 1904–1912,* Vol. I, edited by Andrew McNeillie. I have incorporated two slightly altered quotes from her review: 'that as more and more novels are written by women for women, they increasingly cause the novel as a work of art to disappear', and 'is it not too soon after all to criticise the "feminine note" in anything? And will not the adequate critic of women be a woman?'

Radclyffe Hall's description of Natalie Barney (as the character Valérie Seymour) is taken, with slight alterations, from *The Well of Loneliness*. Léo Taxil is quoted from his 1894 book *La Corruption fin-de-siècle,* although the translation is my own. The line from Renée Vivien's 'Retour à Mytilène' is cited from Lowry Gene Martin II's dissertation, 'Desire, Fantasy, and the Writing of Lesbos-sur-Seine, 1880–1939', although the translations are mine; the description of Aurel's '*Comment les femmes deviennent écrivains*' draws on Cenni's *Gli occhi eroici*.

The expression of Matilde Serao's ardour for Eleonora Duse, as well as the terms '*Nennella*', '*commediante*', and '*la smara*', are taken from Helen Sheehy's *Eleonora Duse: A Biography.* The description of foundling houses (including the mortality rate at the Annunziata orphanage and the term 'children of the Madonna') draws on Anna-Maria Tapaninen's 'Motherhood through the Wheel: The Care of Foundlings in Late NineteenthCentury Naples'. The description of French paternity law is based on 'Seduction, Paternity, and the Law in Fin de Siècle France' by Rachel G. Fuchs. The identification of Eleonora Duse with Madame Robert in Sibilla Aleramo's *L'assurdo* is suggested by Laura Mariani in *Il tempo delle attrici,* and my very loose rendering of lines from Lina Poletti's 'Gli inviti' utilizes the text of the poem reprinted in Cenni's *Gli occhi eroici*. The line from Gertrude Stein's 'Portrait of Mabel Dodge at the Villa Curonia' is quoted from *Selected Writings of Gertrude Stein*, edited by Carl Van Vechten. The description of Eleonora Duse's 1913 interview elaborates a suggestion from Lucia Re's 'Eleonora Duse and Women: Performing Desire, Power, and Knowledge'.

Line 52 of Ovid's *Heroides* XV is quoted from the Loeb edition (*Heroides. Amores*, translated by Grant Showerman). The description of the binding used by Giacinta Pezzana as Hamlet, as well as the comments from Pezzana about getting into character, rely on two articles by Laura Mariani: 'Portrait of Giacinta Pezzana, Actress of Emancipationism (1841–1919)' and '*In scena* en travesti*: il caso italiano e l'Amleto di Giacinta Pezzana*'. The line from Giacinta Pezzana's letter to Sibilla Aleramo in 1911 is quoted from Laura Mariani's *L'attrice del cuore. Storia di Giacinta Pezzana attraverso le lettere*. The reference to the slang term '*gousse d'ail*' is from Gretchen Schultz's *Sapphic Fathers: Discourses of Same-Sex Desire from Nineteenth-Century France*, while Sarah Bernhardt's perspective on the morality of *Phèdre* is based on her memoir *Ma double vie*. 'An idyll by Theocritus' is a quote from Virginia [Stephen] Woolf's journal, published in *A Passionate Apprentice*, describing her voyage in Greece; the sketch of her translation exercises and travels incorporates some elements from her entries in 1905–6. The description of Natalie Barney's stagings of *Équivoque* and *Dialogue au soleil couchant* draw upon Samuel Dorf's *Performing Antiquity: Ancient Greek Music and Dance from Paris to Delphi, 1890–*

1930 (which is the source for Gorgo's line, 'Your life is your poem/Most beautiful,' from *Équivoque*), as well as upon Artemis Leontis' *Eva Palmer Sikelianos: A Life in Ruins* and Ann Cooper Albright's *Traces of Light: Absence and Presence in the Work of Loïe Fuller*. The conversation between Eva Palmer and Mrs [Stella] Patrick Campbell is based on Eva Palmer-Sikelianos' autobiography *Upward Panic*, edited by John P. Anton. Sarah Bernhardt's motto is recorded in her memoir *Ma double vie*.

The *Idylls* of Theocritus are contained in the Loeb volume *Theocritus. Moschus. Bion* (edited and translated by Neil Hopkinson). The line 'Still by the light and laughing sea' is quoted from Oscar Wilde's 'Theocritus: A Villanelle', contained in *The Collected Poems of Oscar Wilde* (edited by Anne Varty). Isadora Duncan's memoir *My Life* provided some elements of the description of the Duncans' undertakings in Greece.

The entries from Alfred Delvau's *Dictionnaire érotique moderne* (1864) are cited from Gretchen Schultz's *Sapphic Fathers* and Nicole G. Albert's *Lesbian Decadence: Representations in Art and Literature of Fin-de-Siècle France*, respectively. The line from Gertrude Stein's poem 'Rich and Poor in English' is quoted from Joanne Winning's 'The Sapphist in the City: Lesbian Modernist Paris and Sapphic Modernity', which also traces the spatial relations of La Maison des Amis de Livres and Shakespeare and Company in 'Odéonia' – as Adrienne Monnier called it – within an eventual lesbian geography of the Left Bank. I have gleaned details about Monnier's bookshop from Martine Poulain's 'Adrienne Monnier et la Maison des amis des livres, 1915–1951'; those about Sylvia Beach come from her own *Shakespeare and Company*. That Eileen Gray 'couldn't understand why he (her father) had to spend such a long time in hot landscapes where even the ground and walls looked parched in villages instead of painting cool green things that were shiny and silky in Wexford', is quoted, with slight variation, from an interview with Gray cited in Jennifer Goff's *Eileen Gray: Her Work and Her World*. The connection between Romaine Brooks' painting *The Screen* (also called *The Red Jacket*) and Eileen Gray's early work is suggested by Jasmine Rault in *Eileen Gray and the Design of Sapphic Modernity: Staying In*; Rault also gives a brief account of Jack. The comparison of Damia to a 'fairground boxer in repose' was made by the dance critic André Levinson, as Kelley Conway notes in *Chanteuse in the City: The Realist Singer in French Film*.

The description of the 1912 staging of Sophocles' *Elektra* in Paris, with Eva Palmer Sikelianos and Penelope Sikelianos Duncan, is indebted to Artemis Leontis' *Eva Palmer Sikelianos: A Life in Ruins*; Leontis also posits that Eva's passion for Greek music and theatre doubled as a pursuit of Penelope. The quote about the 'tightly bound' character of Elektra, whose 'movement must tell to the utmost' is taken with very slight alterations from Virginia Woolf's 'On Not Knowing Greek' (in *The Common Reader*); my representation of the Greek verb '*lupein*' and its implications rests on Anne Carson's 'Screaming in Translation'. 'The Greek Girl' is a section title in Romaine Brooks' unpublished memoirs, excerpts of which are reprinted in Timothy Young's 'The Toll of Friendship: Selections from the Memoirs of Romaine Brooks'.

The explanation of *jus sanguinis* relies on Lucia Re's 'Italians and the Invention of Race: The Poetics and Politics of Difference in the Struggle over Libya, 1890–1913' (from which I paraphrase Pisanelli's claim that 'the principal element of nationality is race'); in noting its colonial impacts, I am indebted to Angelica Pesarani's story '*Non s'intravede speranza alcuna*' ['No end in sight'] in *Future* (edited by Igiaba Scego). Sketches of the racist thinking of figures like Mantegazza and Orano draw on Rhiannon Noel Welch's *Vital Subjects: Race and Biopolitics in Italy, 1860–1920*, as well as on Re's 'Italians and the Invention of Race' (from which I have roughly translated Sibilla Aleramo's lines in *L'ora virile* about wars between countries – and races – and the women who end up supporting them). Yeeyon Im's 'Oscar Wilde's *Salomé*: Disorienting Orientalism' is the source for Wilde's description of Sarah Bernhardt as 'that "serpent of the old Nile"' he envisioned as the ideal Salomé.

The capitalization of words such as 'Beauty' in the description of Isadora Duncan's ideology (as well as the critique of her racial politics) follows Ann Daly's 'Isadora Duncan and the Distinction of Dance'. The framing of Cassandra's line '*Itys, itys*' is indebted to Emily Pillinger's *Cassandra and the Poetics of Prophecy in Greek and Latin Literature*. The description of Ida Rubinstein's costume in *Cléopâtre* draws on Charles S. Mayer's 'Ida Rubinstein: A Twentieth-Century Cleopatra', which is also the source for

Romaine Brooks' portrayal of Ida walking in the snow in her 'long ermine coat'.

Quotes from, and variations on, Virginia Woolf's essays are drawn from 'Mr Bennett and Mrs Brown' (also called 'Character in Fiction', reprinted in *The Essays of Virginia Woolf, Vol. 3: 1919– 1924*, ed. Andrew McNeillie) and 'A Society', from *Monday or Tuesday.* I have paraphrased parts of the first essay in my section 'Virginia Woolf, *Mr Bennett and Mrs Brown*, 1924', and quoted from it (with slight alteration) the famous line 'in or about December, 1910, human character changed'. The line 'a percentage of women died from maladies incident to childbirth' is quoted from Woolf's 'A Society', which describes the insights of the 'Society of the Future' into systemic misogyny. The allusion to 'Girls of the Future Society', taken from Pierre Louÿs' dedication in *Les chansons de Bilitis* (and reprised by Natalie Barney for *Cinq petit dialogues grecs*), is quoted from Tama Engelking's 'Translating the Lesbian Writer: Pierre Louÿs, Natalie Barney, and "Girls of the Future Society"'. 'Objects, Food, Rooms' are sections of Gertrude Stein's book *Tender Buttons.* The allusion to Eleonora Duse's Libreria delle Attrici as a 'room of one's own' comes from Lucia Re's 'Eleonora Duse and Women'. The depiction of Cassandra in Aeschylus's *Agamemnon* is indebted to Anne Carson's 'Cassandra Float Can', in *Float.* The phrase 'the daughters of educated men' is from Virginia Woolf's *Three Guineas.* The paraphrase of Mrs Ethel Alec-Tweedie's *Women and Soldiers*, and the quote, 'Ye Gods! The women have eliminated us. We shall soon be as extinct as the dodo,' are from Laura Doan's article 'Topsy-turvydom: Gender Inversion, Sapphism, and the Great War', as is the reference to Gladys de Havilland's *The Woman's Motor Manual.* Virginia Woolf's characterization of WWI as a 'preposterous masculine fiction' is quoted by Anne Fernihough, in 'Modernist Materialism: War, Gender, and Representation in Woolf, West, and H.D.', referencing a letter from Woolf to Margaret Llewyn Davis in January 1916. Information on Article 14, including the names of women merchants reported in the 1911 census in Bologna, comes from Maura Palazzi's 'Economic autonomy and male authority: female merchants in modern Italy'. The description of Natalie Barney's pacifism is derived from Mary Eichbauer's 'Imagining a Life', although I have slightly altered the quote she cites from Barney's *Pensées.*

'The modern world is perishing under a flood of ugliness' is from Radclyffe Hall's *The Well of Loneliness,* attributed to Pierre Louÿs but presented in the novel as a sentiment that Valérie Seymour would share. The Italian line '*Per voi, per voi tutte, cadute*' is quoted from Lina Poletti's *Il poema della guerra,* while the very free translations of that line, and some few other phrases, are my own; the chant beginning '*Siamo il grido…*' is from the contemporary Italian transfeminist movement Non Una di Meno, which I have translated. 'Oh, Cassandra, why do you torment me?' is a quote from Woolf's 'A Society'.

The line 'when the unfinished, the unfulfilled, the unwritten, the unreturned came together in their ghostly way and wore the semblance of the complete' is quoted from

Virginia Woolf's *Night and Day*. In Radclyffe Hall's *The Unlit Lamp*, the young Joan Ogden is 'discovered hacking at her hair with a pen-knife'. The translated excerpt from Élisabeth de Gramont's article 'Les lacques d'Eileen Gray', originally published in *Les feuillets d'art* in March 1922, is quoted from Jennifer Goff 's *Eileen Gray: Her Work and Her World.*

Noel Pemberton Billing's claim that 'Wives of men in supreme positions were entangled. In lesbian ecstasy the most sacred secrets of State were betrayed' is quoted from Deborah Cohler's *Citizen, Invert, Queer: Lesbianism and War in Twentieth-Century Britain*, which analyses the case of Maud Allan. Cohler's book is also the source for the following lines (from the trial transcript, a private letter, and the Parliamentary Debates of 1921, respectively): 'Clitoris... a superficial organ that, when unduly excited or over-developed, possessed the most dreadful influence on any woman'; 'Lord Albermarle [who] is said to have walked into the Turf [Club] and said, "I've never heard of this Greek chap *Clitoris* they are all talking of"'; and 'beastly subject'. Details from the life of Ada Bricktop Smith, including the phrase 'West-by-God-Virginia', come from T. Denean Sharpley-Whiting's *Bricktop's Paris: African American Women in Paris between the Two World Wars*, with a glimpse of nightlife gleaned from Robert McAlmon and Kay Boyle's *Being Geniuses Together, 1920–1930;* the episode of Josephine's Baker's autograph stamp is recounted in Ada Bricktop Smith's memoir, *Bricktop by Bricktop*, excerpted in Sharpley-Whiting's book.

The question, 'Is it not the task of the novelist to convey this varying, this unknown and uncircumscribed spirit, whatever aberration or complexity it may display…?' is a quote from Virginia Woolf's 'Modern Fiction', included in *The Common Reader*. Virginia Woolf's sentiment, 'I want to make life fuller and fuller', is quoted from *The Diary of Virginia Woolf, Vol 2: 1920–1924*, ed. Anne Olivier Bell. In a diary entry from 1925 (thus in *Vol 3: 1925–1930*), Woolf writes, 'I have an idea that I will invent a new name for my books to supplant "novel". A new ___ by Virginia Woolf. But what? Elegy?'; Vol. 3 is also the source for the quote '(I want to begin to describe my own sex.)' The episode of Rachel Footman at Oxford is paraphrased from Jane Robinson's *Bluestockings* (which excerpts Footman's unpublished 'Memories of 1923–1926'). The sketch of Clarissa Dalloway is derived from Virginia Woolf's *Mrs Dalloway*, which includes the phrase 'interested in politics like a man'.

The line from Virginia Woolf's 1925 letter to Vita Sackville-West, 'if you'll make me up, I'll make you', is quoted from Karyn Z. Sproles' *Desiring Women: The Partnership of Virginia Woolf and Vita Sackville-West.* The Romani phrase '*man camelo tuti*' (and its translation) are quoted from Kirstie Blair's 'Gypsies and Lesbian Desire: Vita Sackville-West, Violet Trefusis, and Virginia Woolf ', originally included in a letter from Violet Trefusis to Vita Sackville-West. The discussion of birds, Cassandra, and madness in Virginia Woolf's writing is indebted to Emily Pillinger's 'Finding Asylum for Virginia Woolf's Classical Visions'. Lina Poletti's Mediterraneanist claim about decentring Europe in conceptions of the classical derives from a line in one of her letters to Santi Muratori, '*rispetto all'Asia-Africa, da cui la Grecia esce, e non più rispetto all'Europa, come si è fatto fin qui*', quoted in Cenni's *Gli occhi eroici*. The description of Nancy Cunard's *Parallax* paraphrases a claim from Oliver Tearle's *The Great War,* The Waste Land *and the Modernist Long Poem*. Nancy Cunard's fond description of the 'glistening pigment' of printer's ink, 'black or red', is taken from her memoir *These Were the Hours*. The following lines are quotes from Radclyffe Hall's 'Miss Ogilvy Finds Herself ': 'Many another of her kind', 'in the end she must blaze a lone trail through the difficulties of her nature', and 'If only I had been born a man!' Eileen Gray's idea of 'the problem of the windows' – i.e. that 'a window without shutters is an *eye without eyelids*' – originally published in an issue of *L'architecture vivante* (1929), is quoted from Jasmine Rault's *Eileen Gray and the Design of Sapphic Modernity*; Rault also gives a detailed description of E.1027 and suggests thematic links to the work of Radclyffe Hall and Virginia Woolf. Three lines from Gertrude Stein's *Composition as Explanation* (given initially as a series of talks at Cambridge and Oxford in 1926, and published by Hogarth Press later that year; the essay was ultimately reprinted in Stein's *What Are Masterpieces* in 1940) are quoted here: 'The composition is the thing seen by every one living in the living they are doing'; 'This makes the thing we are looking at very different and this makes what those who describe it make of it, it makes a composition, it confuses, it shows, it is, it looks, it likes it as it is, and this makes what is seen as it is seen'; and 'It is that that makes living a thing they are doing'. Natalie Barney's praise of Gertrude Stein is quoted from *Adventures of the Mind: The Memoirs of Natalie Clifford Barney* (translated by John Spalding Gatton). From Virginia Woolf's essay 'How Should One Read a Book?' (given as a talk in 1926 at Hayes Court Common School for Girls, and eventually revised for *The Common Reader: Second Series* in 1932), I have quoted the following lines: 'how are we to bring order into this multitudinous chaos and so get the deepest and widest pleasure from what we read?' and 'If a novel bores you, leave it. Try something else... Poetry is too like fiction to be a change. But biography is a very different thing. Go to the bookcase & take out a life of anybody.' The former is quoted from the version in *The Common Reader: Second Series*, and the latter from a holographic draft of the lecture manuscripts reprinted in Beth Rigel Daugherty's 'Virginia Woolf's "How Should One Read a Book?"'

The account of Berthe Cleyrergue's life draws substantially on her memoir *Berthe ou Un demi-siècle auprès de l'Amazone,* from which I have paraphrased (and translated) several short excerpts.

From Colette's *La Naissance du Jour* I have translated the epigraph, as well as a later quote from Colette to a critic. The phrase 'the virile hour' alludes to Sibilla Aleramo's essay *L'ora virile* (1912), which is analysed in Lucia Re's 'Italians and the Invention of Race'. 'Lady Buck-and-Balk' and 'Tilly Tweed-in-Blood' are characters in Djuna Barnes' *Ladies Almanack*. Virginia Woolf's inscription of the dummy copy of *To The Lighthouse* sent to Vita Sackville-West is quoted from Hermione Lee's *Virginia Woolf.* Virginia Woolf's note to Vita Sackville-West about the American publication of the story 'Slater's Pins Have No Points' is quoted from *The Letters of Virginia Woolf, Vol 3: 1923–1928* (ed. Nigel Nicolson and Joanne Trautmann); I have closely paraphrased short sections of that story. The phrase 'that queer amalgamation of dream and reality' is quoted from Virginia Woolf's 'The New Biography', reprinted in *The Essays of Virginia Woolf, Vol. 4* (ed. Andrew McNeillie).

I have quoted a series of brief phrases limning Virginia Woolf's conception of *The Jessamy Brides* and the inspiration for *Orlando* from *The Diary of Virginia Woolf, Vol 3: 1925–1930* (ed. Anne Olivier Bell). Excerpts from Virginia Woolf's notes on 'Suggestions for short pieces' regarding both 'A Biography' and 'A poem' are quoted from Suzanne Raitt and Ian Blyth's 'Introduction' to the Cambridge edition of *Orlando* (which cites the holograph draft of the manuscript). I have quoted some phrases from Virginia Woolf's letters to Vita Sackville-West in 1927 (contained in *The Letters of Virginia Woolf, Vol 3: 1923–1928*), including 'how to read all fiction as if it were one book one had written oneself ', 'it sprung upon me how I could revolutionise biography in a night', and 'Shall you mind?' As is evident, I have described some characters and plot elements from Vita Sackville-West's *A Note of Explanation,* Radclyffe Hall's *The Well of Loneliness,* and Virginia Woolf's *Orlando: A Biography* (from which I have also quoted the last line). Sibilla Aleramo's statement in *La donna italiana* crediting Mussolini with re-orienting 'the female masses to their precise and sacred function as reproducers of the species' is quoted from Carole C. Gallucci's 'The Body and the Letter: Sibilla Aleramo in the Interwar Years'; the translation is Gallucci's. Virginia Woolf's description of Vita as 'divinely lovely, a little tousled, in a velvet jacket', taken from a letter to Clive Bell in 1924, is quoted (with slight alterations) from Raitt and Blyth's 'Introduction' to *Orlando.* The line '(Here another self came in)' is quoted from *Orlando*; the line 'these terrible ones started pointing at her with their shaky, white-skinned, effeminate fingers' is quoted from *The Well of Loneliness.* The defence of *The Well of Loneliness* mounted by Jonathan Cape's lawyers, i.e. that 'throughout [the novel] the relations between the two women were of a purely intellectual character', is quoted with a slight alteration from Adam Parkes' 'Lesbianism, History, and Censorship: *The Well of Loneliness* and the Suppressed Randiness of Virginia Woolf's *Orlando*'. Virginia Woolf's private analysis of *The Well of Loneliness*, 'the pale tepid vapid book which lay damp & slab all about the court', is quoted from Jodie Medd's *Lesbian Scandal and the Culture of Modernism.* Excerpts from the review of *The Well of Loneliness*, penned by James Douglas for the *Sunday Express* in 1928, are quoted absolutely verbatim – I have merely rearranged the sentences – from the reprint of 'A Book That Must Be Suppressed' in *Palatable Poison: Critical Perspectives on* The Well of Loneliness (edited by Laura Doan and Jay Prosser). Vita Sackville-West's letter to Virginia Woolf asking for a copy of *Orlando* is quoted from Raitt and Blyth's edition of *Orlando.* 'Chloe liked Olivia' is, famously, a line from Virginia Woolf's *A Room of One's Own* (1929), originally presented as a series of talks at Cambridge in October 1928.

'*Insieme siamo partitə/Insieme torneremo/Non una, non una/ Non una di meno*' is a chant of the contemporary Italian transfeminist movement Non Una di Meno; the translation is mine. '*Perdere la propria vita*', a phrase taken from a letter that Lina Poletti wrote to Santi Muratori in 1933, is quoted from Alessandra Cenni's *Gli occhi eroici*; the gloss is my own.

ACKNOWLEDGEMENTS

One excerpt of this book was published in *Speculative Nonfiction* (Issue #3: *Erasure,* June 2020); another was published by *Passages North* in July 2021.

Excerpts from *If Not, Winter: Fragments of Sappho* by Sappho, translated by Anne Carson, copyright 2002 by Anne Carson, are reprinted by permission of Virago Press, an imprint of the Little, Brown Book Group, UK. All rights reserved.

The excerpt from *The Albertine Workout*, copyright 2014 by Anne Carson, is reprinted by permission of Anne Carson and Aragi Inc. All rights reserved.

My deepest gratitude to Elly and Sam, who decided this was going to be a novel.